RY

"Incredibly awesome . . . I love ...
—Jaci Bu...

"Maya Banks writes the kind of books I love to read!"
—Lora Leigh, #1 *New York Times* bestselling author

"Maya Banks . . . really dragged me through the gamut of emotions. From . . . 'is it hot in here?' to 'oh my *god* . . . I'm ready for the next ride now'!"
—*USA Today*

"[A] one-two punch of entertainment that will leave readers eager for the next book."
—*Publishers Weekly*

"For those who like it naughty, dirty and do-me-on-the-desk *hawt*!"
—Examiner.com

"A cross between the [Crossfire] or Fifty Shades series and the Wicked Lovers series by Shayla Black."
—*Book Savvy Babe*

"Hot enough to make even the coolest reader sweat!"
—*Fresh Fiction*

"You'll be on the edge of your seat with this one."
—*Night Owl Reviews*

"Definitely a recommended read."
—*Fallen Angel Reviews*

"[For] fans of Sylvia Day's *Bared to You*."
—*Under the Covers*

"Grabbed me from page one and refused to let go until I read the last word."
—*Joyfully Reviewed*

Titles by Maya Banks

FOR HER PLEASURE
BE WITH ME

The Sweet Series

SWEET SURRENDER
SWEET PERSUASION
SWEET SEDUCTION
SWEET TEMPTATION
SWEET POSSESSION
SWEET ADDICTION

The Kelly/KGI Series

THE DARKEST HOUR
NO PLACE TO RUN
HIDDEN AWAY
WHISPERS IN THE DARK
ECHOES AT DAWN
SHADES OF GRAY
FORGED IN STEELE
AFTER THE STORM

Colters' Legacy

COLTERS' PROMISE
COLTERS' GIFT

The Breathless Trilogy

RUSH
FEVER
BURN

The Surrender Trilogy

LETTING GO
GIVING IN
TAKING IT ALL

Anthologies

FOUR PLAY
(with Shayla Black)
MEN OUT OF UNIFORM
(with Karin Tabke and Sylvia Day)
CHERISHED
(with Lauren Dane)

Specials

PILLOW TALK
EXILED

TAKING IT ALL

MAYA BANKS

BERKLEY BOOKS, NEW YORK

THE BERKLEY PUBLISHING GROUP
Published by the Penguin Group
Penguin Group (USA) LLC
375 Hudson Street, New York, New York 10014

USA • Canada • UK • Ireland • Australia • New Zealand • India • South Africa • China

penguin.com

A Penguin Random House Company

This book is an original publication of The Berkley Publishing Group.

Library of Congress Cataloging-in-Publication Data

Banks, Maya.
Taking it all / Maya Banks.
pages cm— (The surrender trilogy ; 3)
ISBN 978-0-425-27298-5 (paperback)
1. Man-woman relationships—Fiction. I. Title.
PS3602.A643T35 2014
813'.6—dc23
2014016869

PUBLISHING HISTORY
Berkley trade paperback edition / August 2014

PRINTED IN THE UNITED STATES OF AMERICA

10 9 8 7 6 5 4 3 2 1

Cover photo of "Daisies" by Nick Veasey/ Getty; "Bluebells" by Nick Veasey/Getty;
"Floral Background" by Irynal/Shutterstock.
Cover design by Rita Frangie.
Interior text design by Kristin del Rosario.

For Carrie, with all my love

TAKING IT ALL

ONE

CHESSY Morgan pulled into a parking spot at the Lux Café in Houston, her eyes widening in surprise when she saw both Kylie's and Joss's cars parked short distances away.

Kylie being there didn't shock her. Kylie was always punctual. But Joss? Joss was perpetually running late. Chessy and Kylie almost *always* had to wait on Joss, who'd dash laughingly inside the restaurant where Chessy and Kylie waited, an unnecessary apology always on her lips for her tardiness.

And, well, who could ever get mad at Joss? Especially for something so insignificant as being habitually late. Joss was just someone who lit up a room with her warmth and sweetness. She'd come a long way from grieving widow after losing Carson to where she was now. Happy. In love. Married to Dash, her former husband's best friend. Chessy was genuinely thrilled for both her friends. Joss and Kylie had both found love. For Kylie, this was huge. She'd made monumental steps in her life, being able to finally overcome the demons from her past that had ruled her present for so very long.

Kylie had more than met her match in Jensen and they made a wonderful couple. Chessy didn't doubt for a single moment that Jensen was absolutely perfect for Kylie.

If only Chessy could say her own love life—her marriage—was as perfect as her friends'.

She let out a sigh and climbed out of her Mercedes SUV, glancing ruefully back at the seven-passenger vehicle. When Tate had surprised her with it, she'd wondered why on earth he'd gotten her something so big, but he'd looked at her with that charming, devilish twinkle in his eyes and told her that it was the perfect car to hold their children. The children they used to talk about having—it had been a frequent topic early in their marriage. They'd spoken of their dreams of a large family and a house full of children, love and laughter. But more recently, Tate had been unwilling to broach the subject of having children.

He was still building his business after going out on his own and having his partner bail on him. He wanted to wait until things were more stable and he was established before having children. But Chessy wondered quietly if that day would ever come. She hadn't had the courage to broach the subject in the last year.

She felt as though Tate was slipping further and further away from her, his career taking over, and she was second or even third or God only knew how far down his priority list she currently was.

"For God's sake, Chessy. Quit being a drama queen. It's not that bad. Tate loves you. You love him. You just have to be patient and see this through. Everything will work out," she scolded herself aloud.

She braced herself to greet her friends as she entered the restaurant and made certain her expression contained none of her dour thoughts. The last thing she wanted was to worry them more than they already were. They'd known for months that things weren't as they should be. She saw the looks passed between them when they thought she wasn't aware. But she missed nothing. Not the worried looks. Not the doubt in her friends' eyes. She knew they were deeply concerned about hers and Tate's relationship. But both women were *happy*. Deliriously so. And Chessy didn't want to drag them down into the mire of her own unhappiness.

She was the "bubbly" one of the group. The one everyone always counted on for good cheer, the happy spark. Except she was absolutely horrible at concealing her emotions. Good or bad, she was utterly transparent. When she was happy, she was really happy. Exuberant. Bubbly. Sparkling even, as her friends often told her. The problem with that was when she *wasn't* happy, she was an open book for her friends to see right through any sort of façade, and no amount of acting ever fooled them for a second.

Still, she gathered herself and pasted on her brightest smile, which made her cheeks ache with effort as she walked up to the booth Kylie and Joss already occupied.

"Thank God you're here!" Kylie exclaimed, immediately grabbing Chessy's hand and dragging her into the curved booth beside her. "Joss is practically glowing and she has that 'I've got a secret' look in her eyes, but she *refused* to spill until you arrived."

Chessy plopped down, having been yanked into the seat by Kylie, and grinned at Kylie's outrage that Joss would hold out on her until Chessy arrived. Some of her earlier ache dissolved, because how could it not when she was with her two best friends in the world? Just being in their presence lifted some of the sadness that seemed to have become a permanent fixture in her life lately.

"Ah okay, I see what Kylie's talking about now, Joss," Chessy said, studying her friend. "You've got a definite 'cat who got the cream' smug look on your face and you *are* positively glowing. So spill. The sisterhood is together and accounted for. Don't make me hurt you, because I can guarantee Kylie will be with me on this. Poor girl has already had to wait for me to get here. We'll sit on you if we have to, so spill already!"

Kylie nodded fervently and all eyes were glued to Joss's radiant smile that spread over her face, lighting up every delicate feature. It was a sucker punch to Chessy's stomach. Joss *did* look radiant. And so happy that it almost hurt Chessy to look at her. But there was no freaking way she'd ruin her friend's moment in the sun by allowing even a hint of her own unhappiness to cloud the gathering of best friends.

"Dash and I are pregnant," Joss said with unconcealed joy. "I'm pregnant," she amended, her face softening, eyes glowing with love and happiness. "We're having a baby!"

Kylie squealed and immediately threw her arms around Joss, hugging her tightly, ignoring startled looks from other restaurant patrons seated in close proximity to the women's booth.

Chessy immediately rose, though her stomach had plummeted, and rushed around since Kylie separated Joss and Chessy. She slid in on the other side of Joss and tugged her away from Kylie's fierce grasp.

"I'm so happy for you," Chessy whispered so she didn't have to choke the words out around the lump forming in her throat.

Joss hugged her back and then pulled away, her gaze piercing as she studied Chessy.

"Thank you," Joss said quietly. "Now perhaps you can tell us what's going on with you and why you look so unhappy. Is it Tate? Have things gotten worse?"

Chessy's heart sank. She should have known of all people she couldn't fool her best friends. And now that Joss was basking in the glow of her news—glorious news—and the realization of a long-time wish come true, the very last thing Chessy wanted to do was dampen the celebration.

She reached down, grasping Joss's hand and squeezing. "This is your moment to shine, girlfriend. We can talk about my woes another time. Right now we need to be toasting the mother-to-be and planning all the fun stuff like baby clothes and possible names! Oh my gosh, Kylie, you and I have to plan a kick-ass baby shower for Joss. The likes of which no one has ever seen. And we're so making the guys get involved. No wimping out because it's a girly activity."

Kylie and Joss exchanged looks, as they often did when they didn't think Chessy could see, and Chessy inwardly winced that she was evidently the cause of so much worry for her friends.

"Do you honestly think for one moment that I would be so wrapped up in the wonderful news of my pregnancy that it would override everything else?" Joss asked, clear reprimand in her tone, though it was the gentlest of reprimands.

Joss was hardly the kind of woman who ever came across bitchy or mean-spirited. She simply didn't have it in her. She was kindness personified and had the biggest, most forgiving heart of anyone Chessy had ever known in her life.

Chessy held up her hands. "I know, hon. I know. Believe me, I do. I'd just rather not rehash it all on a day we should be celebrating. It's not like anything has changed. It's just the same old story and I'm just being a whiny, needy baby. Things will get better."

Joss lowered her voice, her eyes filling with love, so much love, for her best friend that it nearly brought tears to Chessy's eyes.

"I know it had to be hard to hear that I'm pregnant," Joss said gently. "I know you've wanted children. That it was once what you and Tate both wanted and that you still do but he's the one wanting to hold off now. And now you've even questioned the motives for wanting a child now. We've had that discussion recently and agreed that until you and Tate get beyond this current rough patch that a baby would only complicate matters."

Chessy wasn't going to lie to the women she loved most in the world. Her best friends. Her sisters. Her rocks.

"I won't say it doesn't sting a little. Okay, a lot," she amended when she caught sight of the look Kylie shot her. One that said *you aren't fooling anyone, girlfriend.* "It's no secret that I've wanted children. A big family. I want what I was never given as a child. I want a brood of little ones that are secure in the fact that they are loved and wanted with every single part of my heart and soul."

"You want for them what your parents never gave you," Kylie said softly.

Chessy shot her a look of understanding. Chessy and Kylie had one thing in common as far as childhoods went. They were both unwanted, but the similarities ended there. Kylie had suffered a horrific, abusive childhood at the hands of the monster that was her father.

Chessy could never say she was abused, physically or verbally. She simply didn't . . . exist. Not to her parents. Chessy had been a very unplanned child to parents who'd never intended to have children. And as such, they didn't change their lives to adjust to having a child. They simply went on as before, Chessy being an unwanted nuisance. Her childhood had been one of neglect, not abuse, but then some would argue that neglect was indeed a form of abuse. Chessy hadn't been physically harmed, but emotionally? Definitely.

Tate knew of Chessy's childhood, her memories of being lonely and overlooked. It had infuriated him and he'd vowed she'd never feel that way with him. Until . . . now. He'd always made it his priority to put her first. Her wants, her needs, her desires, some of which she expressed, but mostly Tate intuitively understood and satisfied them for her without prompting. He often fulfilled needs she hadn't even realized she had at the time. He'd always gone above and beyond to give her all the things she'd lacked as a child.

God, she wanted that back. She wanted her husband back. Wanted for things to be the way they had been before he'd branched out on his own, forming his own financial planning company with a partner who'd then bailed, leaving him to meet the needs of all their clients.

And in her heart, she knew that Tate was still acting on his desire to see to her every need. He never wanted her to lack for anything he could provide. Financially. She knew his heart was in the right place, but money wasn't what Chessy wanted most. Financial security was all well and fine, but at the expense of her marriage? She just wanted her husband back. The one who saw to her *emotional* needs above all else. *Not* her financial needs. Because money was no substitute for love, no substitute for the man she adored beyond reason. How could she get him to understand that without causing a rift between them? One that may not be able to be repaired. And she simply couldn't countenance that. Nothing was worth losing Tate over. Certainly not her ridiculous insecurities and needy, clingy demands that seemed insignificant in the larger picture. Most women would be grateful for a husband who busted his ass every single day to provide for his wife. How to explain that material things meant nothing to her if they came at the expense of her marriage and the broadening gap forming between them?

"Sweetie, what is going on with you and Tate?" Joss asked, concern creasing her forehead. "We've discussed this so many times and yet I keep getting the feeling that you aren't telling us the whole truth. That you're holding back at least a part of what you're feeling and experiencing. Are you still worried he's cheating on you?"

Chessy sucked in her breath. The very thought, however fleeting it may be, that Tate would ever cheat on her filled her with such agony that she couldn't dwell on it for the pain it caused her. She truly regretted that moment of weakness when she'd shared that fear with her best friends, no matter how little she truly believed it.

"I know he loves me," Chessy said firmly. "I know he wouldn't cheat. He has too much honor. If he wanted another woman, I know he'd be forthright with me and just ask for a divorce."

God, the word divorce sent waves of agony through her heart and soul even though she knew it wouldn't come to that. But panic quaked through her at the very *idea* of her marriage truly ending. It wasn't a thought she could even linger over because of the devastation it caused her.

"But love isn't about causing pain for the person you care about," Kylie quietly inserted.

Lord knew Kylie recently had become very acquainted with pain and love and her own brush with the end of a relationship. If she hadn't kicked Jensen's ass for ending things with Kylie "for her own good" they'd probably still be apart and absolutely miserable without one another.

"He doesn't know he's hurting me because I haven't told him," Chessy said softly. "That's on me. He can't be expected to fix something if he doesn't know the problem *or* the solution. I admit I'm being a coward. A part of me wants to just beg him to stop focusing on business, tell him that I don't care about having a lot of money in the bank, while the other part of me thinks that if I just suck it up and ride it out a little longer things will resolve themselves and I'll have my husband back and everything will go back to the way it used to be."

Joss and Kylie both sighed in resignation. It wasn't as if they hadn't discussed this subject a half a dozen times already. Chessy knew that neither agreed with her thinking or approach to the problem but they loved her and supported her unconditionally. And for that she loved them beyond reason.

Part of her recognized that they had a *right* to be frustrated with her. They listened to her whine about a problem she herself wasn't willing to address, much less try to fix. Chessy knew she had her head firmly in the sand and was in denial over the state of her marriage, but to even contemplate any other alternative meant she had to admit that her marriage was in trouble. And she wasn't prepared to do that. Yet.

"Our anniversary is this Friday," Chessy said, purposely brightening her tone in an effort to relieve the somber turn of the conversation. "Tate has promised me an intimate dinner at the restaurant where we always have our anniversary dinner. No cell phones. No business. He plans to take off early and he said the entire weekend is ours. And," she said, drawing out the word, "he says he has very distinct plans for after dinner, so I can hardly wait. I think having this, one weekend where it's just us, will do wonders for my insecurities and silliness. I never should have let it get to this point. I recognize that I'm at fault for not communicating better with Tate, for not telling him of my unhappiness. But this weekend, when it's just the two of us and our focus is solely on us, I absolutely plan to talk to him about . . . everything."

Kylie and Joss both wore identical looks of relief.

"That's wonderful, sweetie," Joss said.

"I'm so glad you're taking this step," Kylie said. "I agree with you. A weekend with just the two of you is probably exactly what you need to feel better about everything. And talking to him and opening up about the way you've been feeling is a huge step in the right direction. I can't imagine Tate not moving heaven and earth to make you happy again. But as you said yourself, he has to know about the problem if he's going to be able to fix it."

Chessy smiled, her heart lightening and some of the ache slipping away as she soaked in the healing balm of her girlfriends' unfettered, unconditional love. God only knew Chessy was usually the one freely dispensing advice and threatening to kick Joss and Kylie's asses over certain matters when it came to their happiness. It made her a flaming hypocrite that she wasn't taking a dose of the same medicine she dished out to her friends. And that she was quick to tell them what they should do but then shrugged off their advice. *Sound* advice to boot.

Ah well, no more. She was resolving to have the best anniversary weekend ever. She and Tate would rediscover the love she knew they still shared. They'd spend a wonderful weekend together loving and laughing and she would talk to him about her growing unhappiness. It was time for her to stop being a spineless guppy and take a stand when it came to her own life and relationship with a man she loved with all her heart and soul.

TWO

THAT Friday, Chessy sat at the table Tate had reserved at the restaurant for their anniversary dinner, resisting the urge to look at her watch. There were a million reasons Tate could be late. Traffic. Difficulty in breaking free from work. She didn't mind any of it as long as he showed up and their weekend began, just as he'd promised her.

In the beginning of their five-year marriage, Tate had always gone the extra mile to make it a special day for her. One year, they'd eaten here and then he'd taken her home, told her to pack a bag, that they were going to the Bora Bora for an entire week.

She still smiled over the memory of that. Her bubbly excitement over Tate arranging such a wonderful surprise for her. He'd taken her on a reenactment of their honeymoon. Same bungalow set out over the water. Same honeymoon bed. They'd spent most of that entire week in bed, only venturing out to eat or to play in the water.

But in the last two years there'd been no time for such frivolities. They still ate at the same restaurant, but on Monday morning it had been off to work for him as usual.

She glanced at her watch again, breathing a small sigh of relief. He wasn't late. She was merely a few minutes early. Deciding she'd take a quick trip to the ladies room to double check her appearance, she rose and hurried to the bathroom.

She'd paid extra attention to her makeup and hair and had donned a sexy, slinky dress she knew would get a rise out of Tate. With any luck he wouldn't be able to take his eyes off her during the entire meal and his gaze would smolder with all the things he'd do to her once they arrived home.

She shivered in delight as she retouched her lip gloss and patted her upswept hair. Little curly tendrils floated carelessly down her neck and against her cheek. She knew without false modesty that she looked her absolute best.

Hoping that Tate would be at the table when she returned, she closed her clutch and rushed back, her heart sinking when she saw his chair still unoccupied. She slowly retook her seat, scanning the interior to see if he was arriving.

She'd just let out a heavy sigh when her cell phone vibrated. Hoping it was Tate, she opened her clutch and lunged for it. As she glanced at the incoming name she saw it was indeed Tate.

"Tate? Where are you?" she asked breathlessly, trying to keep an accusing note from her voice.

"I'm sorry, my girl." His deep-timbered voice slid like silk over her ears and she got a delicious thrill every time he called her "my girl." "I just got caught up in a last-minute client call but I'm on my way out the door. Give me twenty depending on traffic and I'll meet you there. If you like go ahead and order for us. You know my preference. By the time the food is served, I'll be there."

Chessy couldn't help the frown that curved her lips downward. That wasn't the way things worked in their relationship. Not at all. Tate was her Dominant. Not just her Dominant but her lover, her husband, the man she adored—and trusted—with all her heart.

He always made the decisions. He always ordered her food. Her heart gave a guilty twinge. She was acting like a petulant, pouty two-year-old. He merely didn't want to hold up their dinner, but still, there was a small part of her that registered that lately, with recurring frequency, he'd drifted away from the dominance he'd always held over her. More and more she was forced to act on her own. Make the decisions that Tate always made.

It sounded silly to anyone looking in from the outside. Like she wasn't capable of making her own decisions and was some helpless twit, lost without her husband. But she *willingly* ceded power to Tate in their relationship. He made her feel safe. Cherished. Utterly adored because he took care of her every need. Or at least he used to.

Their relationship—their lifestyle—was her choice. Perhaps the biggest choice of her life. She was an intelligent, smart woman. She had no reservations when it came to know-ing what she was capable of. But she chose to give up power to her Dominant, and submissiveness wasn't for the weak. Not at all. She knew she wielded every bit as much power in her marriage to Tate as he did. Just in a different way.

"I'll take care of it," she said softly. "Drive safe. I can't wait to see you so we can kick off our anniversary and have an entire weekend to ourselves. It's been so long, Tate. I can't tell you how much I need this. How much I need *you*."

There was a lengthy pause and she cursed herself for already putting a damper on the evening before it ever began. It was as if he had no idea what to say in response to what amounted to a *plea*.

"I love you. See you in a minute," she said brightly, to cover up the awkwardness caused by her passionate, needy sound-ing outburst. And, well, the words were truth. She *did* need him. She needed her husband back, even if it was only for one weekend before things went back to the same day-to-day routine.

"I love my girl too," he said gruffly. "Be there as quick as I can."

When she ended the call, her stomach felt as though it had lead in it. And she didn't understand why. He was only going to be twenty minutes late. Thank God he was making it at all. When the phone had vibrated, she'd fully expected him to tell her he couldn't make it. That something had come up and he was cancelling. On their anniversary of all nights.

Was this what their marriage had come to? Her always

expecting the worst? But in her defense, that's precisely what she'd gotten over the last two years. Ever since his partner had bowed out and Tate had to take over the entire client load, Tate had been determined to step up and not lose a single client.

To date, he'd only lost one and he wanted to keep it that way. Which meant being called out at all hours of the day. Clients wanting to meet with him. Or calling him in panic after a bad day in the stock market. It seemed to never end.

In the beginning, Tate had wanted Chessy to accompany him to his dinners with his clients. Had wanted her to play the consummate hostess. They'd even had small dinner parties at their house that Chessy had arranged with Joss's help since Joss was such an amazing cook.

But lately? He hadn't asked her to accompany him for anything. He'd made an offhand remark that it was becoming too much for her and that he didn't want his job to consume them *both*. At the time Chessy had taken it as a sign of his caring. That he wanted to take care of her and not put her in high-pressure situations. But marriage was all about partnership, wasn't it?

She didn't think she'd ever failed Tate or embarrassed him, but now that paranoid side of her wondered just that. If he was somehow ashamed of her, that she was *too* outgoing, *too* bubbly for the staid, moneyed clients he catered to. His not wanting her to be a part of him courting and wining and dining his clients had ended up being yet another rejection, one that at the time hadn't bothered her, but in retrospect made her heart clench. Was Tate growing tired of their marriage?

Did she no longer satisfy him? Had she done something to cause him to lose faith in her? Their relationship? The not knowing was eating her up on the inside and it was growing harder and harder to cover up her growing unhappiness with a bright smile and words of understanding. She was lying to her friends, even though she knew they saw right through her façade. But the simple fact that she *was* lying, keeping so much locked inside her, made her feel like the ultimate fraud.

She swallowed the quick knot in her throat, determined she would not cry tonight and ruin her carefully applied makeup. Joss and Kylie had both come over to lend advice and help her prepare for her anniversary night. She'd needed their support because she was starting to doubt herself and she hated that.

Just because she chose to surrender her submission to Tate didn't make her a brainless twit unable to perform the simplest task unless he was there to direct her. But him always being there, taking care of her, cherishing her, had become her safety net. She knew she'd never fall without him there to catch her. There was comfort in that knowledge. It gave her a sense of security that she'd come to rely on. And lately? She felt like she was operating without that safety net. It was a sad testament of her marriage that she saw more of Kylie and Joss and was more in tune with *their* relationships than she was with her own!

She motioned for the waiter after studying the menu. The truth was she wasn't that hungry and her nerves were on edge because she absolutely planned to address her growing unhappiness with Tate this weekend and she had *no* idea how that would go over.

One part of her thought he'd be horrified that he wasn't providing what she needed. Another part of her feared he'd be
angry with her for not "understanding" the sacrifices he was
making in order to make them financially secure. It was a coin
flip and it saddened her that she was so out of touch with Tate's
thought processes that she had no idea which way he'd go. She
liked to think that he would be understanding and make the
effort to spend more time with her. But the not knowing was
killing her.

The waiter promptly appeared at her table, and in a low
voice barely above cracking, she placed hers and Tate's orders
and asked for a bottle of their favorite wine. A sparkling white
they drank every year on their anniversary. They'd discovered it on their honeymoon and had vowed to commemorate
each year by toasting to an even better next year.

So why did she feel the weight of the world on her shoulders and feel so fatalistic? Why did the last two years of toasting to a "better year to come" make her feel like it had been a
dismal failure, because the ensuing year wasn't better. It had
only grown progressively worse.

She'd never be so stupid as to say it couldn't get any worse,
because it could. What if Tate reacted to her addressing her
own unhappiness by saying he was equally unhappy and
that he wanted out of their marriage? That was the ultimate
worst that could happen, so things could most certainly get
worse, though at this point she wondered if they were even
truly married in their hearts anymore.

Married people didn't operate like they did. At least not

the marriages she was acquainted with. Or rather the relationships. Were Joss and Dash and Kylie and Jensen the excep-
tions to the rule? Or were they the norm? Because Chessy's
marriage didn't even come close to resembling the adoring,
tight-knit couples she was friends with. And she'd never really
looked beyond them because . . . well . . . she was afraid to.
Because she was afraid of what she might discover. So she'd
adopted a head-in-the-sand approach and that wasn't getting
her anywhere at all. It was only making her more miserable.

She refused to look at her watch. Instead she drank in
the occupants of the room and played her favorite people-
watching game, trying to guess the status of the people enjoying their meals.

She picked out one argument that appeared to be in full
swing. Their voices rose before the woman loudly shushed her
significant other and then looked around in embarrassment to
make sure they weren't being observed. Chessy quickly averted
her gaze, not wanting to add to the poor woman's obvious discomfort.

A smile softened her face when she took in an elderly couple holding hands, their arms resting on the table as they
toasted one another with their free hands. Then the older man
leaned in to kiss his wife and Chessy's heart squeezed.

It wasn't until the food arrived at the table that Chessy realized so much time had gone by. She hastily glanced at her
watch to realize that over thirty minutes had passed. She'd purposely waited a bit before placing the order, hoping beyond
hope that Tate would arrive before the food got there.

The waiter gave her a look of sympathy that nearly sent Chessy right over the edge. She smiled brightly. "My husband will be here in a few minutes. Before the food gets cold for sure."

The waiter shrugged as if it didn't matter to him one way or another. He set her plate in front of her and then arranged Tate's across the table. As soon as he left, Chessy reached over and pulled the plate to the chair sitting catty corner to her.

She and Tate always sat next to one another. Never across the table where they couldn't touch, couldn't speak intimately without fear of being overheard.

She sat, feeling conspicuous because the food was in front of her, the smell wafting tantalizingly through her nostrils. Where was Tate?

She pulled out her phone, checking for texts since she'd silenced it once she entered the restaurant. She could very well have missed the vibration signaling an incoming call or text.

There was nothing. Taking a deep breath, she dialed his number and waited as it rang. She frowned when he didn't immediately pick up. Then her gut clenched when it went to voice mail.

Had something horrible happened? Had he been in an accident? He *never* let her calls go to voice mail. Not that she called him much during the day. She knew how busy he was and she didn't want to appear clingy or needy. Even if she was just that. Needing. She needed her husband back.

Her anxiety level reached epic proportions while she watched the food grow colder as more time passed. She should just eat. Let him eat alone if and when he got there. She refused to believe that he could be hurt somewhere, needing help, and she was here waiting for him.

When an hour passed, the waiter hovered, obviously waiting for her to vacate. This was a popular restaurant and they were always full on reservations. An hour was more than enough time to eat and even enjoy dessert and yet her husband wasn't here and two plates of food, wasted, sat in front of her and her stomach was too tied up in knots to even take one bite. She feared if she even tasted the entrée that she'd have to bolt for the bathroom and heave into the toilet.

Tears stung her eyes. Worry warred with anger. The only excuse for being over an hour late when he had said twenty minutes at the most was that he had been in an accident or something equally horrible.

She dug into her clutch, counting out the cash she had, praying she had enough. She didn't have time nor did she want to wait on the waiter to collect her credit card and have to spend precious minutes swiping and then signing the bill.

To her relief she had the cash and even enough for a tip, though the waiter had done little but deliver their food. Uneaten food. She tossed the cash down on the table and strode rapidly to the door, tears pooling in her eyes at Tate's betrayal.

Then she felt guilty because he could have been in an accident. He could be in a hospital somewhere, but why wouldn't she have received a call?

She nearly tripped when the elegant carpet turned into slick marble that led past the upscale bar and to the exit. She was almost to the door when something caught her attention out of the corner of her eye.

She stopped in absolute shock, her mouth open as she stared—at *Tate*. In the bar with a woman, having a drink and smiling broadly at her. And the woman was stunning. Tall, thin, elegant. Obviously of money, and she was touching Chessy's husband, her hand lightly resting on his arm in a distinctly intimate fashion.

God, he was with a woman in the same restaurant that he was supposed to be having his anniversary dinner with his wife. How *dare* he flaunt this woman in this restaurant, *their* restaurant.

Tears flooded her eyes. She was about to turn to flee when Tate looked up, his expression one of shock. Not guilt. It was remorse. She could see him curse, his lips moving as he picked up his wrist to check his watch.

Then he started toward her and she finally made her legs move, momentarily paralyzed by grief and humiliation. She all but ran for the exit, not caring that she'd taken a taxi to the restaurant because she'd planned to ride home with Tate. She had a set of his keys. He could walk for all she cared.

Fury enveloped her even as tears poured down her face, clouding her vision. She hit the parking lot at a dead run, bolting past the attendant. She could see his Escalade in the roped-off area of the valet parking.

"Chessy!"

She flinched when Tate roared her name. But she kept running, thanking God she'd worn a strappy pair of sandals instead of high heels or she'd make an ass of herself and face-plant right in the parking lot.

"Chessy! Godamnit, stop! You can't drive in your condition. Please, just stop and listen to me, please!"

Chessy made it to his vehicle, hitting the automatic door unlock on the key chain. She made it to the door and flung it open, only to have Tate grab the door and reach for her arm.

She whirled, tears streaming down her face. Tate always hated to see her cry. In the past it would have slayed him to ever see her cry. But tonight he looked desperate, and sincere regret lined his face. But at this point, it was too late for regret. He'd pushed her to her limit and there was no going back. She was done.

"Get away from me," she choked out.

She'd never given orders to Tate. Ever. That was *his* role. She was the submissive. He was the Dominant. But now she felt the stirrings of a power exchange. She was taking charge and to hell with what he wanted.

She tried to slide into the driver's seat but Tate pulled her out, cradling her carefully in his arms, as if he expected her to fight. But she had enough pride that she wasn't going to cause more of a scene in a public parking lot than she already had. She went stiff as a board, refusing to meet his gaze as he walked around to the passenger side and deposited her into the seat, pulling the seat belt over her and securing it with quick, brusque movements. Then he looked her directly in the eyes, his gaze hard and unyielding. A look she would have died for, one she'd craved for such a long time. Why did he have to finally haul out his dominance when he'd royally fucked up and she no longer cared?

"Don't you dare move," he growled.

Usually such a tone would have Chessy quivering in anticipation. It was a tone he used when he was commanding her. Owning her. Using her body as his own. His possession. To do with as he liked. But now? She was just pissed enough to tell him to shove it up his ass.

She stared woodenly through the windshield as Tate carefully disengaged the keys from her hand and then closed her door. In a matter of seconds he was in the driver's seat starting the engine, almost as if he were afraid she'd leap from the car. And she'd given it serious consideration, but then she'd have to figure out a way home, which meant having the restaurant call her a cab, or she could call Joss or Kylie. Either would come at a moment's notice.

But then she would be faced with the humiliating fact that her best friends would know her anniversary had been a complete disaster. Hell, for that matter they may have suspected it would be a cluster fuck from the very start. It wasn't as if they hadn't expressed enough concern over Chessy's faltering relationship with her husband.

Tate pulled out of the parking lot.

"Please don't cry, Chessy," he said softly. "I'm so damn sorry. Time got away from me."

"Who was she?" Chessy asked coldly, ignoring his words

and his apology. Words meant nothing at this point. Actions spoke far more clearly than words, and his actions had been reprehensible in her mind.

Tate gave her a startled look. "She's a potential client. A very important potential client, one I'd like to get on board as quickly as possible. She wanted to meet face-to-face, and I arranged to meet her at the bar of the restaurant so that when we finished I could have dinner with you."

"Yes, well, dinner was delivered and perfectly cold and you were an hour late," Chessy said in an icy tone.

"What's going on with my girl?" Tate asked softly. "You've been different lately."

She gave him her best "duh" look and then pinned him with a piercing stare. "Wow. Observant of you, Tate. I've been different for an entire year and you just now notice? At a time you missed our anniversary dinner because you were schmoozing some rich floozy in the bar of the restaurant we were supposed to have dinner in. Think about that for a moment, Tate, and imagine if the roles were reversed and you were sitting there over cold entrees and then you saw me in the bar of the same restaurant with another man."

His gaze grew hard and he nearly growled. "I'll never let another man touch you unless I command it."

Chessy wanted to weep at what they'd lost. That he'd bring up a kink they both enjoyed and hadn't participated in for two years. Two long years. And in the last year, he'd given up any semblance of dominance. It was like an alien had invaded his body and her Tate was gone.

"I'm not happy," she said, finally getting to the heart of the matter. "I haven't been happy for a long time."

Tate looked shocked. Genuinely and utterly shocked. "What are you saying?" he asked hoarsely. "Are you telling me you want out of our marriage?"

He looked so horrified that for a brief moment she had hope, but then she remembered all the missed dates, him leaving early at gatherings of their friends because someone had called. And he'd missed his anniversary dinner because he was wining and courting a potential client.

Potential client her ass. That woman was on the prowl and Chessy damn well knew it. She was a woman and she clearly recognized the signals the woman was giving off. And Tate had done nothing to ward her off. Hadn't avoid her touch. Tate would lose his shit if another man took such liberties with her unless Tate commanded him to do so. To pleasure her while he watched. Always in control. She couldn't even remember the last time they'd been to The House.

The House was a place where people could indulge in any hedonistic fantasy. No judgment. No condemnation. Damon Roche, a very wealthy businessman, owned The House and he was very discerning when it came to membership. Hell, for all Chessy knew their membership had expired or they'd been taken off the guest list since they hadn't been in two years.

She took in a deep breath. Damn it, this was not how she'd envisioned having this talk with Tate. She'd wanted to have a wonderful anniversary dinner followed by a night of love-making. At this point she wouldn't have even cared if it

involved dominance. She just wanted that intimate connection to her husband back.

And then, after a wonderful weekend, with no cell phones,
business shit or anything else, she'd wanted to very carefully
broach the subject of her growing unhappiness.

Damn him for forcing her hand after the debacle that was
their anniversary.

"I don't want out of our marriage, Tate. I want our marriage to *change*," she said firmly, proud that she was able to lay
it out without faltering or breaking down into tears.

Tate gave her another look filled with utter confusion and
then swore when he nearly veered into the other lane. He yanked
the wheel, righting them and avoiding a collision—barely.

"Just drive," she said wearily. "This isn't something we
should be discussing in a damn car. We'll talk about it when
we get home."

She wanted to weep over the fact that she was giving all
the commands. She was issuing the orders. This wasn't the
way their relationship was supposed to work and yet he was
forcing her to take control. She could positively feel the power
shift in their relationship and it wasn't something that gave
her any satisfaction.

THREE

TATE pulled into the driveway of their house that was in an exclusive gated community in a suburb of Houston. He glanced sideways at Chessy, something he'd been doing all the way home despite her short directive to just drive and they'd talk later.

The evidence of tears—more tears than just from the restaurant, which meant she'd been crying on the way home—ravaged her delicate features. It was like being sucker punched and having no idea how to respond to the attack.

He was absolutely useless when Chessy cried. He hated to see her unhappy and he'd move heaven and earth to fix whatever was making her unhappy.

But hell, apparently it was *him* who was making her unhappy. What the hell did he do about *that*? He was utterly baffled by Chessy's outburst. For one horrible moment he'd thought she was telling him she wanted a divorce.

He hadn't been able to breathe for the terror gripping him. The thought of being without Chessy? It didn't bear thinking about.

"Come inside so we can talk, baby," he said in a low voice that was almost pleading. Hell, it *was* pleading. He was damn near begging.

She stared ahead, her gaze fixed on the windshield, never wavering. It was like looking at an ice sculpture.

"Chessy," he prompted. "Please come inside with me. There's a lot I don't understand right now. I need my girl to talk to me so I can fix this."

Slowly she turned, her eyes swamped with so much hurt that an invisible hand clutched Tate by the throat and squeezed until he could barely breathe. Where had things gone wrong? How could he not have seen this coming?

Yes, he'd noticed that she'd been different in the past year, but she'd never given him any hint that she was unhappy or that he wasn't satisfying her. She always had a bright smile, warm with love for him. She was always understanding when he was called away for business when they were together. Her difference had been a moment's puzzlement quickly swept aside by her sunny smile and sweet disposition.

Had it all been a lie? Or was he just completely blind to his wife's dissatisfaction?

"Do you *want* to fix it?" she asked in a challenging tone. "Seriously, Tate. Do you even care? Do you want to fix what's wrong or do you just want things to continue on like normal? You leaving get-togethers with our friends. You receiving phone calls at all hours of the evening—after work, mind you. We can't even make love for that damn phone going off, and you're so tied to it that one would think if you actually let it go for an hour that the world would end."

Tate sucked in his breath at the bitterness in her voice. The hurt crowding into her face and bleeding over into her impassioned statement. Or rather her question. Did he want to fix it? Of course he did. But first he had to know what the hell he was supposed to fix.

He reached across the seat to take her hand, half afraid— okay a lot afraid—that she'd recoil, that she would refuse to let him touch her. She went rigid but didn't yank her hand away. He gently pried her fingers apart with his thumb and then laced their hands before lifting hers to his mouth as he leaned over.

"Listen to me, baby. I love you. You mean the world to me. Always have. Do I want to fix things? Damn right, I do. But first I have to know what I'm up against. And that means that we have to go inside and you have to talk to me. Will you do that, please?"

His words felt all wrong. His entire demeanor since the night had ended in shambles had not been him. Nor was it indicative of his relationship with Chessy. She was his. In every way that counted. She'd gifted him with her absolute submission, and as her Dominant—and the man who loved her with all his heart—his responsibility was to cherish her, protect her gift, ensure her happiness.

He felt like a complete failure. He hadn't been dominant tonight. Chessy had been in control, dishing out commands to him when he was usually the one giving her instructions. It was the way their relationship worked. Always had.

And yet tonight? Hell, thinking back, it went way beyond just tonight. When was the last time he'd truly exerted his dominance? He used to control every aspect of Chessy's life. It may seem extreme to someone on the outside looking in, but it was what worked for them. He wanted her submission and she wanted his dominance. She'd never shied away from his control. Never protested. Never gave any sign she was anything but happy with their agreement.

But when had he last demonstrated that dominance?

It was a sad testament that he couldn't even remember. Couldn't point to a time or moment over the last year when he'd acted as her Dominant.

The pieces were coming together in his mind, and he didn't like what he was seeing. He hated the idea that he'd failed Chessy. Miserably. She was unhappy, and his girl was always happy. She lit up a room like a million rays of sunshine. She had such a tender, loving heart and she spread that love to everyone she encountered.

People were always at ease with Chessy. It was why he'd made certain to bring her to dinners with prospective and current clients because she made others relax, be more open. She was like a magnet, drawing people to her effervescent personality. Later he'd worried that keeping up with his pace was too much for her, and he never wanted her to feel the pressures of his job. That was his to bear. Never hers. So he'd told her he wanted her to back off. Spend time with her friends instead of always planning a social gathering.

And now the light had gone out in her beautiful eyes. All because of him and his dismal failure to provide for her needs.

He tightened his grip on Chessy's hand, waiting for her response. She was taking way too long to respond, her brow wrinkled as if she was waging some kind of internal war. God, whatever it was, let him come out the victor and let her acquiesce to his plea to talk this out.

"I'll talk," Chessy finally said.

But her tone was fatalistic. Like she'd already decided the outcome after they discussed their relationship and why she was so unhappy. Had she lost that much faith in him? The idea devastated him.

"But it has to be in neutral territory," she added. "We have no business having sex with this wall between us. I don't want our physical attraction to hinder our discussion." Her gaze swept downward, sorrow creasing her face and tugging her lips into a sad frown. "That's assuming you even still want me," she said in a tone tinged with grief. "It's been so long since you've instigated any sort of sex that the reasonable conclusion is you no longer desire me or find me attractive."

Tate damn near swallowed his tongue as protests immediately formed on his lips. Goddamn it but there was so much wrong with her statements that he didn't even know where to begin.

They *never* used the word sex when it came to their love-making. *Never.* Sex was for people not emotionally involved to the degree Chessy and Tate were. At least that was his thinking on the matter.

And not want her? He was flabbergasted. What could he have possibly done to plant such a ridiculous notion in her head? She was the most beautiful woman in the world to him. Other women? Simply didn't exist. How could he want for more when he had a gorgeous, loving, generous, tender-hearted submissive wife he came home to every day?

Okay, so maybe they hadn't made love in a while. A long while. He winced inwardly again as he pondered and tried to remember the last time they had truly made love.

There had been hasty sessions. No buildup. No extended foreplay. Totally selfish on his part because he'd had sex with her and then he was off to work or to a meeting with a client.

Yes, he'd just used the word sex to describe their lovemaking. Because, well, what he'd done lately amounted to just that. Selfish sex. Not seeing properly to her needs. Not exerting his dominance. Something she didn't just want but *needed.* Yet another dismal example to mark on his growing list of failures.

"We'll talk wherever you want," he said around the knot in his throat. He was ceding power to her. A complete reversal of roles. He didn't like it one bit, and by the look on Chessy's face, neither did she.

But what was he supposed to do in this situation? It would make him a flaming asshole if he whipped out his dominance and forced her submission and then used his dominance to manipulate her.

The hell with that. He wanted her to have complete and utter control in *this* situation. He didn't want her to feel threatened by anything. He was laying himself open and putting himself at her feet if that's what it took to pull out everything she needed to say. It was apparent their relationship was in real trouble, and that Chessy had been unhappy for quite some time.

That gutted him.

"Let's go in then," he said in a neutral tone even though his heart was flayed open and fear—an alien sensation— gripped his entire body. He'd hit the panic button the moment his gaze had met Chessy's at the restaurant and he'd seen the utter devastation in her eyes. He'd known then that he'd pushed her too far. And what woman could blame her? On a night when his attention should have been focused solely on her and celebrating another year of marriage, he'd bailed to court a prospective client.

And he now realized just how that situation had to have looked to her. Him smiling and wining a beautiful woman just yards away from where his wife waited for him to show for their anniversary dinner. Food cold, her giving up, all because time had slipped away from him and the urgency of sealing the deal with a client had taken over his priorities. Yeah, he'd fucked up and now he had to work fast to pick up the pieces. Because it wasn't just tonight, though he realized it was likely the last straw for her. Her unhappiness extended for a lengthy period of time and he'd been blind to it all. Or perhaps a small part of him had known and he hadn't wanted to admit it because to do so would be admitting he'd failed her.

She didn't wait for him to come around and open her door. She simply pushed it open and quickly got out and started for the house, then hastily unlocked the door without looking back. But she wasn't fast enough that he didn't see the tears streaking down her cheeks.

Fuck.

He hurried after her, worried she'd give up on talking to him and shut him out completely. A part of him was terrified that she would go in and pack her stuff. Or his. She had to know he'd never let her move out. This was her house, her security. If anyone ever had to leave, it would be him, and God, he didn't even want to think about that happening.

Whatever was wrong between him and Chessy he would fix or die trying. She was his world. How could she not know that?

Because you haven't proved that to her lately, dumbass.

He shook off the self-chiding and walked into the sprawling living room with twenty-foot ceilings, and to his relief he saw Chessy standing at the liquor cabinet, her stance rigid as she poured a glass of . . . what the hell was she pouring? Chessy wasn't much of a drinker. She had wine with the girls and at get-togethers. It was something she and Kylie shared. Neither ever drank much. Kylie came from an abusive background with an alcoholic, misogynist father, but Chessy came from a much different background. Neglected. Not physically abused, but her childhood had shaped her, had given her insecurity about her place in the world. And he'd vowed never to make her feel like her parents had. Now he had to face the very real prospect that he'd broken that vow.

Chessy threw back the drink, swallowing in a big gulp, and then promptly coughed and sputtered. Tate was behind her in an instant, her perfume wafting tantalizingly in his nostrils.

The dress she'd chosen to wear was meant to seduce. She'd known, had he showed up for dinner, that he wouldn't have been able to keep his eyes off her. That he would have hurried them through their dinner so he could take her home and peel that delectable dress off her body and then take over as a Dominant to his submissive.

She'd made a lot of plans for their anniversary it would seem. He'd caught a glance of the open master bedroom on his way to the living room and all the equipment he used and had chosen by his own hand was lying neatly on the bed for his perusal. To pick and choose the instruments he would use this night. Until Tate had to fuck it all up by allowing what was supposed to be a very special night for his girl go completely down the drain. How the hell would he make this up to her?

When she heaved and coughed again, her eyes, already watering, kept watering as she tried to correct which pipe her drink had gone down.

Tate instantly began patting her back and then rubbing smooth circles around her back, massaging. "You okay, Chessy? What the hell were you drinking anyway?"

She shrugged. "I just grabbed the first bottle I saw and went with it."

Tate reached around her and grabbed the bottle at the very front where she'd carelessly shoved it back in.

"Jesus, Chessy, you don't need to hit the hard stuff in order to talk to me. Remember me? Your husband, but more than that, your best friend? When have you ever had to ply yourself with alcohol just to talk to me? Is it so bad?"

She burped and then covered her mouth. It amused Tate though. Chessy was the epitome of polite and discreet. She would have been mortified to ever burp in a public place. He just thought they were cute. Little "Chess burps" he called them since they weren't a complete blowing-out-the-windows kind.

"Because what I have to say isn't good," she said in a tone that told him the healthy dose of alcohol was already working its way down her body and loosening her tongue. Or at least he hoped so. But at the same time, *what* she said registered with him and froze his insides. Completely paralyzed him and his tongue seemed dry and swollen, impacting his ability to even speak.

Because what I have to say isn't good.

The words rang in his ears, like a continuous video feed endlessly cycling, repeating itself until he nearly shook his head to make it stop.

"Come and sit down on the sofa with me, Chessy. You don't need to be standing and pacing after downing that alcohol. We can work this out, baby. You have to know I love my girl more than anything in the world. Whatever it is, I swear we can work it out."

His impassioned words seem to hit her, and she stood, absorbing them. He could see the wheels turning in her mind, the uncertainty in her eyes, and worse, doubt. Doubt clouded her beautiful eyes, and that hurt him because he was used to her having complete faith in him. In their marriage and relationship.

This was new territory for Tate and he didn't like it one bit. In all other aspects of his life, he was decisive, take charge, take no prisoners. And until tonight, he would have believed that he was still Chessy's Dominant and that he was taking care of her needs.

"Chessy?" he prompted softly, reaching to touch her arm.

She flinched and visibly recoiled and he swore under his breath. When had she gotten to the point of not being able to bear his touch? Was he hurting her so badly that she couldn't be in the same room with him?

She turned, wobbling unsteadily as she headed for the sofa. He wouldn't even allow himself relief over that small victory because he knew he still had a veritable mountain to climb once they settled onto the sofa and Chessy poured her heart out.

If she would.

She sank onto the couch, her entire body sagging as a weary look entered her eyes. She looked defeated.

He went to her, sitting beside her. It killed him to maintain any distance but he was afraid of her rejection if he so much as touched her.

"Talk to me, baby," he encouraged softly. "Please. Give me a chance to fix this."

Her eyes watered and tears gathered rapidly as she finally turned her gaze to meet his.

"I'm not sure it *can* be fixed," she said, her voice choked with emotion. "I used to think it could be. I was certain everything would be all right. I told myself to just be patient. Let things ride out and everything would go back to normal when you were secure in your business. But I'm tired of waiting, Tate. I'm tired of faking a smile and saying 'it's okay' every time you have to dump me for a client when I'm bleeding on the inside. I've pretended for so long that it's become second nature and I can't do it anymore. I just can't."

The utter despair in her voice flayed open his heart. He caught his breath, unsure of even what to say to her. This wasn't a simple fix. Not something that could be worked out in one night or even two. Their relationship was in deep trouble, and he was only just now recognizing the magnitude of all he'd done to her over the past years.

"My friends look at me with pity," she continued on, her gaze falling away from his.

She stared forward, so much pain in her features that it was a physical hurt for him to witness.

"They know I'm terrible at faking happiness. They see through me and they know I'm unhappy. They know the situation with you is bad. Even Dash and Jensen are giving me pep talks, for God's sake. It's humiliating. And I don't know how to fix it. Now I don't even know if I can."

"Chessy, baby, don't say that. Nothing is unfixable. We can overcome this together, I swear it."

She yanked her head so that her eyes were boring straight into his. "You dumped me for a prospective client on our anniversary. I sat there for an hour over cold food after you *promised* me you'd be there, that you'd only be twenty minutes late, and you lied," she said accusingly.

Tate reared back with a frown. "What did I lie to you about?"

Her gaze was full of scorn and rising fury.

"You just don't get it, do you?" she raged. "You call me from work and say you were detained and that you'd be there in twenty minutes. You never said a damn word about meeting a client—a gorgeous female client who was all over you—at the same restaurant where your wife was sitting alone, waiting for her husband. You lied to me. Lies of omission are still lies. You tried to hide from me that you were entertaining a potential client on my goddamn anniversary and you stood there in the bar with her, smiling and laughing, while I was just a few yards away realizing that I'd been stood up by my husband on our anniversary. A day that used to mean something to you. And now? I have no idea where I stand with you, Tate."

"How long have you felt this way?" he asked softly, cutting to the heart of the matter.

He had to back up, before the debacle of tonight, and figure out where he'd gone wrong.

She sighed, a heavy sigh of weariness and defeat. "Forever? Or at least it seems that way. I can remember the way it used to be and I guess that's what upsets me the most. I know what we're capable of, but in the last two years, you've drifted further and further away from me, and while I used to be at the top of your list of priorities, I doubt I even rate in the top five at this point. You certainly don't act as though I have *any* priority in your life."

She turned to look at him, stark fear in her eyes. Dread, as though she were preparing herself for what she was going to say next.

She huffed out her breath and squared her shoulders before lifting her gaze to lock with his.

"Are you cheating on me, Tate? Is that what all the 'business calls' have been about? Is that where you're spending your time instead of with me?"

He was so flabbergasted by her question that momentarily all he was able to do was stare openmouthed at her. Then, he'd had enough. This could go on no longer. Sitting there while she tortured herself was killing him inch by inch. He was dying on the inside at her pain and agony. The *hell* he'd let her suffer under such misapprehensions any longer.

And then her next words stopped him cold, panic hitting him like a freight train. She lifted her head, all the life gone from her eyes. They were dull, defeated, like she was through fighting a fight he hadn't realized she was waging. Tears burned hot and jagged at the corners of his eyes, his jaw locked like iron, her words tiny darts right through his heart.

"I want out, Tate. I can't take *this* anymore."

FOUR

CHESSY clamped her hand over her mouth in horror as she blurted out the damning words and registered the shock and devastation in Tate's eyes as they hit him with the force of a punch in the face.

Damn it, she hadn't meant it how it came out! It sounded like she was asking for a divorce. One minute she was focusing on how to fix things—*Tate* was focusing on how to fix the problem—and she'd jumped from simply laying out her frustration to telling him she wanted out.

"You want a divorce?" Tate asked hoarsely, his eyes shiny with moisture. "God, Chessy, are you so desperately unhappy that you won't even give me a chance to fix what's wrong between us? I fucked up. I readily admit that. But you can't just quit on us like that. Unless . . ."

He drifted off, pain intensifying in his expression as though whatever he was thinking was the absolute worst and that he couldn't bear to put it into words.

He ran a hand raggedly through his hair and then down his face, wiping at his eyes.

"Unless you no longer love me, no longer want me," he ended in a whisper.

"That wasn't what I meant," Chessy said in a desperate voice.

God, this was such a complete disaster. Nothing was going the way she'd planned. But then nothing in the last two years had gone according to her plan.

"Then what *did* you mean?" Tate asked cautiously as he stared directly at her.

Her hands fluttered in front of her as she lifted them and then let them fall uselessly into her lap. She bit into her bottom lip, closing her eyes as she tried to sort through her frayed emotions. Her nerves were shot. The alcohol was making her fuzzy. And all she wanted to do was go to bed and bury her head underneath her pillow.

She wanted to call a redo of the entire day. Hell, the entire last two years.

"Chessy?"

She opened her eyes, trying to hold back more tears. She refused to be accused of manipulating him with the one thing he hated most: her tears of upset.

"I just meant that I wanted out of our current situation. I *hate* it!"

Her hands trembled against her thighs and she pressed her fingertips into her flesh, against the material of the sexy dress she'd worn for her husband tonight. A dress that had decidedly gone unnoticed. It had been a monumental waste of money.

Tate gently reached into her lap and tugged at both her hands until he pulled her upright from her position on the couch and forced her into closer proximity to him. His gaze was serious, his eyes grave and earnest as he stared at her.

"I love you, Chessy. I don't know how much you believe that right now, but I love you. I always have. That hasn't changed. It never will. But I need to know if you still love me, if I've killed your love for me with my neglect."

She closed her eyes again. Shouldn't she feel relieved by his impassioned declaration? Isn't this what she wanted? Affirmation that he did love her? Still wanted her?

But he'd neatly dodged the question of his fidelity, perhaps because there had been so much else addressed in her hysteria. She'd seen the shock in his eyes when she'd blurted that she wanted out, that she couldn't take it anymore.

Perhaps it had been swept aside in everything else that had been said, and she was too afraid to push him for an answer.

"I've always loved you," she said wearily. "But loving someone isn't enough when you aren't getting one hundred percent from them any longer. I feel as though I've been doing all the giving, making all the concessions, and that may sound selfish, but it's the way I feel. It may not be fair, but it's how I feel so there's nothing to be done about it."

"Baby," he said gently. "I can fix this. You just have to give me the *chance*. I never want to be without you. I'm sorry if I haven't made you feel that way lately."

"I'm too tired and strung out to have this discussion tonight," she said, her shoulders sagging. "I just want to go to bed. We can't have this conversation when I'm not on equal footing, and anything I say right now is likely to be all twisted up because I'm so upset, and that does neither of us any good."

She saw the frustration, the beginnings of a raw edge of temper, but he held it back, not reacting to her firm dictate. Or perhaps he saw how truly close to the edge she was and didn't want to push her right over.

He dropped his hands from hers and turned halfway from her, his gaze directed forward so his profile was presented.

"If that's what you want," he said in a low voice. "But we're going to talk tomorrow, Chessy. No more putting this off. It's been put off long enough and I realize that's my fault."

She got up from the couch before he could do or say anything to change her mind and headed for their bedroom to collect her things.

Tate watched his wife exit the living room in the direction of their bedroom. He breathed a sigh of relief. At least he could hold her tonight if nothing else. But damn it, he wasn't ready to call it quits for the night. There was so much left unsaid, unresolved. He wasn't the type to delay anything. And spending an entire night with his future hanging precariously on the edge of destruction? Not ideal.

But he couldn't afford to push Chessy. She was clearly at

her wits end. His fuck-up on their anniversary had pushed her too far. Finally too far. He was damn lucky she hadn't left his dumb ass already.

He hauled himself off the couch, mentally preparing for the night ahead. He hoped like hell that Chessy didn't close herself off to him, lie rigidly in bed or, even worse, cry herself to sleep. His heart would be cut to ribbons.

When he got to their bedroom door, he nearly bumped into her as she came out holding a pair of pajamas and her toiletries. He frowned, dread creeping up his spine.

"Where are you going?" he demanded.

She lifted her chin, forcing her gaze to meet his, a defiant look in her eyes. At least she wasn't crying. A small victory at best.

"I'm sleeping in the guest room tonight," she said quietly. "I need some time alone. To get my thoughts together before we get into this tomorrow."

It was like a fist to his gut. As she shoved past him and walked toward the guest room at the far end of the hallway, his breath left him and he couldn't squeeze air back into his lungs to save his life.

He stood there staring helplessly at her, knowing he should go after her and at the same time recognizing she'd given him an ultimatum of sorts. Hands off. Give her space.

Numbly, he walked into their bedroom, knowing he'd never sleep tonight. How could he when Chessy was sleeping down the hall from him and their marriage was in serious jeopardy?

They'd never slept apart. Not when they were in the same house. He'd gone on very few out-of-town business trips, most of them in the last couple of years, and that was the only time they'd damn well slept apart. Even then he'd always called her and they had talked on the phone way beyond bedtime. Because he'd missed her, missed having her in his bed, and he'd given up precious hours of sleep when he needed to be alert and aware the following morning for important meetings. Didn't that count for something?

A small part of him registered that he should be angry. That he'd made countless sacrifices to ensure that the woman he loved more than life had the world at her feet. And yet he couldn't bring himself to be anything but remorseful when he took in the extent of Chessy's unhappiness.

Chessy who usually lit up a room when she walked in. Chessy who had a smile that could knock a man to his knees a mile away. Chessy who'd always been nothing but sweet and understanding, smiling, eyes bright and supportive. Had he given her the same support she'd given him? The same understanding?

The answer to those questions bleakly registered a resounding "no" with him. He knew he'd fucked up and there was no way he could turn this back on her because she'd been nothing but loving and supportive of him even amid his neglect of her needs and wants.

He clenched the back of his neck and rubbed absently as he paced helplessly around their bedroom. He couldn't make himself shower or get ready for bed. All he could see was an empty bed, one she should be in, her scent enveloping him as he slept.

She was his security blanket. The only solid thing in his world where everything else was uncertain. He'd taken her for granted, had shit on her repeatedly over the last two years, and he'd never realized the extent of his neglect. Until now.

He'd done what he'd vowed never to do: Made her feel unwanted. Invisible. Just as her parents had done. Self-loathing ate at him, digging a yawning chasm in his heart and soul.

How could he possibly imagine a future without her? He was scared shitless. Fear like he'd never experienced gripped him by the balls and had a stranglehold on his throat.

Never, *never* would he forget the look in her eyes when he'd glanced up from his potential client—hell, what was her name even? He couldn't remember. All he could see running in an endless cycle was Chessy's stricken, devastated look when she'd seen him in the bar with *another* woman. On their anniversary night when Chessy had been forced to leave after cold food had gone wasted and she'd withstood the humiliation of being stood up. *On their anniversary.*

God, she'd asked if he was cheating on her, and he'd never even given her an answer. And even he had to admit how bad it looked for him. To have been with another woman in the same restaurant where his wife waited. What kind of flaming bastard did it make him to have pulled a stunt like that? At the time he'd thought it was the best way to have his cake and eat it too. Court a prospective client over drinks for fifteen minutes and then walk a few yards farther into the restaurant where his beautiful wife waited and then they'd kick off their anniversary weekend and have two whole days to love and celebrate another year.

Was she even now lying in bed in the guest room worrying and dying a little with each breath over the thought that he'd been unfaithful to her? He couldn't stand the idea of her thinking it a minute longer. He wanted to charge down there, confront her now and get everything out of the way so they *both* slept easier tonight.

But that was his selfish, inconsiderate side rearing its ugly head, and it was clear he'd been selfish for far too long in their relationship. She'd asked for time and, goddamn it, no matter how it ate at him, no matter that he wouldn't sleep a single minute, he'd give her the time she asked for. But in the morning? Things were going to be sorted out.

Then again, he knew this wasn't something to be resolved with one simple conversation or a few hours of heart-to-heart communication. It would take time and effort on his part to win back her trust—and her *love*. The two went hand in hand in his book. All solid marriages enjoyed both. Love *and* trust. One couldn't exist without the other. She hadn't really answered his question as to whether she still loved him. All she'd said was that she'd always loved him. Past tense.

That scared the holy hell out of him.

He couldn't imagine his life without Chessy. He loved her with his heart and soul. But he hadn't shown her his love in a very long time, and actions spoke far louder than words, a token "I love you" from time to time. He'd taken advantage of *her* love and he'd put her second, maybe even third or fourth on his priorities, a fact that shamed him to his soul and a mistake that would likely haunt him for the rest of his life.

FIVE

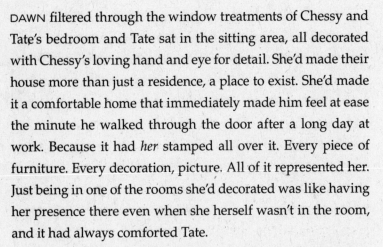

DAWN filtered through the window treatments of Chessy and Tate's bedroom and Tate sat in the sitting area, all decorated with Chessy's loving hand and eye for detail. She'd made their house more than just a residence, a place to exist. She'd made it a comfortable home that immediately made him feel at ease the minute he walked through the door after a long day at work. Because it had *her* stamped all over it. Every piece of furniture. Every decoration, picture. All of it represented her. Just being in one of the rooms she'd decorated was like having her presence there even when she herself wasn't in the room, and it had always comforted Tate.

More than that, just coming home to her was the best part of his day. And yet he hadn't let her know that in a long time.

He'd assumed she knew. And assumptions had gotten him into huge trouble.

He left their bedroom with purpose, having been up all night thinking of the best line of attack. It was the wrong word but this was most certainly going to be a battle. He'd be a fool not to think it would be the biggest battle of his life and so he'd planned accordingly.

He tiptoed down the hall and silently cracked the door of the guest room to peek in on Chessy. He saw her in bed, the covers kicked off and tangled at her feet as if she'd slept restlessly. He let his gaze travel up her body to her face, which was turned his way, and winced at her tear-ravaged face. Jesus, she had cried herself to sleep, if she'd slept at all until recently.

There were definite shadows under her eyes, bruises against her pale, beautiful skin.

Silently, he retreated, heading for the kitchen to make breakfast, the first in his plan of "attack," for lack of a better word to use. Wooing? Courting her again? Making her feel loved and special to him? Yeah, all of that.

Normally he'd serve her breakfast in bed, but she wasn't in *their* bed. And he didn't want her hiding there the entire day, refusing to face him, their marriage, and refusing to save it, because damn it, he wasn't giving up without one hell of a fight.

It was game on, and he'd had the better part of the night to reflect on all his mistakes. He planned to start rectifying them now.

He quickly cooked breakfast, her favorite. A cream cheese

bagel with scrambled eggs topped with cheese and skillet-fried ham all piled on the bagel to make a supreme breakfast.

He made himself one as well even though he wasn't remotely hungry, but he wanted a semblance of normalcy when he went to get her out of bed. She'd likely resist but it was time for him to take back the reins and right their relationship in the only way he knew how. Reassert his dominance, something he'd failed miserably on for a long damn time. He just hoped to hell he wasn't too late.

Not wanting the food to chill, he set their plates at the breakfast nook and quickly walked down the hall to the guest bedroom. When he eased the door open, he saw that she was awake but staring dully out the window, her gaze unfocused and tired, deep bruises underneath her eyes.

"Chessy," he said softly.

She blinked and turned her gaze to him, obviously surprised to see him standing there.

He walked into the bedroom and over to the bed, sitting on the edge close to where she lay. He trailed one hand through the loose curls that were in disarray over the pillow.

"I've made breakfast for us and then we need to talk. Get up. Don't bother getting dressed. Just come into the kitchen so we can eat."

He inserted firmness into his tone and her eyes widened at his obvious command.

She started to get up as if on autopilot, used to obeying his orders, but then she hesitated and dropped her gaze, sorrow swamping her features.

"Chessy, get up," he said in a more forceful tone. "Breakfast is getting cold."

When she lifted her head again, there was so much hope in her eyes that it broke his heart. This is what he hadn't been giving her. His dominance, his love, his absolute adoration of this woman. He could kill himself for causing her one ounce of pain. But all he could do was pick up the pieces and try like hell to put them all back together again.

He held out his hand to help her the rest of the way from bed. She quickly glanced at him, wary, but she hesitantly reached up and slipped her soft hand into his.

Heat immediately scorched up his arm, desire sliding up his spine and back down, spreading rapidly through his balls. His dick hardened to the point of physical pain. Damn it, they still had combustible chemistry. Why hadn't he been acting on it lately? The few selfish nights of sex where he took but didn't give back was hardly the lovemaking she deserved.

He watched her closely, observing her body language as she rose from the bed, her hand held tightly in his. As though he were afraid of losing her, wanting to hold on to something tangible and not let her escape.

A strong surge of triumph slammed into his chest when he saw her nipples tighten through her thin pajama top and her cheeks were flushed with the same answering desire.

He had hope. She hadn't lost her desire for him. It was a start.

Wordlessly, he led her out of the bedroom and into the kitchen. The words he wanted so badly to say would have to wait. He had a distinct plan. Have breakfast together, regain a sense of normalcy and then he'd lay it out to her. Put himself at her feet and bare his very soul to her.

A small smile escaped her when she saw the plates on the table and realized he'd cooked her favorite. But she didn't utter a sound as she sat down, her shoulders hunched, her gaze firmly plastered downward. Avoiding his. As if she couldn't bear to face him yet.

"Eat, baby," he said quietly as he took his own seat.

Though his words were said softly, there was authority behind them. A command. One of a Dominant to his submissive.

She sent a shy look in his direction, one of uncertainty, and yet hope registered once again on her features. Was she battling with herself over whether to accept his gestures? He hadn't even *begun* his line of attack. If she thought he believed that all could be solved by merely a breakfast—her favorite—and a few commanding words here and there, she was mistaken. He well knew the seriousness and the direness of this situation and he was well prepared for all he wanted to say.

Finally she cut into her bagel, taking a forkful and putting it to her mouth. With so much on top, it required a knife and fork to eat.

He dug into his own, swallowing it with difficulty. It was tasteless, stuck in his throat, and he wanted to leave it uneaten, but he could hardly sit there while she ate and not eat himself. He wanted these quiet moments while they were eating to put her more at ease for the ensuing conversation they would have.

She fiddled with her fork and then cut small pieces with her knife, but he could tell her heart wasn't any more into it than he was.

"Can't eat, baby?" he asked gently.

She lifted her gaze to his for the first time since they'd begun eating. There was an almost pleading look in her eyes as she shook her head.

"I can't," she said in a low voice. "It sits in my stomach like lead."

"Mine too, my girl. What do you say we toss breakfast and then go into the living room and talk. There's a hell of a lot I want to say and the waiting is agony."

She sent him a startled look at that, her lips parting in surprise. Hell, did she honestly think this wasn't hell for him? That she was the only one suffering?

He rose from the table, pushing back the plate he'd clean up later. He held out his hand as he'd done in the bedroom, waiting for her to take it so they could go into the living room and talk. Finally talk this out. He had a hell of a lot to say and the words were burning his lips, dying to burst free.

When they entered the living room, she started to break free of his hold and head for the fluffy armchair that was her favorite. He tightened his hold on her hand and steered her toward the couch instead. He firmly sat her down at the end so the arm of the couch would support her and she'd be comfortable and then he sat right next to her, their thighs touching, and he turned himself sideways, pulling up one leg onto the couch so he sat facing her profile.

"Look at me, Chessy."

She turned slowly, her face pale, fear in her beautiful eyes. He swallowed back the knot in his throat because this was not the time to hesitate or stand down. He had to pull a full-court press.

"First thing I want to say to you, because it was never addressed last night."

She sent him a faintly puzzled look but at least he had her full attention now.

"I have never been unfaithful to you, Chessy," he said in a clear, distinct and earnest voice. "I have never even *entertained* the thought. I love *you*. You are the only woman I ever want to be with."

Chessy's breath intake was swift and sharp. She stared at him for a long moment, searching his face, as if for the truth in his words.

"Then who was that woman last night?" she choked out. "On our anniversary, who was the woman who was *all over* you in the bar of the restaurant we were supposed to eat at?"

The bitterness in her voice made him wince. He'd never expected their marriage to come to this. Not only was she questioning his fidelity, but she was also questioning every aspect of their marriage. And all of his shortcomings and failures over the last two years.

"She was a potential client," he said, looking her straight in the eye. "I don't know what the hell you thought you saw, but *I* was not all over that woman. I was having drinks with her and discussing the possibility of her transferring her portfolio to me. She'd be a big coup. Her husband died and left her a lot of money. Most of it in stocks and bonds, and she's unhappy with the financial advisor her husband used. So yes, I was having drinks with her. I told her I could only meet with her a short time as I had another commitment. I got delayed. Time got away from me. I had *no* idea so much time had passed, baby. I would never purposely do anything to hurt you. You *have* to believe that."

"But you *have* hurt me," she whispered. "Over and over again. I can't even count on two hands the times you've left me for a client. When we're at friends', with Dash and Joss or Kylie and Jensen. When I'm alone at the house on a weekend because you're off golfing with clients or taking them to dinner. Without me. You used to include me in your dinners and social affairs but then you quit. Are you ashamed of me? Did I *fail* you in some way?"

He was shocked by her outburst. God, by the magnitude of hurt she was feeling. All piled up and finally exploding last night—and now. It flayed his heart open and he was bleeding on the inside for all he'd done to this precious woman.

"God *no*, Chessy! Fail me? Me *ashamed* of you? You are the most beautiful woman in the world to me. You light up the entire room when you enter. Ashamed? Jesus Christ. I didn't want to burden you anymore. I could see how it was affecting you being called upon so many times, always going out, or entertaining in and you taking care of all the details. I could see the toll it was taking on you. I never wanted that for you. I wanted you to be financially secure and for you to do whatever the hell you wanted in your free time. Not always having to rush around because of the obligations I had. They weren't yours to bear."

"I never minded," she said in barely above a whisper. "I felt important to you. Like we were a team. I wanted to support you. Be there for you. And then it was the only way I got to spend time with you because you were always gone, always on the phone, never here with me. And then I lost that too. I lost *you*."

"You haven't lost me, damn it! Chessy, I love you. I can't say that enough. Nor can I say I'm sorry enough. I wish to hell I could say that I saw when everything went all wrong, but it just happened gradually and I took for granted that you'd always be here. My wife. The woman I loved."

"Don't you turn this around on me," she said, fire sparking in the eyes that had been dull and filled with sorrow just minutes ago. "Don't you *dare* insinuate that I haven't been here. I've been here every damn *day*. Waiting for my husband to come home. To be here. To fulfill my needs. You're supposed to be my Dominant, Tate! And even my friends and their significant others can see you aren't living up to your promise to me when I gave you my submission."

Tate's lips thinned into a tight line. "What the hell do you mean about Dash and Jensen seeing *anything*?"

Chessy gave him a tired look. "They're both dominant and they treat Joss and Kylie like *queens*. I've heard from them time and time again that in return for the gift of my submission you're supposed to put my needs above all others. That you're to cherish me and my gift absolutely. Respect it. Recognize how precious such a gift is. And they said you're failing miserably. Now how do you think that makes me feel to have my marriage picked apart and judged by my best friends and their husbands, or rather husband and lover in Kylie's case."

Tate let out a low growl. "They have no right to judge anything. What we do is our business and our business alone. Our marriage is not up for public speculation. Ever."

Chessy's accusing eyes found his. "It seems that if you were living up to your promise and acting as a true Dominant, not to mention husband and lover, that no one would *have* fodder to point out your shortcomings."

The shot hit home and left him devoid of speech for several moments. She was right and it hurt that he had no comeback. No excuse.

"There's no one else in this relationship except you and me," he finally said in an even voice. "I readily admit that I've royally fucked up and I intend to rectify that starting now. This is our anniversary weekend and I intend to salvage it."

She looked at him for a long moment, hope stirring in her eyes. "How?" she whispered.

"It goes beyond a simple weekend," he continued, briefly ignoring her question. "There's a hell of a lot more I have to make up for and a weekend won't do that. I have to start over, from the beginning, and make damn sure I never let you down again. Going forward you will be put first in everything, Chessy. I don't expect you to believe it right away. I have to regain your trust and, God, I hope your love as well. I'm not letting you go without a fight."

Chessy's expression softened and she offered him the first smile he'd seen in so very long. He couldn't remember the last time she'd smiled, and that hurt him. He couldn't look back and pinpoint a time. And now he realized just how long she'd been miserably unhappy. He'd ignored it. Ignored the signs, so wrapped up in his job and ensuring his business grew and flourished after his partner had bailed. All at the expense of the one person he loved most in the world.

"I do love you, Tate. So very much. I've never *stopped* loving you."

"Thank God," he whispered fervently, relief pouring over him.

"I don't want to leave you," she said as fervently as he had. "That was *never* an option for me. I hope I never gave you that impression. God, it's the very last thing I ever want. I can't imagine my life without you—your love. I just want . . . *us* . . . back. That's *all* I want. Your dominance, your love, your *priority*. That isn't too much to ask, is it? Am I being selfish? I've fought with myself for *two years*, feeling guilty—and selfish—for craving your attention and love when I knew you were working so hard to keep your business going. But I can't do it anymore. I don't *care* if I sound selfish. I want us back!"

He pulled her into his arms, praying she didn't resist. He hugged her tightly, wrapping his arms around her, encompassing her until she was fully against him, her soft body molded to his. Finally she relaxed against him, her rigidity gone. She let out a soft sigh and rested her cheek against his chest.

"You aren't being selfish," he said fiercely. "Everything you've said is what I should have been giving you. It's *my* failure, not *yours*. I swear to you, Chessy, everything is going to change starting now. I know I fucked up our anniversary night, but I want a do-over. Everything starts now. We have the weekend just to ourselves. I'm turning my goddamn phone off. I don't give a fuck about business. Not if it means I don't have you."

He pulled her gently away so he could look into her eyes, judge her decision. They were full of hope—and relief.

"Baby, I know a weekend can't fix what's between us. I know I have to regain your trust and faith in me and that's going to take longer than a few days, but I swear to you that if you give me the chance, I'll get us back. That's what you said you wanted, wasn't it?"

Slowly she nodded.

"Then that's what I'm going to work on," he vowed. "It—and you—will be my foremost priority. I know you'll have to wait and see to judge my sincerity, but I will *not* give you any reason to doubt where you are on my priorities from this point forward."

Then she smiled and he couldn't breathe. It was so radiant, lighting up the room. His old Chessy, the one who sparkled and shone just by *being* was back, even if just for a moment. The light that he'd effectively stomped out repeatedly over the last while. God, all he wanted to do was take her to bed and make love to her.

"That's all I want, Tate," she whispered. "Just you. Nothing else. I don't care about money and financial security if I don't get to enjoy it with the man who holds my heart."

The man who holds my heart.

The sheer magnitude of that statement was humbling. He very nearly went to his knees in front of her to beg her forgiveness all over again.

"Kiss me," he whispered, so choked up he could barely get the words out.

He gently cupped her face, framing it in his hands, and he lowered his mouth to hers, drinking in her sweetness and the sweet little sigh she breathed into his mouth.

He stroked her cheeks, caressing, unable to get enough of simply touching her, tangling his hands in her wayward curls.

"Will you make love with me, Chessy? Right here and now? Let me seal my promise to you?"

Her intake of breath was swift and her gaze lifted to his, hazy with desire, her pupils dilated in familiar fashion. Thank God she still wanted him. That her heart was big enough for forgiveness. He didn't suffer any illusion that another woman would have walked away a long time ago. But his girl had a heart the size of the state they lived in.

"I want that," she whispered, leaning her cheek into his palm as if seeking his touch. "So much, Tate."

He slid one arm underneath the bend of her legs and then anchored his other around her waist, effortlessly lifting her to cradle her in his arms.

For a long moment, all he did was stare into her eyes, absorbing her acceptance like a parched desert soaking in its first rain in months.

And then he slowly walked toward *their* bedroom.

SIX

CHESSY relaxed her body against Tate's, absorbing his strength, his solid, muscled frame as he walked them through the doorway of their bedroom. She rested her head on his shoulder and splayed her fingers out across his chest just below the hollow of his throat.

How many weeks—months—had she yearned for this? To be made love to, with or without all the accouterments of dominance, by her husband. Her entire heart, body and soul ached for him. To reconnect in the most intimate of ways, to say with their bodies all they couldn't say with mere words.

She was almost afraid of his phone ringing. It was only with the fiercest of restraints that she didn't search for it, looking to see if it was attached to his hip as it always was. She forced herself not to think about it and to savor his promise that finally, finally he was focusing on just the two of them. No business associates, no clients—potential or otherwise. Just her and him and trying to rebuild all that they had lost.

He gently laid her down on the bed, standing over her, a fierce gleam in his eyes. His gaze was predatory as it raked over her, undressing her before he even touched her rumpled pajamas.

A delicate shiver worked its way over her body. Delicious anticipation. So much wanting and desire pent up inside her that she felt near to bursting.

Then he reached down and hooked his thumbs in the waistband of her pajama bottoms and slid them slowly and reverently down her legs. He tossed them aside and then carefully unbuttoned her top from the bottom up, parting the material so her breasts were bared.

He lifted her just enough that he could pull the top free and it went the way of her bottoms, disappearing from view. All that was left was the lacy, sheer panties that she'd purposely worn the evening before in anticipation of their anniversary.

Tate stared down at her, his eyes glowing in appreciation, taking in her near-naked body lying on the bed below him.

"You're so beautiful," he whispered. "The most beautiful girl in the world to me."

She was sure she glowed as she smiled up at him, absorbing his words into her heart. She held up her arms for him, inviting him to lower himself onto her body. He took only long enough to strip out of his clothing before complying with her silent request.

His cock pressed against the V of her legs as his body blanketed hers. He nuzzled his lips against her neck and then kissed and sucked a line down to her breasts, shifting his body downward so he could feast on her.

He circled her nipple with his tongue, coaxing it to a rigid bud before sucking it firmly between his teeth. He flicked his tongue over the tip, his teeth grazing the tender flesh. She squirmed beneath him, breathless with pleasure.

She caressed his shoulders, enjoying the ridges of his muscles, tracing with her fingertips, the flesh solid and firm beneath her touch.

Then he went lower still. After giving each breast equal treatment, his mouth trailed down her belly in a damp line. He nuzzled into the soft tuft of hair between her legs and then he ran his thumb down the seam of her pussy. He parted the delicate folds and licked from her opening up to her clit.

Her hips arched, a soft moan escaping her. Tate knew so well how to please her. Every touch. Every kiss. Every caress. He knew her body better than she knew it herself. He always sensed what she needed even before she did and immediately gave her what it was she wanted. She never had to ask.

His tongue slid inside her, lapping gently against the walls of her vagina. He sucked as his tongue withdrew, causing her to clench in protest, wanting that delicious sensation not to end.

His hands slid underneath her ass, cupping the globes firmly as he lifted her higher so he could devour her with his mouth. Already she could feel the fluttering in her womb that signaled the rise of her orgasm.

"My girl is close," Tate said against her clit, his breath blowing over the quivering bud. "Do you want to come now or do you want me inside you?"

As if he needed an answer to that question. She always wanted him inside her. Wanted them both to fall over the edge together.

"Inside me," she said breathily. "I need you, Tate."

Still, he teased and tormented her, bringing her right to the brink and then retreating, allowing her to ease back from the edge. Just when she thought she'd scream in frustration, he slid up her body, opening her legs wide as he settled between them. He nuzzled her breasts, teasing them to rigidity before finally sliding inside her.

Her breath caught, unable to escape her chest as he pushed inside her. He was met with slight resistance as she stretched to accommodate him.

"Take me," he growled.

It was a command he often gave her, one that sent delicious chills over her body. It was a game they played. As though she were reluctant to take him whole and he was determined to get there.

He withdrew and then thrust hard, seating himself fully, her gasp echoing through the room.

"All of me," he commanded. "You'll take all of me."

"Yes," she whispered. "Take me, Tate. You own me."

He withdrew again and hammered forward, his hips pressed against her behind as he strained to reach maximum depth.

"How much can you take, Chessy?" The silky words slid over her ears, sending an uncontrollable shiver over her body. "No mercy. I'm going hard. I want you to come for me. Let go."

Then he began thrusting hard and fast. The slap of flesh against flesh filled her senses. Her entire body tightened as her orgasm swelled and built, an inferno erupting all around her.

She sobbed his name as the room blurred around her. But through it all, she could see his face, his eyes intently boring into hers, demanding her submission. She gave it freely. For this man she'd give anything at all.

His body came down on hers, his forearms propped against the mattress on either side of her body. His hips undulated, rising and falling. Their breaths mingled and his mouth found hers in a heated rush that left her breathless. His tongue mimicked the motions of his cock, fucking her mouth just like his cock fucked her pussy.

She hitched her legs higher, tilting her pelvis up so she could take even more of him. She wrapped her legs around his waist, anchoring herself to him and then lifted to meet every thrust, matching his motions so they moved in perfect unison.

"I love you," Tate said into her mouth. "I'll always love you, Chessy. I need you to believe that."

"I love you too," she breathed.

Then she closed her eyes, her body so taut she felt near to breaking. His words mixed with the deep thrusts unraveled her at the speed of sound.

She reached for his shoulders, digging her fingers into his solid flesh.

"That's it, baby. Give it to me," Tate said in a soothing tone.

And then she simply burst. Pleasure bloomed and exploded around her. Her body seemed to fly in a hundred different directions all at once.

She was panting, trying desperately to draw air into her starved lungs. And then Tate tensed above her, his brow creased into an expression that bordered on pain. He thrust hard and then again and then he stilled, his hips pumping spasmodically against her body.

His release flooded her, hot and silky. He moaned as his hips twitched, each surge of cum causing another spasm.

Then he finally lowered his head to hers, so their foreheads touched and their noses bumped.

"God, I've missed you, baby," Tate said in a voice full of regret. "I'm so sorry. So damn sorry."

"Shhh," she whispered. "Not now. Not when everything is so perfect. Let's put the past behind us where it belongs. We have so much to look forward to."

He kissed her lingeringly, their tongues dancing and teasing.

"I'll always put you first from now on," he vowed. "You'll never question your place in my heart or soul."

SEVEN

KYLIE Breckenridge stared at her cell phone, her brow creased with indecision as she fixated on Chessy's contact number. She vacillated between calling Chessy directly or calling Joss to see if Chessy had been in touch. But she knew if Joss had heard anything at all, she would have called Kylie by now. And, well, Kylie didn't want to risk interrupting Chessy if things had gone really, really well and the two were even now in anniversary bliss. Even though her gut told her that months of accumulated unhappiness wouldn't be fixed in a single night's time.

She sighed and resisted the urge to hit Send to call Chessy.

Warm hands slid over her shoulders and an instant shiver that never failed to comfort her skated over her skin. Heated lips followed the hands, sliding deliciously down her neck until she moaned softly, arching into Jensen's mouth.

"What has you worried, baby?"

She turned her head to look back at Jensen as he sat up in bed next to her. She was angled toward her nightstand where the phone had rested until a few moments ago, one leg pulled up on the edge of the bed while the other dangled to the floor.

Biting her lip in consternation, she lowered her gaze back to the phone before allowing it to slide from her hands onto the mattress.

"I'm worried about Chessy," she admitted. "She was so excited about her anniversary last night and I really expected to hear from her this morning but . . . nothing. Not a word. I thought about calling Joss, but surely if Joss had heard something she would have let me know. We're both worried about her and not hearing from her . . . well, it concerns me."

Jensen's smile was sweet and full of understanding. He leaned in and rested his forehead to hers, the corners of his mouth tilted upward in amusement.

"If it were my anniversary, I'd still be in bed with my wife, either making love to her or just having finished. You worry too much, baby. If I had to guess, they're making up for a lot of lost time and if Chessy laid out her concerns like you told me she planned to, I can't imagine Tate not having a serious come-to-Jesus meeting with himself and reprioritizing his life to make Chessy front and center. You not hearing from her is a good thing. Think about it. If things had gone bad, you'd have heard from her by now. Her silence likely means that they're focusing on each other as they should. As *Tate* should."

Kylie sighed again but relaxed, some of her tension and worry easing under the matter-of-factness of Jensen's reasoning.

"You're right. I know you're right. I just can't help but worry. Chessy has been so miserable lately," she said quietly. "And I hate that. Chessy just . . . shines. Except when she's not happy. Joss and I have worried ourselves sick because we can see how unhappy she is. And it has to be hard for her. I mean look at Joss. So gloriously happy. Pregnant with her first child. The love of Dash's life. And then there's . . . us."

Jensen's eyes flickered, his expression growing intently serious. "Us? Now this I want to hear."

Kylie flushed but smiled at the gentle teasing in his tone. "It's just that we're all so . . . *happy*. And then there's Chessy. It has to be so hard for her, seeing all of us, and being so *un*happy herself."

His gaze grew even more gentle. He tipped up her chin and brushed a kiss across her mouth and then followed it with his tongue, lapping gently at her lips. When he drew back, his gaze was hooded, eyes dark with desire that elicited a prickle of chill bumps over her skin.

"And are *you* happy with us?" he asked, his tone serious.

She melted at the slight insecurity she heard in his tone, which he tried to hide, but she knew every aspect of this man. Was still learning to a degree, their relationship still young and on the fringes of something new and exciting.

"I'm very happy," she whispered. "I never thought I was

unhappy before. Resigned, yes. But unhappy, no. I thought I'd accepted my place in life. Just a few best friends. My head in the sand, never moving forward, always stuck in the past. But you taught me to look ahead. To feel optimism for the future. I'll always love you for that."

Fierce satisfaction lit his features and he curled his hand behind her neck, pulling her down to him as their lips met in a heated rush. She went down on top of him, her hands splayed over his muscled chest, fingertips pressing deep into his flesh.

He kissed her hungrily, his mouth feeding ravenously from hers. His free hand slid up her side and around to cup her breast until her nipples were taught and rigid, tingling, wanting his touch, his mouth.

"You have no idea what your happiness means to me," he said as he pulled his mouth from hers. "That I make you happy . . . Kylie, you can't possibly know how much that humbles me. That you trust me. After what I did . . ."

Pain and regret immediately swamped his features and Kylie fiercely put her fingers to his mouth.

"Jensen, no. That's behind us. You'd *never* hurt me. I know that. You have to know it too. You have to believe it like I believe it. Trust yourself as much as I trust you. I *love* you," she added softly. "No one believes in you more than I do. I just wish you'd have that same faith in yourself. I don't *want* to tie you to the bed at night because you're afraid you'll have a nightmare and hurt me. Having to do that hurts *me*. Seeing the look on your face when I tie your hand to my headboard. It guts me. Because I *know* it's unnecessary. But until *you* believe that, until you can have the same faith as I do, I'll do whatever it takes to keep you with me. In my bed, my life, my heart."

Her impassioned words rendered him speechless, his lips parting, the unfurling of hope—real hope—in his eyes. Had she finally been able to reach him? To cut through his blinding fear of ever lashing out at her in an unguarded moment and causing her physical hurt?

"I'll work on it," he said hoarsely. "We have that appointment with the counselor. I know how hard that was for you. What a monumental step it was for you to be willing to bare your soul to someone other than me or your best friends. I can only be willing to do the same, Kylie. If you can do so much, if you can work up the courage to seek help, then I'm going to be right there beside you every step of the way. I swear it."

She curled into his side and threw one arm over his body as he gathered her closely against him with his arm. She turned her lips into his chest and pressed a kiss right above his heart.

"I'm still worried about Chessy, but I'll give it another day before I call her. If I know Joss, she's every bit as worried about Chessy as I am, but maybe you're right. Maybe they're working it out and having a glorious anniversary weekend. I'll get all the juicy details later," she added with a smile.

Jensen groaned. "Just don't venture into the TMI stage. There's only so much I want to hear about another woman and her husband. I'd much rather focus on what I have in *my* arms."

"Good," Kylie said smugly, with confidence she'd never possessed until recently. Not until this man. "Because I'll kick your ass if you ever start visualizing another woman."

Laughter rumbled through his chest.

"You're more than enough woman for me, baby. You keep me on my toes, and swear to God, you were made for me. There was never a more perfect match than us."

Contentment spread through Kylie's heart as she snuggled further into Jensen's embrace. Yes, the future looked bright indeed, despite her concern for her best friend and her marriage.

But Jensen was probably right. Chessy and Tate were likely even now enjoying their weekend and reconnecting as Chessy had hoped they would.

Joss Corbin dug her toes deeper into the bottom of the sheets and lay as still as possible so her already churning stomach would hopefully quiet.

She glanced at her phone, which was lying to the side of her just underneath the pillow, and frowned. It was late afternoon and she'd expected to hear from Chessy by now with a full report on her anniversary evening out with Dash.

She and Kylie had both exchanged a flurry of texts the evening before, worrying that Chessy's night would not go as well as she planned. The silence was killing her. Silence could be good. Or it could be bad. And she hated to think of the worst-case scenario, which was Chessy at home, miserable, and unwilling to seek support from her two best friends because of embarrassment or shame.

God only knew Chessy had suffered enough of both lately.

Dash entered the bedroom carrying a tray of dry toast and

a glass of apple juice, though the thought of the sweet juice turned her stomach even more. Even now, watching as he closed the distance between the doorway and the bed, her stomach twisted into knots and she had to breathe through her nose to stifle the urge to make a run for the toilet.

Dash sat down on the edge of the bed and positioned the tray over her lap as she scooted up on the fluffy pillows arranged against the headboard. His eyes were shadowed with worry and concern as he took one of her hands and pressed a kiss to her open palm.

"Are you feeling any better yet, honey? Has your stomach settled at all?"

Even as he spoke, he slid his free hand underneath the tray and rested his palm over her still-flat abdomen. Warmth from his touch seeped into her skin, doing wonders for the turmoil caused by morning sickness—an ailment she hadn't suffered until her pregnancy had been confirmed.

After a call to one of the nurses at her obstetrician's office, the nurse had laughingly told her that it wasn't uncommon not to suffer the symptoms of pregnancy until the pregnancy was confirmed. Apparently it was 95 percent psychological in Joss's case. Or perhaps it had just been too early in her pregnancy for morning sickness to rear its ugly head.

Other symptoms had presented themselves from the very start. Fatigue, and her breasts were so tender that at times it was unbearable to touch them. Something Dash had been extremely careful about when they made love.

She gave him the warmest smile possible, considering how sick she felt, and cupped his jaw after he'd kissed her palm.

"I'm feeling better," she said truthfully. "Usually within an hour of me waking up the nausea mostly goes away and I'm fine the rest of the day. You taking such good care of me and ensuring I eat has gone a long way in helping me cope with this."

"You never have to worry that I'm not going to be here every step of the way or that I won't give you my utmost care," he said in a low growl.

Her smile broadened. "I love you. And I'm so excited, Dash. You can't imagine how happy I am about our baby. It's such a dream come true. You. Us. Our son or daughter. I never imagined being so happy again and you've given me so much."

His eyes glowed with warmth—and love—as he stared tenderly back at her. "I'm so happy that I have to stop and remind myself to be grateful for the precious gift of you and our child," he said gruffly. "I love you too, Joss. Always have, always will. As much as I want our baby to be born and as much as I can't wait to grow our family and watch as our children grow up in front of our eyes, I plan to savor every moment of your pregnancy. Watch you swell with our baby. I'll never forget these moments. Other than the day you told me you loved me, the day our child is born will be the most precious moment of my life. I hope you never doubt that."

"Never," she said with fervor. "I'll never forget, Dash. Just as I hope you'll never forget how much I love you."

He stroked her cheek and then motioned toward her phone.

"No word from Chessy yet? I know how worried you and Kylie were. And well, I admit to having some major concerns myself. I have no idea what the hell is going on with Tate but I hope he pulls his head out of his ass soon."

Joss grimaced as she glanced toward her phone as well. "Not a word. Which could be good or bad. I'm hoping for good. I'm hoping they were able to work everything out and that Chessy finally confronted him with her unhappiness. I want so much for her, Dash. I know how hard it was for her when I told her I was pregnant. I almost *didn't* tell her, but it would have only hurt her more and made her feel that much more conspicuous about her troubles with Tate."

He rubbed his hand from her belly down the inside of one thigh before stopping to squeeze her knee.

"You did the right thing, Joss. Chessy would never want you to withhold such wonderful news out of worry over her. And you have the right to be happy. She'd never begrudge you that."

"I know," Joss said quietly. "I just love her and want so badly for her and Tate to resolve the issues in her marriage so she can be happy again. Just like Kylie and me."

Dash smiled. "She will be. Just like her best friends. Now try to eat some toast, baby. You need something in your stomach before you get up and move around. I figured we'd take it easy today. Enjoy the weekend together. Maybe sit on the couch, you in my arms, and watch some movies. I'll cook dinner for us tonight if you're up to eating something more substantial by then."

She sighed blissfully. "You take such good care of me, darling. I love you for that."

He leaned in and kissed her on the nose and then patted the top of her thigh. "Eat up. I don't want to leave you to take my shower until I know for certain you're going to be able to keep down your toast."

EIGHT

CHESSY awoke, the late afternoon sun filtering through the bay window of their bedroom. She was surrounded by warmth and strength. Tate's body was wrapped around her, arms anchoring her to him, one leg thrown possessively over hers while her head was pillowed on his broad shoulder.

She let out an imperceptible sigh, not wanting to wake him and spoil the first moment of true contentment she'd felt in a very long time. All felt right with the world. She wasn't a fool to think that everything had been miraculously fixed with Tate's magic peen, but it was a start.

Their lovemaking had been a coming together of two lost souls. Or at least hers had been lost until now. She'd been bereft of his presence for so long and she couldn't remember the last time she'd awakened in his arms, or that they'd spent the better part of a *day* in bed.

He was always hurrying out to work in the mornings with barely a kiss on her forehead and a gruff "hope my girl has a good day" before he was off, with her never even knowing when she'd see him again.

It was hard not to focus on those not so great times even when here and now the world seemed perfect. He'd certainly nailed it when he'd said that their relationship couldn't be fixed in a single weekend, but the ever-optimistic side of her knew that it was *something*. That he was giving her something he hadn't been giving her in over a year. Himself. His absolute priority and attention. His love that in her darker moments she'd thought she had lost. But he'd been utterly sincere last night and this morning, especially this morning when neither of them was so volatile and overly emotional. She knew Tate hadn't liked going to bed the night before with things still unresolved between them but she also knew she was right for putting it off until a time when they both had the night to reflect and better think of how and what needed to be said.

"Is my girl awake?"

Tate's voice rumbled from his chest and she smiled against his chest where her lips rested.

"You're smiling," he said.

Her smile broadened. This was the old Tate. Always so in tune with her every movement, her every thought. She closed her eyes, simply savoring the moment, drinking it in. It very nearly brought tears to her eyes but she refused to allow them because she feared he'd take it the wrong way and they'd be right back at square one.

Instead she simply nodded, confirming what he already knew. He hugged her to him more tightly and brushed an affectionate kiss on the top of her head.

"Not that I'm not loving exactly where I am and having you naked and in my arms, but I promised you a do-over of our anniversary dinner out, and if we're going to make it, we need to get up and moving. I need to get cleaned up and I was thinking about a dual shower, one where I wash and pamper you. And then we have dinner and then come back home so I can make love to you all over again."

"Mmmm," she said against his chest. "That sounds wonderful, Tate."

"I'm glad," he said gruffly. "I owe you so much more, but I promise that you're going to get that from me twenty-four-seven from now on."

She pushed up to her elbow so that she looked down at his contented, sleepy eyes as they gleamed back at her.

"I believe you," she said quietly.

Relief brightened his eyes, fire quickly replacing any signs of sleepiness. "Thank you for that, Chess. You have no idea what your forgiveness means. And your willingness to give me another chance."

She reached down and lovingly cupped a hand to his face, stroking the chiseled line of his cheekbone with her thumb.

Then she leaned down and kissed him. For once she was in a position of control, her over him, taking the initiative.

His hand immediately went to the back of her head, tangling in her hair, but he was careful to allow her to direct the kiss. It was almost as if he were still treading in very careful waters, and if he only knew that wasn't what she wanted from him at all. She *wanted* him to assert his control—his dominance—over her again. She craved it with everything she had in her heart and soul.

She was born for this man. Born to be his submissive and he her Dominant. It was a need that defied reason or explanation. Some things just were and for her that was their relationship. She hated to even use the word marriage because it was so . . . traditional and quaint and in a lot of ways outdated. What they had between them went far beyond the edges of most married couples' faith and trust in each other. The things she offered Tate, the things he demanded of her, could well be grossly misunderstood by outsiders unfamiliar with the dominance/submissive lifestyle and how deeply emotional and connected—profoundly connected—those bonds were. Yes, she had a kick-ass diamond wedding set but that wasn't what made her Tate's girl.

She literally put her entire safety, her well-being, into Tate's hands. And in return, there was not a more cared for woman on the earth. Well, when things were normal between them . . . Their relationship defied convention and neither of them gave one damn. They made the rules. No one else. And most of the rules were made by Tate.

There wasn't a handbook on "how to be a proper Dominant" out there. Tate would have laughed himself silly over the idea that he needed some "how-to" book in order to live his life and satisfy his cherished submissive. Maybe those sorts of guides worked for other couples, and if they did, more power to them. But that wasn't the way it worked between Chessy and Tate. It never had been.

Tate made the decisions and he didn't give a flying fuck if he was thumbing his nose at propriety or paying homage to others who lived the same lifestyle.

In the very beginning of Chessy and Tate's relationship he made it very clear what he wanted and told Chessy that this may not be the way she thought such a relationship would work, but he'd be damned if he playacted some cookie-cutter "Dom" scene from an instructional manual. Over his dead body would he have others directing his relationship with his wife! His cherished submissive.

"What's my girl thinking?" he queried softly, taking in her pensive expression.

"That you don't bear the sole blame for the current state of our relationship."

When he would have immediately launched a protest, she gently put her fingers to his lips to silence him.

"Just moments ago you were grateful that I still loved you, that I forgave you and that I was willing to give you another chance. But Tate, the same goes both ways. I could have said something much sooner than now. I could have been honest with you earlier on. I think I should also be asking your forgiveness and for another chance to make things right between us. I let the lines of communications completely give way between us. Yes, you share responsibility in that. Communication is a two-way street. But I should have been bolder in asking for what it was I wanted—demanded—from you much like you demanded certain things from me in our relationship. I was just . . . afraid," she said, her voice going lower and lower until she trailed off into a husky whisper.

"Afraid of what, baby?" he asked gently.

She found his gaze again, swallowed back her nerves. "I was afraid that if I pushed, then you'd realize I wasn't what you wanted anymore. That you didn't need me. That I was just a burden—an unwanted burden. I was afraid you'd walk away. And so I tried to be as undemanding and understanding as I could even though I was dying on the inside. But then it all became too much and I could no longer be that person anymore. I had to take the risk, because the reward for not taking the risk was no reward. It was *hell*."

The stark way she said the last made Tate suck in his breath like someone had punched him directly in the stomach.

"Do you have any idea how much it guts me to have to listen to you say that? About me? Your husband, your Dominant, your lover? All I can look back and see is that I never made it *possible* for you to come to me with your unhappiness. How could you have told me if I wasn't willing to hear it?"

He rose up to his elbow, planting it in the pillow so they were now nose-to-nose.

"I will never walk away from you, Chess. Not going to happen. I don't know why the hell you haven't walked away from *me*. No other woman would love me, continue loving me, in the face of such emotional neglect. I've spent the entire afternoon while you've been sleeping all curled up next to me thanking *God* that you still love me and actually forgive me for nearly destroying the most precious thing in my life. You, baby. You. And I almost *did* destroy you, and me along with you. Because I cannot imagine my life without you. I don't *want* to imagine my life without you. If I have anything to say about it at all, you and I are going to grow old and gray together and loving every single minute of it. There is no Tate without Chessy and I hope to hell there's never a Chessy without Tate."

She smiled at the poetic rendering of their relationship. So simple and yet so elegant and beautiful. No Chessy without Tate and no Tate without Chessy. It certainly fit her way of thinking when it came to the man she married and loved with all her heart.

"I love you," she said, thinking—no, *knowing*—he needed to hear it again. As emotionally fragile as she had been over the last long months, she now realized he was every bit as emotionally fragile right now. Now when he understood all he had to lose.

He touched his forehead to hers and just rested it there,

NINE

ONE playful shower and one Tate-induced orgasm when he paid a little extra attention to the area between her legs later, Chessy sat at her vanity while Tate carefully ran a comb through her towel-dried curls.

Her entire body was quivering in the aftermath of the powerful orgasm. She'd had to sit because there was no way her legs would have supported her straight out of the shower. The result was a small puddle of water on the floor where it had drained off her body and from her hair, but it was the last thing on her mind.

She smiled up at Tate in the reflection of the mirror and then closed her eyes, savoring one of her favorite things that Tate had done so often over the years. Tend to her hair. She was a total tactile person, loved being touched and loved having her hair brushed or simply played with.

their breaths mingling, eyes closed as they savored the intimacy of such a simple gesture.

"I love my girl too," he breathed. "And now I'm going to get my girl in the shower and give her a washing she's not going to forget any time soon, and I mean every part from head to toe and especially the parts in between are going to get very special treatment."

She couldn't count the times in earlier years when she and Tate would simply lie on the couch, her head in his lap as he idly ran his fingers through her strands as they watched a movie. It would always count as one of her best memories.

Her eyelids fluttered open and her smile disappeared for a brief moment. Before she could recover, Tate was already frowning back at her in the mirror, a questioning look in his eyes.

"What's wrong, baby? Did I hurt you? Am I not being gentle enough with your hair?"

She laughed. "As if. You're a master at combing a woman's hair. If you ever get tired of financial advising, you can always start up a salon. You'd have women coming in droves just for those hands of yours. Which, by the way, are totally mine. I'll chop them off before allowing another woman access!"

He looked befuddled for the briefest of seconds and then threw back his head and laughed. But then he sobered and focused his stare back on her.

"What were you frowning about then?"

She fidgeted uneasily on her vanity bench, not wanting to bring up a bad subject. But Tate wasn't going to allow her to dodge his question. Quietly he rotated her, picking up her legs and swiveling her body until she faced him. Then he got down on one knee and cupped his hand to her face.

"Tell me."

She sighed. "I know I shouldn't ask. I mean, that's not the way our relationship works, and I don't want you to get the idea that I want our relationship to change. That I don't want your dominance and for you to make the decisions. But . . ."

"Ask, baby," he prompted gently. "I think we both know we're at a fragile point in our relationship where the rules are temporarily changing. They have to. Because I need to know what your needs and wants are. I'd want to know that regardless of whether it's now or two years ago. I've always wanted you to communicate your needs to me. How else can I fulfill them?

"Yes, it's my job as your Dominant to often know your wants and needs before you do even, and it's my job to provide those for you. But I've been a complete dumbass and as a result—and it's painful for me to admit, but I'm man enough to own up to my failures—I am out of touch with your desires. I hate even saying that. But you're going to have to help me until we're back on track. That open line of communication we were just discussing in bed a while ago? That has to be in place going forward."

She nodded her understanding, breathing out her relief. They would be okay. She could feel it. Tate was going to extraordinary lengths for a man so used to being in control of every aspect of his life. But he was right. They were in anything but control right now and it would take them both to right the ship and get back to smooth waters.

"I just wanted to know where you planned for us to have dinner tonight," she said in a low voice. "I don't . . . I don't want to go back to where we were supposed to have dinner last night. I don't think I could handle it. There was a lot of humiliation in last night for me. I don't want to even remember it. I'd rather just go somewhere else and truly start over again."

The look of love, understanding and self-recrimination all crowding into his eyes made her emotional and she had to swallow hard at the knot forming in her throat.

He leaned forward and pressed his lips to her forehead and left them there a long moment. When he pulled away, he framed her face in his hands and stared her directly in the eyes.

"I'd never do that to you, my girl. I thought we'd go to a place we've never been before. I've heard good things about it. I've already made a reservation. I placed one online before I got you up this morning. I want a fresh start too. It'll be a new beginning all the way around."

Relief and love coursed through her veins. To her dismay, a tear rolled down her cheek and collided with one of his hands. Damn it but she'd been determined not to cry. She'd done entirely too much of that the night before. As it was, it was going to take her best makeup job to disguise the shadows under her eyes before they went out to dinner. And she wanted to look her best for Tate tonight. Just as they wouldn't be eating in the same restaurant, neither would she wear the same outfit she'd worn the night before.

But Tate seemed to understand that she wasn't upset. His expression grew even more tender and he leaned in and kissed away the path of the single tear that had trickled onto his hand.

"I love you, Chess. Please don't ever forget that."

"I love you too," she whispered. "Now shoo so I can finish getting ready. How much time do I have?"

He checked his watch and then helped her to her feet,

patting her lightly on the behind. "Forty-five minutes before we need to leave, so get a move on, baby. I'll go get dressed and meet you in the living room."

She sent him a brilliant smile, one she could feel in the tightening of her cheeks, and she was rewarded by an answering smile from him that took her breath away. There was so much promise in that smile that she was besieged by a surge of giddiness. She all but skipped to her closet to pick out what she would wear. Her hair still needed to be blown dry, but she'd save that for after her wardrobe had been selected and then she'd do hair and makeup before dressing.

TEN

TATE gazed at Chessy's bright smile as they sat in a corner table of the new steakhouse in the same suburb of Houston they lived in. It was a mere five-minute drive from their house, and while they were certainly acquainted with most of the restaurants in the fast-developing Woodlands, this was a place that had just opened a few months before and already promised success judging by the number of people in the spacious interior.

Some of the awful weight that had pressed on his heart had eased and he was feeling optimistic about his and Chessy's future. How could he not rededicate himself to this beautiful woman and vow to put her first before all else? It was no less than she deserved and he'd made her a promise five years ago when she'd given him her heart—and her submission—to cherish those gifts absolutely.

That he'd failed was a burden he'd carry with him to the grave, but it wasn't too late. There were no lengths he wouldn't go to in order to secure her love and faith once more.

He gazed at her shining eyes and his mind drifted, an image of her bound in a position of utter submission, the hands of another man caressing her under Tate's watchful eye. Another man commanding her, via Tate's command, preparing her for Tate's possession.

It was a kink they both enjoyed, had made it a point to participate in at The House on a regular basis before Tate got so involved with his business. Then The House and the activities had fallen by the wayside, something Tate intended to correct soon.

But first he had to cement his recommitment to her. Ensure that she knew in her heart she was first in his heart. And then he'd plan a night of utter decadence. All focused on Chessy and her pleasure. It would be a gift to her. His gift.

"Oh no," Chessy whispered, her eyes suddenly stricken.

Her words and expression yanked Tate from his erotic reverie and he frowned as he took in her obvious distress.

"What's wrong?" he demanded, looking around to see what could have caused her to be upset.

"Kylie and Joss must be so worried," Chessy said anxiously. "They knew all about our anniversary plans and I was supposed to call them this morning to check in. I completely forgot about it."

Tate smiled, though he could feel the tightness in his features. Yes, Joss and Kylie were Chessy's best friends, and as such, he supposed they shared everything. Too much for Tate's liking. It was obvious that not only his wife's closest friends had been scrutinizing his marriage but also Dash and Jensen. A fact that didn't sit well with Tate. He was a very private person and the idea of his personal life being the topic of conversation, not to mention judgment, of others dug under his skin.

But in this case the truth hurt and if he wasn't so guilty of neglecting his wife then the scrutiny of others wouldn't hit so close to home with him. It was a cross he had to bear. But he'd be damned if he hung his head when in the company of Chessy's friends. *His* friends. They weren't just his wife's friends. Hell, he'd inserted himself into Dash's relationship with Joss when Dash had nearly blown everything all to hell. Tate had been furious with Dash, rightfully so, but the hypocrisy that was so evident was appalling.

He and Dash went way back. As had their relationship with Carson, Joss's first husband. Only Jensen was new to the mix, but all evidence pointed to him being a solid addition to the close-knit group of friends. He made Kylie happy, and of all people, Kylie deserved happiness.

"I'm sure they aren't worried," Tate said in a reassuring tone. "The fact that they haven't heard from you is good, wouldn't you think? If things had gone badly, you would have called them. I'm sure they take silence as a good thing. They likely think we're still in bed, and were it not for the fact that I promised you a do-over of dinner, that's exactly where we would be right now."

Her cheeks turned a delightful shade of pink and her eyes blazed with quick desire. It made him want to haul her right out of the restaurant and not stop until they were back home in their bed, her naked and underneath him.

"You're right," she admitted. "They were just so worried about me." Her features twisted and she grimaced with her admission. "Lord knows I gave them cause to worry. I seriously thought my marriage was over."

Tate's gut clenched and it took everything he had to sit there in a semblance of a relaxed posture as she stated so matter-of-factly that she'd thought their marriage was over. Unable to keep from touching her, he reached for her hand and lifted it to his mouth, pressing a tender kiss to the inside of her palm.

"Never that, baby. I can only say, again, how sorry I am for not putting you first. But I won't make that mistake again."

"Let's not rehash it all over again," she said, her lips in a determined line. "Let's put it behind us where it belongs and start over from right here and now."

"Now that sounds like an excellent plan," he said in satisfaction. "Would you like dessert? I know what I want, and it's not on the menu."

She flushed again as she let her hand drop from his hold. Then she shook her head. "I'd rather go home," she whispered.

Tate held up a hand for the distant waiter before the words were fully out of her mouth. He handed the server his credit card and watched as he hurried away to total the bill. He drummed his fingers impatiently on the table as he waited for the check to return. The minute the waiter reappeared, Tate scrawled the tip, added it to the amount and then hastily signed the slip, shoving it aside as he stood.

He hovered over Chessy, helping her to her feet as she collected her purse, and then he guided her toward the exit to the parking lot where he ushered her into the passenger seat of his car.

He immediately reached for her hand, anchoring it to his in the console between the two seats. Something so small and seemingly insignificant as her touch was something he'd missed. Not until now had he realized just how much he'd missed seeing her, talking to her, touching her. No amount of money or financial security was worth the loss of her love.

"I love you," he said, glancing briefly in her direction.

Her warm smile of complete happiness took his breath away.

Already he was planning their evening at home. Reasserting his dominance was something he knew she wanted but was difficult for him. Because for all practical purposes it should be him on his knees in supplication before her, begging her forgiveness all over again, not her kneeling in submission before him.

But his dominance was not something she just wanted. It was a need. For both of them. And getting back to the roots of their relationship was essential for peace of mind for both of them. It was important that Chessy felt safe and secure in their marriage once more. Tate would do whatever necessary to ensure her happiness.

When they pulled into the concrete drive, Tate came to a stop outside the garage where Chessy's Mercedes SUV was parked and he cut the engine.

When she would have opened her door to get out, he squeezed her hand to hold her in place.

"Go inside to the bedroom. Undress and kneel on the carpet in front of the fireplace and wait for me," he said, injecting a note of authority into his tone.

Her eyes widened, hope spreading like wildfire through her expression, and then her eyes became half-lidded as smoldering desire replaced her momentary surprise. She expelled a soft sigh, one of relief as though she'd waited for just this event. The moment when he retook the reins in their relationship. Shame crawled up his neck and spread over his chest, tightening until he could barely draw breath. No wife, regardless of whether she was in a position of submissiveness or not, should ever be faced with a failure of a husband.

When he loosened his grip on her hand, giving her silent permission to go, she fumbled with her seatbelt and hurriedly got out of her seat. He followed her up the short sidewalk to their front door and unlocked it before pushing it open for her to precede him.

He purposely delayed, giving her time to go into the bedroom and ready herself. And well, he had to mentally prepare himself for what lay ahead because it was difficult for him to be commanding and authoritative when all he wanted was to cherish her, wrap her in his tenderness and make up for all the pain he'd caused her.

While he could bring himself to command her and to delight in her submissiveness, there was no way in hell he'd touch her precious skin with a crop or his hand. Even the beauty of pleasurable pain had lost its luster and for the time being he couldn't swallow the thought of indulging in something that had before always brought them immeasurable satisfaction. There would be no blurring the line between pleasure and pain tonight. He wanted only to bring her pleasure. To reestablish their emotional connection by reforging the physical bonds between them.

When enough time had passed that he could be assured she would be prepared for him, he walked slowly to the bedroom, holding his breath in anticipation of his first glimpse of her. Beautiful. Naked. Kneeling in magnificent submission as she waited for him and his command.

His pulse accelerated as he pushed open the already ajar door and then he saw her.

His breath left in one long exhalation and he was suddenly unsteady on his feet. He gripped the frame of the door until his knuckles were white as his gaze slowly traversed her beautiful body.

She was the picture-perfect image of complete submission. Kneeling on the soft rug in front of the fireplace, her body silhouetted by the light shining from the bathroom, his wife rested, awaiting him. His command. But speech escaped him. He could barely form a coherent thought much less put to words a description that did her any justice.

Long flowing hair fell down her back, a section artfully arranged over one shoulder and playing an erotic game of peekaboo with one dusky pink nipple. His mouth watered as he imagined tasting the twin peaks. Running his tongue over the puckered ridges and sucking them until they were hard and aching.

He could almost hear her low moan of pleasure. It only brought home to him just how long he'd gone without hearing the sounds of her satisfaction. How remiss he'd been in providing the pleasure she deserved.

"Forgive me, Chessy," he whispered in a voice he knew she wouldn't hear. It wasn't as though he didn't feel she deserved the plea for forgiveness, but he was determined to forge ahead and not bring yet another reminder of how much he'd failed her. Not tonight when so much promised to be right. Finally right again.

As though sensing his quiet perusal, her chin tilted up, her gaze finding his. Their eyes locked, hers simmering with need and desire. He was sure his were a perfect match to hers.

"You're beautiful," he said, so she'd hear.

Her eyes reflected her pleasure at his words.

"I'm glad you find me beautiful," she said in a low voice that hummed deliciously over his ears, sending awareness deep into his body.

"Do you doubt your beauty to me?" he asked, though he knew it wasn't well done of him to ask such a question. How could she believe he found her beautiful still after five years of marriage when his actions had pointed to just the opposite?

Would a man who still loved his wife and thought her to be the most gorgeous woman in the world treat her the way he had?

Yes.

He winced at his frank admission. But yes, he did still love his wife, and yes, he thought she was the most beautiful woman on earth, and yes, he'd treated her as though neither were true.

"No," she said without hesitation. "You've removed all the worry I had that you no longer desired me or found me beautiful. When you look at me like you're doing right now, I *feel* beautiful."

He crossed the distance between them and gently threaded his fingers through her hair, stroking and allowing the strands to spill over his hands like the finest silk.

"I'm very glad you feel beautiful, Chessy. Because you are. And in no way should the way I look at you be the measure by which you consider your beauty. You're beautiful inside *and* out. A more loving, giving woman I've never known. And you're *mine*," he said with ultimate satisfaction. "I'm never letting you go. Never doubt how beautiful you are to me. To others. You shine, baby. When you walk into a room, everyone stops to look at you. You're a joy to watch. Your kindness and compassion glow from the depths of your soul. I don't deserve you. I never have. But thank God you're mine anyway."

She angled her head, nuzzling her cheek into his palm as he gently stroked the satiny-soft skin with his fingertips, simply enjoying the way she reacted to his touch. So responsive. So honest. There was no holding back for her. It was one of the many things he loved so much about her.

She had no inhibitions. She didn't just live life. She attacked it. What she enjoyed, she enjoyed wholeheartedly with zest and fervor that attracted people to her. Others just flocked to Chessy, her personality a magnet that held people in her thrall.

It was one of the main reasons he'd taken her to so many business functions in the beginning. Before he felt guilty for using her to further his career. It sounded worse than it was. The word *used* wasn't a pleasant one. But he'd benefitted from her ability to have people—especially men—eating out of her hand. Not that women weren't similarly drawn to Chessy's warmth and genuine sweetness. But he wasn't an idiot. He knew his wife's effect on the opposite sex. Just as he knew she'd never in a million years even entertain the thought of straying. Not his girl.

She put people at ease. Made them feel as though they'd known her forever. She exuded genuine warmth that couldn't be faked. There wasn't an insincere bone in her body.

And she was *his*.

He bent at the waist so he could brush his lips over the top of her head, inhaling the scent of her hair deeply into his nostrils. Desire surged hotly through his veins, giving him a heady sensation. He felt drunk, intoxicated by her essence. He was the most fortunate of men. He accepted it, knew it for the truth it was. Most men in his position never *got* a second chance at perfection. The opportunity to make amends for many wrongs performed. He wouldn't waste a single moment. He'd grab on with both hands and be on his knees, grateful and humbled by his wife's forgiving nature.

"Tell me what you'd like tonight," he murmured next to her ear.

His mouth pressed against the shell of her ear and he nuzzled softly, grazing his teeth lightly over the delicate skin and then sucking at the tiny lobe.

She shivered and he grew harder, his erection straining at the pants he still wore. It was a scenario they'd enacted before. He, the Dominant, asking his submissive how to please her. Yes, he was in absolute control, but in essence he was hers, his pleasure hers, his desire whatever she desired.

"My hands . . . behind my back," she whispered, her eyes closing when he traced the edge of her ear with his tongue. Her breath hitched and he smiled as he drew away just enough to take in every facet of her expression.

"Me on my hands and knees . . . you behind me," she continued in a shy, faltering voice.

He loved that even as uninhibited as she was in bed, she was still adorably shy when expressing her fantasies. It was the perfect blend of good girl meets bad and a glimpse of her inner vixen who came out to play during intimacy.

"You taking me hard," she said breathlessly. "Not stopping even if I beg you for mercy. Refusing when I say no. Your hand twisting in my hair, pulling as you thrust into me. You demanding me to remain still and to take whatever you give me."

His own eyes closed. He took long, measured breaths to still his racing pulse. All the blood in his body pooled painfully in his groin, his dick so hard that it had reached the point of pain. He couldn't move for the material of his underwear abrading the sensitive head of his penis. Already there was a bead of moisture coating the tip. He was imagining being balls deep inside her, plunging and straining even harder to go deeper. Him holding her in place to meet his thrusts, his hand, as she'd whispered, tangled in her hair, forcing her to take whatever he dished out.

It was one of the many roles they played during sex. Their love life was wide open and wonderfully diverse. If it could be imagined, they enjoyed it. He knew how damn lucky he was to have such a wonderfully responsive lover. Wife. Best friend. It was cliché but, in his case, so very true.

"I like the way my girl thinks," he said in a husky, passion-laced voice.

"Think my man is up to giving his girl what she wants?" she asked with a teasing glint to her eyes.

He tipped her chin up with one fingertip and brushed his mouth over hers. "I think I can manage. It's a hardship but I can swing the sacrifice."

"Good," she whispered against his lips. Then she slid her hand up the inside of his thigh to cup his bulging erection. "I'd hate for this perfectly good hard-on to go to waste."

ELEVEN

CHESSY ran her fingers lightly over Tate's erection and then grew bolder in her caresses. Her husband was very well endowed. Not enough to make the logistics impossible but certainly enough for her to never complain in that department. Too much, and a girl had major appendage issues. Too little? And it was inevitable disappointment.

She liked her man just as he was and had no complaints about his prowess in bed or in domination. She was positively giddy with anticipation over Tate taking control back. Reasserting his dominance and his mastery over her body. Nobody knew her better than Tate. Though she hadn't had many lovers before meeting Tate, she'd had enough to know perfection when she found it. At the time, being young and hopelessly naïve, she'd lamented the fact that Tate hadn't been her first.

She'd had this ridiculous romantic notion of gifting him not only with her submission but her virginity as well. Now she was glad he *hadn't* been her first because there was no doubt in her mind that he was miles above any of the other men she'd been with.

She was also secretly, and not so secretly, smug and delighted that Tate had admitted he'd never had a woman—a submissive—who was so perfectly suited for him. They were just meant to be, as corny as it sounded to say it aloud. But nothing about her relationship and ensuing marriage caused her any embarrassment. She was proud of who and what she was with him. He'd never given her any reason to feel shame for her desires and she loved him deeply for that. For always praising her boldness when it came to embracing her needs and desires.

"Baby, you're killing me," he groaned. "And I want to give you everything you want tonight. It will be my honor—and privilege—to give you whatever you need from me. My love. My control. Whatever makes you feel safe and cherished."

The words coming from him hit the very heart of her. A part of her soul that had been long denied. Emotion clogged her throat, making it impossible to breathe around the growing knot. Tears burned her eyelids but she furiously blinked them back, determined not to give him any misapprehension about her willingness—and desire—to see the night through in absolute decadence and splendor.

"I *do* feel safe and cherished with you, Tate. Please don't hold back with me. I'm not fragile. I won't break. I need you. I need *us*. Like we were. I need things to go back to normal. I want your control back, that feeling of absolute safety and security I feel when I'm with you."

He cupped her face in his hands and kissed her again, long and lingering this time, his mouth utterly possessive. As though they'd never drifted apart and were taking up right where they left off before he became so distant to her.

He reached down and took both her hands in his, gently pulling her to stand before him.

"Then go to the bed. Belly down, arms stretched toward the headboard and feet on the floor at the end. Get as comfortable as possible while I get the rope to bind you."

Another shiver, almost violent in its intensity, quaked through her body, leaving desperate need in its wake. She stumbled precariously, like she was drunk on alcohol, as she weaved her way toward the bed.

Tate was with her the entire way, helping to position her to his liking on the bed. She eased down onto her belly, resting her cheek against the soft mattress. She planted both feet firmly on the floor, her toes curling into the sheepskin rug at the foot of the bed. Then he left her, his absence a keenly felt void as she waited for him to return with the bonds that would render her helpless and at his absolute command.

She didn't have long to wait. It was as if he were as impatient as she was to reclaim this part of their relationship. She closed her eyes, relaxing under his patient touch.

He pulled one arm up first, ensuring she was comfortable with gentle questions to gauge her reaction. First he looped the rope around her left wrist, testing the strength of the knot before securing it to the headboard, stretching her arm high above her head in the process. Then he repeated the motions with her right arm until she was spread wide on the bed, arms outstretched and reaching high toward the head of the bed.

She was completely vulnerable, unable to move except to rise up on tiptoe, flexing the arches of her feet and then back again. She tested the strength of the bonds, a quiver of delight tumbling around her belly when the ropes held fast and she was unable to move but the barest of inches.

"You are so absolutely beautiful," he said in a reverent, awe-filled voice. "More beautiful to me than even five years ago when we first married. I know I've failed miserably in making sure you *know* how beautiful—and important, *all*-important to me—but with every passing day, you grow even more gorgeous to me. There'll never be another woman for me, Chess. No one who owns every part of my heart and soul like you do."

If he didn't stop, she'd lose the battle to keep her tears at bay. The words he'd spoken to her, obviously from the very heart of him, ever since their crisis on their anniversary night, were heartfelt. An unobscured window to his very soul.

She bit into her lip and closed her eyes, not wanting to see what he would do next. Instead she reached out with her heightened senses and anticipated his next move. Would he torment her endlessly, drawing out her pleasure to its maximum peak? Or would he move in, rough and dominant, instantly possessing her body and rebuilding the faltering connection between them?

So much was at stake here. This night. It wasn't merely kinky sex meant to satisfy their more acute sexual tastes. This was truly a turning point in their marriage, whether he reestablished his control or they shifted to a different kind of relationship entirely.

She flinched when he pressed a kiss to the small of her back and nibbled his way over the plumpness of both cheeks and then ran his tongue up the cleft of her ass until she was trembling with desperate need.

Would he fuck her ass? Or would he slide into her pussy, hard and pulsing? Perhaps he'd first thrust into her pussy and save her ass for last. Anal sex was something she didn't merely endure. It was something she found extremely erotic and she embraced that dark need. She was completely unashamed of her desires and had never felt any inhibitions about letting Tate know what turned her on. Every kink they indulged in, she was a full and active participant. Just because he was the Dominant didn't mean her role in their lovemaking was passive. Far from it.

His mouth left her and his fingertips replaced his lips, tracing delicate lines down and then around her anal opening, teasing her mercilessly until she was already precariously close to begging. Not for him to stop. But to please give her more. To end her desperate journey to sexual fulfillment.

"I'd love to draw out your pleasure all night," Tate said, strain evident in his voice. "It's certainly what you deserve. But I'm very close to coming already. Once I get inside you I'm never going to last for more than a few minutes."

"Please don't make me wait," she begged. "Don't make *us* wait. I want you so much, Tate. I don't know how long *I'll* last once you get inside me!"

He chuckled low in amusement, his hands growing bolder in their exploration of her most intimate areas. "My girl is greedy tonight. I like that."

She almost growled in frustration because despite his earlier words of not being able to last long, he was taking his sweet time working her up to inevitable release.

It wasn't unnoticed by her that instead of using a flogger to mark her back and behind, he covered every inch of the area he'd usually kiss with leather with his mouth instead. A long sigh escaped her. This was a very different Tate tonight, but she didn't mind in the least. She knew in her heart that he couldn't bring himself to break out the flogger because he was instead showing her his love and tenderness in a completely different way. One she found ultimately satisfying.

His teeth grazed the small of her back, eliciting tiny chill bumps dancing over her skin. Then he followed with his tongue until she was straining against the bonds with impatience.

And then finally, just when she was prepared to beg him to put an end to it, he spread her buttocks, pushing upward so he had access to her pussy, and positioned himself just at her opening.

She could feel his broad head pushing inward, inch by delicious inch. Then he stopped and a strangled sound of need erupted from her throat.

"Does my girl want this?" he asked in a teasing voice.

He withdrew partially and she moaned her protest.

"Tell me what you want," he said in a gruff, demanding voice.

"You," she choked out. "All of you. Please, Tate. I need you."

He rewarded her with a forceful thrust that seated him to the very hilt. His hips pressed against the insides of her thighs and he held himself there a long moment as his groan of pleasure mingled with her sigh.

"God, Chessy," he said in a strangled voice. "You feel so damn good."

She made a humming sound deep in her throat. It was all she could muster. Words escaped her as indescribable pleasure rocked over her body. Her fingers curled into tight fists, held firmly by the rope securing her to the bedpost.

Slowly, he withdrew, the walls of her vagina protesting, trying to suck him back in like a greedy fist. Then he slammed forward again, forcing her feet from the floor where they were planted. She gasped at the fullness of his possession. So deep. He was hard as stone, stretching her pussy to its maximum width.

His fingers curled around her hips, lifting her to meet his thrusts. She closed her eyes, completely giving herself over to the ecstasy shuddering through her body. He knew exactly how to please her, how to torment her with delicious, edgy pleasure. Knew just how close to bring her to the edge before pulling her back only for her orgasm to rebuild, bigger and more cataclysmic.

How he managed to last as long as he did was a mystery to

her. She could feel just how close he was to hurtling over the cliff. His fingers tightened in her flesh, his thrusts became more frantic but yet he'd slow, pulling them both back.

Her need had become desperate. She was nearly sobbing at the overwhelming pressure, the promise of something utterly beautiful and all consuming.

"Say my name," he said hoarsely.

"Tate!" she cried.

"Who owns you, Chessy? Who do you belong to?"

"You," she sobbed. "Only you, Tate."

"Then come for me."

He thrust hard, forcefully, harder than before, purposely driving her to the brink of insanity. She was mindless, writhing against the bonds that held her tight. She turned her face into the mattress, screaming as her orgasm welled and burst like a cascade of fireworks.

He began coming, flooding her with his release. His semen made his thrusts smoother and easier. Impossibly, he drove even deeper, her body opening and welcoming him like a long-lost lover. And in essence he was. This was their renewal. A reunion of souls.

He strained against her, his hips pumping hard and fast while the rest of his body remained solidly glued to hers. His hands left her hips and slid up her spine, soothing her in the aftermath of her explosive orgasm. And then he lowered his body, his cock pulsing deeply in her vagina.

He blanketed her with his warmth and strength. She could feel his heartbeat, fast and furious, against the small of her back. And then his cheek lowered, lying against her skin. Trapped between him and the mattress, her own heart raced.

Turning his face, brushing against her hypersensitive flesh, he pressed his lips to her spine.

"You're my girl, Chessy. Never doubt that," he whispered, the words wrapping around her heart, squeezing with love and renewed hope.

They were back!

"Give me the words, baby."

"I'm your girl," she said dutifully.

"And who does my girl love?"

"You," she said. "Only you."

"Who owns you?" he growled.

He pushed further into her, his cock still turgid inside her even after his release. Her body shuddered, chill bumps prickling across her skin.

"You do," she whispered.

"Who loves you?" he asked in a softer voice.

Her heart surged to overflowing. Tears pricked her eyelids and she closed her eyes briefly to hold them at bay.

"You do."

"Who knows you're his world? The one who's gifted with your submission?"

"You, Tate. Only you."

He kissed her skin again, a soft benediction as his words whispered over her flesh.

"I love you, Chessy. Only you. Remember you're my girl."

"I love you too, Tate."

She had to stop because tears were running freely down her face, wetting the mattress her cheek rested on.

"Chess?"

The concern in his voice made her scrub her tear-stained face into the mattress. She didn't want to fall apart now of all times.

He withdrew carefully, mindful not to hurt her. Then he immediately untied her hands, tossing aside the rope.

"Chessy?" he asked again as he climbed onto the bed beside her. "Talk to me, baby. What's wrong? Did I hurt you?"

He pulled her into his arms, positioning her on her side, and used his arm to pillow her head. Then he slid his hand over her damp cheek, wiping away the tears. He leaned over, kissing away every bit of moisture from her face before cupping her jaw and tilting her chin upward so she met his gaze.

"What's wrong, baby?"

The concern in his eyes was nearly her undoing and damn it but the tears started all over again. She gave a quiet hiccup, the strain of trying to keep her emotions at bay making her chest ache.

It was as if a dam had suddenly burst and tears ran like a river as she stared back at her husband. They were back. It was as if the last two years had been erased and all that mattered was here and now. Her in his arms. Him taking back control.

"Chessy, you're starting to scare me. What the hell is going on? Talk to me."

"Nothing's wrong," she finally managed to say in a faltering voice. "Everything is *right*."

He heaved a visible sigh of relief and touched his forehead to hers. "You nearly gave me a heart attack, baby. I thought I'd done something wrong. Or hurt you."

She shook her head as he wiped another trail of tears from her cheek. "I love you so much, Tate. I've waited so long for this. It seems like I waited for an eternity. And now we're back. I've missed you—this—so much."

He gathered her more closely in his arms and kissed her tenderly. "You've always had me, Chess. I know it doesn't seem like it. I haven't acted like it. I haven't given you what you need—what you deserve. But I swear all of that is going to change starting now. I don't want to lose you. I can't envision a future without you."

She snuggled into his arms, tucking her head underneath his chin. "You'll never lose me, Tate. I don't want to be without you either. I'm afraid you're stuck with me."

He chuckled, the sound rumbling from his chest and vibrating her cheek. "I'll suffer the inconvenience of me being stuck with you."

TWELVE

CHESSY entered the Lux Café wearing a broad smile and with a skip in her step. Kylie was there, and as usual, excluding the last time they'd met for lunch, Joss was running late. Kylie lifted one eyebrow when Chessy all but danced up to their booth. But there was relief in her eyes when she stood to hug Chessy.

"Thank God," Kylie said fervently. "Joss and I have been so worried, Chessy. We didn't hear from you all weekend! Jensen swore that was a good thing but I wasn't so sure until now. You're positively glowing!"

They were interrupted as Joss hurried up to the table. Like Kylie, there was concern in Joss's eyes but as she studied a beaming Chessy, her eyes brightened and a smile lit up her face.

"You look so happy, Chessy!" Joss said in a hushed whisper.

TAKING IT ALL 119

"Let's sit," Chessy urged. "I don't want the entire restaurant to hear the sordid details of my anniversary weekend!"

"Ooohh, sordid!" Kylie crowed as she pushed into the booth and then motioned for Chessy to slide into the middle from the other side so she'd be flanked by Joss and Kylie.

Chessy complied and then Joss scooted in next to her.

"We're dying to hear the down and dirty," Joss said. "When we didn't hear from you I knew it had to be a good sign because if things went badly you would have called us."

Chessy smiled and nodded. Then she let out a wistful sigh. "Oh you guys, it was wonderful. Just like old times. I had my Tate back."

"So did you spill your heart?" Kylie asked. "Tell me you didn't back down and not bring up your issues."

Chessy shook her head. "No, I didn't back down," she said softly. "It actually began a total disaster."

Joss's mouth dropped open and Kylie's eyes narrowed.

"How was it a disaster?" Joss exclaimed.

Chessy winced. "He didn't show for our dinner. I was on my way out and I saw him in the bar with another woman."

"Oh. My. God," Kylie said, fury evident in her voice. "What the hell? On your anniversary?"

"It wasn't pretty," Chessy admitted. "I jumped to some major conclusions and walked out. He came after me and we had it out."

"I bet," Joss murmured.

"But it's okay now," Chessy said. "I know I gave y'all an abbreviated version but I'd rather not rehash it. The woman was a potential client. He met her in the bar so he could come straight to dinner and time got away from him. When I confronted him with how unhappy I am, he was horrified. He's apologized a million times. And he promised to put me front and center from now on."

"Do you believe him?" Kylie asked softly.

Chessy nodded. "He was so sincere. And so upset and *afraid*. Afraid I was going to leave him. Honestly, guys, it scared him to death. That more than anything told me that he still loves me and wants me. And well, he spent the rest of the weekend proving just that."

Color rose in her cheeks, her skin flushed and warm.

Joss and Kylie exchanged knowing smirks.

"Did he break out the flogger?" Joss teased.

Kylie looked appalled, which made Chessy laugh. Kylie couldn't comprehend the lifestyle that both Chessy and Joss lived, but she accepted it with good nature, even if she couldn't envision herself in such a relationship. She shook her head and shot an accusing look in Joss's direction.

"You did that on purpose to get a reaction out of me," Kylie said in a sour voice.

Chessy laughed and Joss looked delighted.

"You're shining today," Joss commented. "It's like looking at the old Chessy. I'm so glad to have you back, hon. I've hated seeing you so unhappy. I'm so glad you and Tate have made amends, or rather he's making amends. Good for you for confronting him and laying it out to him. I'm not sure I'd have the courage to do something like that."

Kylie snorted. "So says the woman who told Dash off when he pulled his stupidity."

Chessy laughed again and then all three women burst into laughter. God it felt good to feel so light again. The weight of the past two years had become oppressive. Just finally being able to confront Tate with her unhappiness had been so freeing.

"Okay, so he didn't break out the flogger," Joss said, a twinkle in her eyes. "So what did he do? I want all the gory details."

Kylie rolled her eyes and then made a show of plugging both ears. "I'm too innocent to hear this."

Chessy snorted. "Oh please. Like you and Jensen don't perform your own X-rated sex shows? Ever hear of the saying 'doth protest too much'? Well that's you. It's always the quiet ones you have to watch."

Kylie blushed and Joss hooted with laughter. "You nailed her, Chessy. Look at that face. That's the look of a cat who's definitely gotten the cream."

Chessy choked on her drink and nearly spurted water from her nose. "Oh my God, you said cream. I'm dying over here."

Kylie groaned. "Dear Lord. You both have to stop. Is everything a sexual innuendo with you two?"

"Yes!" both Chessy and Joss said in unison.

They immediately hushed when the waiter arrived to take their order. As soon as he left, they burst into laughter again. Tears streamed down Joss's face and she hastily wiped her eyes with the table napkin.

"You two are incorrigible," Kylie grumbled. "Let's leave my sex life out of this."

"This is a novelty," Chessy teased. "You having a sex life, I mean. A few months ago you would have been appalled by the notion. It's high time you got in on the action."

Kylie lowered her head and beat her forehead against the table. "What did I do to deserve this?"

"Hmmm, I'd say Jensen is very rewarding," Joss said, a dreamy look on her face.

Kylie's smile was rueful. "I can't argue with you there. But can we please move on to a different topic? Chessy still hasn't filled us in with all the juicy details."

Chessy grinned. "Let's just say that Tate and I are well on our way back to the way things used to be. At first he held back his dominance. I think he was too focused on making sure I wasn't going anywhere. After the horridness of our anniversary night, he kicked it into high gear. He made love to me like whoa. No dominance. Just tenderness that was so sweet it made my heart ache. But at the same time I wanted his dominance. I didn't want our relationship to change. I just wanted us back, you know?"

"Yeah, I know," Joss said softly.

"I get it," Kylie admitted. "Jensen is dominant in all aspects except our sex life. There . . . he gives up complete control to me. But one day . . . One day I'd like to be able to give him control there too. We're both going to therapy. I'm hoping it will help me trust him more. That sounds so awful. I do trust him. In my heart I know he'd never hurt me. But it's hard. And more than me knowing he'd never hurt me, he has to believe that too."

Chessy reached for Kylie's hand and squeezed. "I understand completely, sweetie. And you'll get there. Rome wasn't built in a day, you know. Jensen is so perfect for you. So patient and understanding. The fact that he's willing to give up control in the bedroom is amazing. It proves just how much he loves you to deny that part of himself."

Kylie's eyes became watery. "But I don't want him to have to deny any part of himself. And that's what bothers me. I want him to have control but I'm not there yet."

"You'll get there," Joss repeated. "Give it time. You've only been together a short time."

"So Tate didn't . . . dominate you?" Kylie asked. The words came out strangled, as if she didn't know what label to put on Chessy's relationship with Tate.

Chessy's smile was gentle. She let go of Kylie's hand as the waiter delivered their entrees. Only when he was gone did she address Kylie's question.

"At first no. I think he didn't think it was appropriate. In fact, he very much humbled himself. For a moment it was as if he was the submissive and I was the Dominant, which is laughable since I'm the furthest from a Dominant you can get. I think he felt awkward about just falling into our old routine. It was an apology, I think. He was so reverent and careful. It was wonderful, don't get me wrong, but I wanted—needed— his dominance. And so after our dinner do-over, that's when he retook control."

"I'm glad for you," Joss said sincerely. "I've hated seeing you so unhappy, Chessy. I'm sure now that you've let Tate know how you feel that you'll see a change in the way he treats you."

Chessy winced. "That sounds so bad when you say it like that. Like he was abusing me or something."

"Neglect is akin to abuse," Kylie said softly. "You should know that better than anyone."

Chessy's heart clenched at the subtle reminder of her childhood. Not abused, but unwanted. She wasn't sure which was worse. Both were unforgiveable for a parent to subject a child to. She'd spent her entire childhood ignored, dismissed, unloved and a nuisance to parents who'd never wanted a child.

Tate was well aware of the circumstances of her childhood. He'd been the first person she'd ever confided in. As soon as she'd turned eighteen, she'd left her home and worked her way through college. Her parents hadn't even bothered to show up for her high school graduation much less her graduation from college.

Her phone chimed, signaling a text message. Grateful for the interruption so the conversation didn't dissolve into a dissection of her childhood, she dug into her purse and clicked on the text. It was from Tate.

Have an important client meeting at 4:30. I'll be home no later than 6. I promise. I'll bring supper. Love my girl.

Chessy's heart sank, dread tightening her chest. When she looked up, her friends had worry in their eyes. Chessy forced a bright smile. After all, how long had it been since he just texted her with his plans much less to say he loved her and that he'd bring home dinner. She'd revel in that aspect and set aside her paranoia. The last thing she wanted to do was ruin a perfectly good day when things had gone so well the past two days.

"Oh, that was just Tate telling me he was bringing supper home."

She left out the rest because she didn't want to see knowing looks in their eyes.

THIRTEEN

AT five minutes after six, Chessy was pacing the living room checking her watch. A worried frown tugged at her lips. Surely he wouldn't be late the very first day back at work after their come-to-Jesus anniversary weekend.

She sucked in a deep breath and tried to talk herself down. He had a client meeting at four thirty. Then there was rush-hour traffic. Not to mention he was picking up takeout. There were plenty of perfectly normal reasons he could be a few minutes late.

She checked her watch again. He was only seven minutes late. Not the end of the world. Damn her for being so paranoid. She could be flexible. He didn't have to be at her beck and call every waking moment, nor did he have to be accountable to her for doing his job.

But it worried her. What if this weekend had been him hitting the panic button and saying and doing whatever it took to appease her? What if he had no intention of changing his routine?

Guilt crushed through her chest when she heard the sound of his car pulling up. How could she have doubted him? She forced herself not to rush to the door to greet him. There was no way she wanted him to know how worried and paranoid she'd been with no reason.

A moment later, the front door opened and Tate appeared holding a plastic bag with the take-out containers inside. He was juggling his briefcase and his suit coat as he kicked the door shut with his foot.

Chessy hurried over to him to take the bag and then leaned up on tiptoe to kiss him on the cheek.

"Sorry I'm late, baby," he said, regret lining his brow. "The restaurant messed up my phone order and I had to wait for them to remake it. I got your favorite."

Her heart melted at the very real worry in his eyes. She felt so guilty for doubting him, for worrying that he wouldn't keep his word.

She carried the bag containing the take-out order to the breakfast nook where she'd already set out plates and silverware while Tate tossed his suit coat over the back of the sofa.

"You want wine?" she asked. "I put a bottle out a little while ago, but if you'd prefer something different, I'll get it."

He snagged her waist and pressed a kiss to her lips. "Whatever you picked out is fine. Have I told you lately how beautiful you are?"

A giddy thrill assailed her. Her heart turned over in her chest as she smiled broadly up at him. She wrapped both arms around him and leaned into his embrace.

Her smile became dreamy, love surging through her heart. "I'll never get tired of you saying so."

"Mmm, what about I love you and you're my girl?"

She sighed. "Even better. Sit down while I pour you a glass of wine. Tell me about your day and your client meeting. Did it go well?"

A brief look of discomfort crossed his face before he turned swiftly to pull out his chair. When he was settled, he met her gaze again, no hint of the previous discomfort evident, leaving her to wonder if she'd imagined it.

"Oh, the usual," Tate said in a casual tone. "The meeting was with a potential client who's considering transferring a large portfolio to my firm. It would be quite a coup if it comes to pass."

She set his glass of wine in front of him and then slid into the seat next to him. "That's wonderful, Tate. You've worked so hard. It doesn't surprise me that you're landing bigger and bigger clients."

He caught her hand and pulled her over to sit on his lap. He thrust a hand into her hair, cupping the side of her head as he tugged her down to meet his lips. "Your confidence in me and support of me means everything. Knowing my girl is behind me makes me feel like I can own the world."

She smiled and cupped his face in her hands, returning his kiss with one of her own. "I have no doubt you could do just that if you set your mind to it."

"I'd much prefer to own *you*."

"You do, Tate. I belong to you. Always. Heart, soul, body and mind."

"I have a surprise for you," he murmured. "Well, two actually."

She couldn't control the surge of delight that made a broad smile curve her lips. She *adored* surprises and Tate well knew it. It didn't matter how simple or elaborate. *Anything* Tate gave her was treasured and met with utter delight.

"Tell me!" she said, all but pouncing on him. She jiggled and bounced on his lap in excited anticipation.

He laughed and patted her hip. "Hop up so I can get the first one. It's in my jacket pocket."

She scrambled off his lap and perched on her chair, waiting impatiently as he strolled leisurely over to the couch to retrieve his coat. He dug into his pocket and pulled out a beautifully wrapped small box with a shiny silver bow. Her eyes widened and she nearly bounced out of her chair when he walked back over.

He slid the box along the tabletop until it rested in front of her.

"Happy anniversary to my girl," he said huskily. "I intended to give it to you Friday night, but we got . . . sidetracked."

She caught her frown before it appeared. Just thinking back on their emotional, gut-wrenching anniversary night was enough to remove all her present joy. So she focused instead on here and now and the fact that her husband was *back*.

She reverently opened the wrapping, taking her time so she didn't tear it. He chuckled as he watched her, shaking his head.

"I've never understood why you don't just rip into it. It's just paper, Chess."

"But it's beautiful paper," she protested. "I hate to tear something so pretty."

He laughed again but fell silent until she got to the box underneath. With shaking fingers, she opened the lid and shook out the velvet jewelry case inside. She sucked in her breath when she finally managed to reveal the contents.

Inside was a radiant, sparkling diamond bracelet that caught the light and twinkled brilliantly. She held it up, viewing it in awe, and tears burned the edges of her eyelids, making the bracelet blur in her vision.

"Ah hell, Chess. Don't cry."

She gave him a watery smile and then sniffled. "I can't help it. It's gorgeous, Tate! I love it. Put it on for me, please. My hands are shaking so badly I'll never be able to get it latched."

He laughed but complied, carefully looping the tennis bracelet around her left wrist. It made her look and feel decadent with the gorgeous diamond wedding ring and now an equally beautiful diamond bracelet. She felt as lit up as a Christmas tree.

When he was done, she held up her arm, twisting it this way and that, watching in fascination as it caught the light and sparkled just like the Christmas tree she'd just thought she resembled.

Then she threw herself back onto his lap and kissed him ferociously. "I love it," she said fervently. "I absolutely adore it! Thank you. You've made this the perfect anniversary weekend and Monday!"

A brief shadow crossed his face, as he no doubt remembered the inauspicious start to their anniversary. Sorrow and regret brimmed in his eyes before she kissed him again, soothing away the painful reminder to them both.

When she finally drew away, she remembered that he'd said he had *two* surprises.

"What's the other surprise?" she asked, excitement once more bubbling to the surface.

He smiled and tenderly pushed a strand of her curly hair from her cheek. "It's not immediate, rather it's a surprise I've planned for us."

"Oh, I like it when you say *us*," she said dreamily. "What is it? Tell me, tell me!"

He chuckled. "My girl is so impatient."

She mimicked strangling him by wrapping her fingers around his neck and adopting a ferocious scowl. "Stop holding out on me and *spill*."

He kissed the tip of her nose and then pulled away so he could gaze into her eyes.

"I know it's been a long while since we visited The House. So I've planned a night for us. Two weeks from now on a Friday night. I've even already hand-picked the man who will participate in our fantasy."

Her pulse immediately began to race and she couldn't

control the surge of wicked anticipation that licked like flames over her skin. Images from the past, the immeasurable pleasure they'd both enjoyed, raced through her mind. Another man touching her, pleasuring her, at Tate's behest. Under his command, always in control, stepping in only when Chessy neared her orgasm. Those belonged to him. It was one of the two things he wouldn't allow another man. The other was that another man was never to kiss her on the lips. Some may think it was an odd "rule" but Chessy understood completely.

Kissing on the lips was decidedly more intimate than being kissed in other places. It signaled a more emotional connection, one only found between her and Tate.

"Is it someone I know?" she asked in a low voice. "I mean is it someone you've chosen before?"

He stroked her cheek. "Is my girl worried? We don't have to do this, Chess. I wanted to do something special for you. For us. I know it's something we enjoyed in the past and I'm just sorry that I've let it go as long as I have without giving you something that brings us both pleasure."

"No, that isn't it at all," she denied. "I was merely curious. If I shouldn't be asking or if you don't want me to know, that's fine. But when on earth did you have time to pull this all together? Did you plan it before our anniversary?"

She was genuinely curious to know whether he'd planned it before or after the debacle of their anniversary night.

"You have the right to know anything that affects you," he said firmly. "To answer your question, no, this isn't someone we've played with in the past. I spoke to Damon and he gave me a few names of men who didn't mind playing the Dominant when in actuality I would be in total command of every aspect. I arranged to meet them this morning. It's why my client meeting was so late in the day. I wish I could say that I had planned this prior to our anniversary. It's something I should have been more aware of, and I'm sorry for that. But I picked a man I thought would give you the most pleasure while allowing me to dictate what he does and doesn't do. When I showed him your picture I thought he was damn near going to swallow his tongue."

He laughed as he said the last and Chessy smiled.

"So he liked what he saw?" she asked innocently.

"Oh yeah. He liked."

A thought occurred to her, one that had her blushing to the roots of her hair. Her entire face was literally on fire.

"Tate, tell me you didn't show him one of *those* pictures," she whispered.

Those pictures being ones Tate had taken of her in different sexual positions and in various stages of undress. Bound hand and foot. Some naked and spread-eagled, her hands and feet splayed wide and restrained in all directions.

They were beautifully erotic, but only intended for Tate. It made her sound like the ultimate hypocrite, being willing to allow another man to touch her. To flog her, mark her, give her pleasure. So why object to Tate ever showing such pictures to another man?

Except that to her those pictures were personal and were meant to be shared only between her and her husband. It didn't *have* to make sense to anyone but her.

Tate's expression grew serious. He cupped her chin, rubbing his thumb gently down her jawline.

"I would never betray your trust," he said gravely. "Those pictures are for me and only me. I showed the man—James—one of my favorite pictures of you from our vacation in the Caribbean. The one of you in that sexy sundress smiling brightly enough to outshine the sun. There isn't a man alive who wouldn't be on his knees to have a woman like you. And that certainly includes me. You're mine," he said in a thoroughly satisfied voice.

She smiled then, feeling awful for having questioned him in the first place. It was baffling to her, this new turn in their relationship, where she seemed to question him with growing frequency.

She'd never questioned him in the past. She always, without fail, abided by his decisions. Accepted without reservation whatever he chose. So why now? She bit into her bottom lip, knowing *exactly* why she had begun to question him, even if she hadn't openly acknowledged it until now. She couldn't quite shake the sense of betrayal even though Tate was going above and beyond to make amends. Maybe these things just took time. They'd both already admitted that it would take more than a weekend to set to rights two years of unhappiness and the fear of their marriage dissolving.

"I'm sorry," she said quietly.

His look of surprise took her aback. "What are you sorry for, baby?"

"For questioning you. For not trusting you."

His expression softened and warmth entered his eyes. He put his arms around her and rubbed up and down her back in a soothing pattern.

"I'd say you have reason for both," he admitted. "I haven't *acted* like someone you could trust or not question over the last two years. It's me who should be apologizing to you, *not* the other way around."

"You already have. More than enough times," she said firmly. "And my apology still stands. I gave you my trust before we were even married. I gave you my love and then my submission and then my life when I married you. I'll never regret any of those choices, Tate. I want you to know that. As far as I'm concerned the past is in the past. We've moved beyond that point and I have complete faith in you that you'll keep your promise of putting me first from now on."

"You have the most loving, generous heart," he said in a voice thick with emotion. "I don't deserve you. I don't deserve your forgiveness and I damn sure don't deserve your trust after I've failed you at every turn."

She put her fingers to his lips to hush him before he could continue.

"I'd much rather hear about this night of decadence you've promised me," she said with a wicked grin. "Or am I not allowed to know?"

He smiled back at her, the shadows erased from his eyes. This moment felt so much like old times. Her sitting on his lap and them just talking, teasing and just . . . *being*. It felt utterly perfect.

"All I will tell you is that I will personally choose what you wear to The House and, just a warning, it's going to be positively sinful. At least for the time you're wearing it, that is," he said in a deliciously evil tone that sent a rush of anticipation flooding through her veins.

"Except for the shoes," he murmured thoughtfully. "I plan to find out where Kylie got her killer fuck-me shoes because I'm buying you a pair just like them so that when I fuck you the *only* thing you'll be wearing are those shoes. It will give my 'helpers' plenty of leverage to hold you down so you're utterly helpless to my every whim."

Helpers? Her mind was ablaze trying to imagine such a scenario. In all of the fantasies they'd played out at The House over the years, apart from Tate and whatever man he involved to fulfill both hers and Tate's decadence, that was where it ended. Tate and whomever he deemed deserving to put his hands on what Tate considered his property. And now he had used helper in the plural. *Helpers.* Meaning more than one!

"Uh, Tate, I know I just apologized for questioning or trusting you, but can you tell me a little more about this trip to The House? You mentioned helpers, meaning more than one, and you specifically singled out James as the one who'd flog and mark my skin until it's rosy and evenly marked so that when you take me you see those marks and while you didn't administer them yourself, they were still put there by your command. I see the satisfaction that brings you."

Tate nodded.

"But adding more than this guy James? What exactly are

you planning for me—us—that night, or is all that top secret and I find out when I get there?"

"If you're afraid or unsure then we don't go. Period. There is no way in hell I'd ever force something on you that you were not completely on board with, and with me, seeing me, knowing in your heart that I am the only true Dominant for you, I think you'll be more than satisfied with the plans for the evening."

"You're such a tease," she groaned. "I want to know more! I'm dying to know all the dirty details."

He chuckled but evidently decided to give her more information. Or perhaps it would only end up being a tease fest where he whipped her up into an even more frantic state of anticipation.

The one word that had never escaped her lips, much less her mind, was *fear*. She was never afraid when Tate was there, even if a few feet away. He may have a desk job but the man was completely serious when it came to his workouts. She teased him all the time about being the most gorgeous, well-dressed fashion plate to go to the office and talk to clients on the phone all day.

Oh there was more to it. She was making light of his job. She knew he had many important dinners, lunches, after-work drinks, calls at all hours of the night. And in the beginning she hadn't minded. Each accomplishment made her prouder and prouder. But somehow along the way his job—his struggle after his partner bailed—had faltered at first and so Tate had thrown all of his time and energy into making it a solid success. Endless and countless lunches, dinners, golfing. Meetings for drinks. It had become all-consuming.

"I will lead you into the common room by your collar."

Her hand automatically went to her throat where the delicate jeweled collar rested.

"I'm having another specially made just for that night, and it will be ready this week. I'll pick it up when I also go pick up what you'll be wearing to the event. And those killer fuck-me shoes. Those are at the top of the list.

"But every man in The House that night will know you belong to me. The leash is also being fashioned, yet another thing to do on my shopping trip. Well, and there's the lingerie I had to get my girl because just imagining you with that outfit the damn mannequin was wearing gave me a hard-on that lasted thirty fucking minutes!"

Chessy could hold back her laughter no longer. She shook against him, her giggles muffled by his shirt.

But Tate was still being serious. "I have the perfect earrings and necklace. It is my intention to drape you in jewels and nothing else. Every eye in the common room will be on you. You'll wear your hair down. I love your curls. And you may as well just forgo makeup because I guarantee, before the night is over, there will be none left."

He said the last with a smirk that told her he'd be getting as much pleasure from their role-playing as she would.

One of his favorite scenarios was to have another man fuck her ass while Tate fucked her mouth. And yeah, that would definitely ruin a makeup job, and if such hedonistic pleasure awaited her she was more than happy to forgo being fully made up for the evening.

Her thoughts turned dreamy again. So far she'd remembered all the pleasure Tate had received as if she were a plaything, brought out for boys' enjoyment and then put away with no regard for her whatsoever. And it certainly wasn't true.

Tate, even though he was a forceful Dom, was also exceedingly gentle and tender, often interpreting her body signals before she even knew what her body was telling her. He always seemed to know exactly what she wanted more of. Or less of. Or what made her wild with want and need. He was so in tune with her body. Hell, he was in tune with her damn thoughts most of the time. But then her friends had always told her she was as transparent as glass.

When she was happy she shone. Brought light and warmth into any room. But when she was unhappy? It was equally evident. All the light that surrounded her on a seemingly endless basis just burned out. Deep shadows had formed underneath her eyes and she was already getting lines across her brow from worrying and stressing.

"I don't need to know any more," she said warmly. "I do trust you, Tate. My curiosity always gets the better of me. You know that. I'm more than happy to wait. I don't want to ruin the surprise for you since it's obvious you've spent most of the day today preparing for this outing."

"And how do you feel about going, Chess? Be straight with me. Does it make you scared or nervous?"

She immediately shook her head. "As long as you're there with me the entire time. That the commands come from you. As long as I know you're in complete control, then yes, absolutely. I want to go. I'm not scared or nervous. Not when I have you."

"God I love you," he breathed into her mouth. "And I promise that our night at The House will be a night you'll never forget."

FOURTEEN

CHESSY'S impending night out at The House was met with completely opposite reactions from Joss and Kylie. Kylie tried very hard to hide her confusion and the fact that she didn't understand the lifestyle her two best friends had chosen.

And while Joss was, in reality, a newcomer to the submissive lifestyle, it had been a want, a desperate need that went years back. It was the one thing her husband hadn't ever been able to give to her and Joss loved him too much to ever pressure him. So her need had gone unrequited. Until Dash. Her dead husband's best friend.

Now, *Joss* understood completely Chessy's excitement over a night at The House. It was a place Joss and Dash had frequented before Joss learned of her pregnancy. Dash would never do anything that could cause possible harm to their child, not that he'd ever cause Joss to come to any harm either, but he guided her with a fiercely protective dominance. Something Tate and Dash had shared in theory but not in practice over the last two years.

But Chessy and Tate were picking up the pieces and both were deeply committed to repairing their fragile relationship. It was all she could ask for. Just for Tate to reevaluate and recommit himself to her. Even her own commitment was being renewed. Stronger. More everlasting this time so that nothing would ever come between them again.

The women were enjoying a later than usual lunch the day before Chessy and Tate's upcoming evening at The House and Chessy was brimming with hope and optimism. Not that she'd ever look to another man to somehow fill a gap in her marriage to Tate. Just the opposite. The nights at The House had occurred frequently in the first few years of their marriage. It was something they embraced—enjoyed—and it brought them even closer. For some couples such a thing would certainly drive a wedge between them. Jealousy always had the potential to overshadow all else when another person was introduced into a relationship. But she, or rather Tate, had never exhibited any signs of jealousy—but then Chessy had never had to contend with another woman in the picture. She was honest enough with herself to acknowledge she would likely be insanely jealous were another woman to touch Tate, but then Tate had never even entertained the idea, to Chessy's knowledge. He seemed content with their current arrangement. In fact, he seemed to derive as much pleasure from the act as Chessy did herself. It was no coincidence in her mind that when they *stopped* exploring the darker side of their desires,.the rift had begun.

Any time a marriage lost both an emotional *and* a physical connection it was no longer about a kink they both enjoyed. It had become a matter of survival. The survival of their love and their marriage.

As soon as the waiter delivered their entrees and they were afforded complete privacy, Chessy asked the question she was sure was also burning a hole in Joss's brain. Chessy reached for Kylie's hand and squeezed.

"How did your first counseling session with Jensen go?"

Kylie's expression became shuttered and she briefly glanced away. Then, as if realizing that Joss and Chessy were her best friends and confidantes, she looked back up, vulnerability shining in her eyes.

Chessy tightened her hold on Kylie's hand while Joss reached for Kylie's other.

"You don't have to tell us," Joss said in a low voice. "The last thing we want is for you to be uncomfortable. We were both worried and we knew since it was only the first time that things may not have gone as well as you'd like. So say as much or as little as you're okay with. Chessy and I love you. You're our sister in our hearts. We just want you to know that you can always talk to us about anything and we'd never betray your confidence. Even to Dash or Tate."

As Joss spoke, she glanced Chessy's way as if gauging whether she was speaking for the both of them and if Chessy was in agreement with all Joss had to say.

Chessy nodded immediately. "Absolutely. We just want you to know we love you and we worry about you. You and Joss are my best friends in the world, and God knows you've both nursed me through my frequent misery and bouts of self-pity."

Kylie gave them a watery smile, which prompted Joss to shove a table napkin into the hand Joss had only just let go. It was a well-known fact in the group that Kylie hated crying. Especially in public. It would mortify her if she knew someone saw her losing control in a room full of people.

Kylie accepted the napkin and wiped hastily at her face. "At least I didn't wear makeup today," she said ruefully.

"You're too beautiful to need makeup," Joss said firmly.

Chessy smiled her agreement.

Kylie laughed, her tears replaced by mirth. "You're both so full of shit but I love you for it." Then her expression sobered once more and she breathed out a sigh. "The therapy session went okay. I mean I guess as well as it could go considering that for me it was akin to bloodletting. The therapist wants to see us individually first before she sees us together. Monday is Jensen's turn and then I suppose the therapist will compare notes on our insanity and try to put the puzzle pieces together or try to figure out how two equally fucked-up people ever belong in a relationship together."

Chessy scowled. "That better be sarcasm or your twisted

sense of humor coming out because you and Jensen are perfect for one another."

Kylie smiled. "I may have inserted a *little* sarcasm."

Joss snorted. "Ya think? Come on. Give us the real scoop. Unless of course it's too personal and you'd rather not get into it."

Kylie rolled her eyes and shook her head. "I think we've established that I seem to have no personal boundaries when it comes to the two of you. Just recently, as I recall, we were shitfaced drunk in Joss's living room and I was blurting out what a stupid-head Jensen was and then I revealed my grand seduction plan of making love to him and *then* tying him to the bed. If I survived telling you guys all of that I think a visit to my therapist pales in comparison."

Chessy and Joss both dissolved into laughter.

"She does have a point," Chessy admitted. "Even Dash was privy to that particular outburst. But it was a brilliant plan. I have to give you that."

Kylie groaned and briefly covered her face with her hands. "Did you have to remind me that Dash was there to witness my drunken humiliation?"

"Hey, it worked, did it not?" Joss demanded. "I'd say you pulled that plan off spectacularly."

A satisfied smile curved Kylie's lips upward, effectively erasing all the earlier conflicting emotions that had shone in her eyes.

"Yeah, it worked," Kylie said in a faraway tone that told both the other women she was taking an X-rated trip down memory lane.

Then she shook her head as if coming down from the clouds, her expression growing somber once more.

"We discussed my childhood and my inability—or rather my inability until I met Jensen—to form relationships with men. And the fact that in particular I feared dominant, strong men. She made me feel . . . *normal*."

The last was said in a bewildered tone as if Kylie had never until now considered herself remotely normal.

"Sweetie, of course you're normal," Chessy defended. "After what you endured at your father's hands I'd say you *wouldn't* be normal if that didn't affect you well into your adult life. Think about it. The one man in a little girl's life she's supposed to be able to trust above all others, the one who is supposed to protect her at all costs, betrayed you horribly. He abused you horribly. No woman—I don't care if she's Super Woman—could escape that kind of horror unscathed."

"Besides, you've merely been discerning when it comes to men," Joss said with conviction. "That doesn't make you abnormal. That makes you picky, and all women should be picky when it comes to choosing the man they'll trust and give their hearts to. Can you imagine your life without Jensen now? What if you'd hooked up with some other guy? You wouldn't have what you have now, so fuck normal."

Chessy's and Kylie's mouths both dropped open in unison. Then Chessy burst into laughter until tears streaked down her cheeks. She coughed and wheezed into her napkin while Joss gave them both looks of bewilderment.

"Well, that's one way to put it," Kylie said ruefully. "And it mirrors what Jensen himself has said. I believe his exact words were 'fuck normal.'"

"I always knew he was a smart man," Joss said in a smug tone that matched her expression.

"It's just so funny to hear you dropping F-bombs," Chessy said, still laughing. "Not that you haven't before. It's just not your normal MO."

Joss rolled her eyes. "I swear you two seem to think I'm some Miss Goody Two Shoes."

"Oh no, we became well aware that you're the closet bad girl of this group," Kylie said dryly. "I might have considered you Little Miss Sunshine at one time, but that was *before* you told us at lunch that you were going to The House and wanted to hook up with a dominant man. I think it's safe to say that we certainly reevaluated any assumptions we'd made about you in the past."

Joss's cheeks turned a delightful shade of pink and Kylie and Chessy both burst into laughter.

"Busted!" Chessy crowed.

Kylie turned her gaze in Chessy's direction in a swift change in topic, once more putting the focus on Chessy, and likely relieved to have it off herself. But that was just Kylie. She'd certainly come a long way but it didn't mean she liked being thrust into the spotlight. Even by her best friends.

"So, uhm, you've sort of said in the past what it is you and Tate do at The House, but I'll be honest, I mostly tuned you out. I know that sounds horrible, but my virgin ears could only take so much!"

"Oh for the love of God," Joss muttered. "So says a woman who tied her boyfriend to her bed. The only difference here is that our husbands tie *us* to the bed."

Chessy smothered her laughter with her hand. "Busted again, sweetie. No response to that one, huh."

"So are you going to spill or not?" Kylie persisted, purposely ignoring their needling. "I guess today is a day for morbid curiosity because I confess, I can't wrap my brain around Tate actually sharing you with another man. No matter what your past difficulties may have been, he is and always has been forbiddingly possessive of you."

Chessy was determined not to show any self-consciousness in this discussion. No, it wasn't a conversation she'd have with just anyone, but Kylie and Joss weren't just anyone. They were her best friends. Her sisters, as Joss had so eloquently put it. And she wasn't in the least ashamed of her and Tate's sexual preferences.

"It sounds more complicated than it is," Chessy said ruefully. "Basically Tate chooses a man to dominate me but who is dominated by Tate."

Even Joss blinked over that explanation and then Chessy realized how it had come across. She groaned. "Okay, that is *not* what I meant."

"This I gotta hear," Kylie said in a dry tone.

"Tate chooses a man who would ordinarily act as a Dominant and not take instruction, especially from another Dominant. The man's task is to . . . please . . . me. Tate tells him what to do and how to do it. Tate watches from the sidelines. That's a figurative expression, by the way. Tate is always right there over-seeing every aspect of what goes on. But he directs the action."

Kylie's expression grew thoughtful but she didn't interrupt Chessy's explanation.

"The other man takes me through the paces."

Chessy glanced around uneasily to ensure no one was sit-ting close enough to their booth to potentially overhear and lowered her voice for the remainder of her explanation.

"The man undresses me, slowly, at Tate's command. From there, it's whatever Tate wishes to see or experience."

Kylie frowned. "And not about what *you* want?"

"Oh yes," Chessy said with a radiant smile. "Tate is very aware of what I like, what gives me pleasure. But he likes to surprise me. He never tells me beforehand what to expect. Me not knowing heightens the anticipation. Sometimes the man will bind me to cross bars, arms and legs spread wide. He'll flog me or use leather. Other times he'll secure me over a spank-ing bench and after the man has 'sufficiently prepared' me, Tate will take over and fuck me while my skin is still heated from the kiss of the whip." She could feel the blush working its way up her neck at the blunt way she'd described the scene.

Kylie sent a suspicious glance Joss's way. "You don't seem the least bit shocked or appalled. Just what have you and Dash been up to anyway?"

"Oh, much the same," Joss said cheerfully. "Only without the other guy, and well, not since we learned I was pregnant."

Kylie shook her head. "Clearly I'm the boring one in this group."

Chessy smiled mischievously. "Oh, I don't know. Tying a guy to your bed can't exactly be considered *boring.*"

"Y'all are never going to let go of that, are you?" Kylie asked with an exasperated sigh.

"Nope!" Joss said, a huge grin on her face.

"I think y'all are the ones who need therapy," Kylie grumbled. "I'm looking more 'normal' all the time."

Joss checked her watch and then glanced up at the others in chagrin. "Sorry to eat and run but I have to leave if I'm going to make my OB appointment."

Chessy made a shooing motion with her hand. "You go on. Lunch is on me today."

Joss paused on her way up from the table and pinned Chessy with a pointed stare. "Kylie and I will expect *all* the juicy details Saturday, and if we don't hear from you, we're totally coming over."

FIFTEEN

CHESSY'S phone rang, Tate's ring tone, and she answered quickly. It was around the time Tate usually got off of work and she hoped he wasn't calling to say he would be late.

"Hello?"

Tate's voice was gruff and laced with thick desire.

"I want you naked and kneeling in the living room when I get home."

Her pulse fluttered and sped up, leaving her breathless and nearly unable to respond.

"I'll be waiting," she whispered.

"Love my girl."

"I love you too."

"See you in ten minutes," he said.

Chessy ended the call and then ran for the bathroom,

knowing she didn't have much time. She brushed out her hair as much as she was able. The humidity was particularly high today and the result was her hair being much curlier and less manageable than usual. But then, Tate loved her curls.

She checked her appearance with a critical eye, wanting to look her best. She applied light lip gloss, though it was silly considering it would most certainly be wiped off within minutes of Tate's arrival.

She stripped out of her clothing, tossing it in the laundry basket in the bathroom, and then she hurried back to the living room and settled into a kneeling position on the soft rug in front of the fireplace.

The wait seemed interminable, but then finally she heard the sound of Tate's car pulling up to the house. Her breath caught in her throat and she expelled it in long, shaky breaths.

With their visit to The House coming up the next day, she wondered what Tate had planned for tonight.

The front door opened and then Tate appeared in the living room, his suit coat over one arm, briefcase in the other.

His look of intense appreciation gave her a heady thrill. His eyes glowed with open lust. The fact that after so many years of marriage he still looked at her with the same desire he had when they first married gave her fierce satisfaction. But Tate wanting her had never been the issue.

He slowly laid his things down on the couch and immediately loosened his tie, but held on to it instead of discarding it with the other stuff.

His walk toward her was slow and leisurely as if he were

taking in every bit of the moment. When he finally got within touching distance, his hand gently threaded through her hair and then he roughly pulled her head back and his mouth crashed down over hers, feeding hungrily from her lips.

"Consider tonight a preview of what's to come at The House," he murmured.

Her blood surged and her nipples beaded into tight knots.

"Just be warned, I plan to work you hard," he said. "Remember your safe word."

"I remember," she whispered.

He pulled her arms behind her back, her still in a kneeling position, and he tied her wrists together with his tie. Then he walked around to the front of her and hastily unzipped his pants, pulling his cock free without removing his clothing.

"Open," he commanded.

He shoved his hand into her hair and angled her head back as he grasped his cock with his free hand. She instantly obeyed, opening her lips just as he thrust fully into her mouth. He was rough and she reveled in it. She wanted to sigh her satisfaction that they were returning to the roots of their relationship. Finally.

"Let's see how much you can take," he said gruffly.

He began to thrust hard, hitting the back of her throat with the broad head of his cock. Her cheeks puffed outward and she inhaled sharply through her nose to keep up. But she was determined she would endure whatever he chose to do.

"Very nice," he complimented as he continued to push himself as far as he could go.

Precum wet her tongue and made his thrusts easier to take. His taste filled her mouth and she sucked greedily, wanting more. Wanting him to come down her throat and bathe her face with his release.

But evidently he had other plans.

Just when she was sure he would ejaculate into her throat, he pulled out abruptly and released his hold on her hair.

"I'll be back for you," he said in a low voice. "Do not move."

She nodded her obedience and he left the room, leaving her to wonder just what he was cooking up. The fact that he'd said it was a preview of their night at The House had her nearly light-headed with anticipation.

It was several minutes before he reappeared. And he was completely nude, his erection straining upward so it was flat against his abdomen. Whatever he had planned, he was as excited as she was.

He reached down to untie her hands and then, to her surprise, he secured the tie around her eyes so she was blindfolded. He took her hands, easing her to her feet.

When he was certain she was steady, he curved his arm around her waist and led her toward the bedroom. A moment after they entered, he pushed her against what she realized was the special spanking apparatus that was normally stored in the spare bedroom.

He pushed until she was completely bent over the inwardly curved leather indention of the piece. Then he looped rope around one wrist and pulled until she was at full stretch and tied it to the bottom of the leg that supported the equipment.

He repeated the process with her other wrist before moving to her ankles.

He tied both to the legs so she was completely immobile and powerless. Only then did he remove her blindfold so she could see—limited as her sight was.

"I'll give you only the choice of what you will be flogged with," he said in a rough voice that never failed to excite her.

This was her Tate. Her Dominant. What she'd missed most in the past. His dominance. Her utter submission. And the fact that as careful as he was with her in all aspects, now he would be rough and unyielding, pushing her to her very limits.

"Leather," she whispered. "The leather belt."

She wanted that sharp edge of pain tonight. She didn't want a gentle workup to something more. She wanted it all.

"My girl is feeling very adventurous tonight," he murmured. "Leather it will be."

Soon she felt the sensuous caress of the leather as he trailed it down her spine and then over her buttocks. He teased her, not giving her what she wanted right away. He continued to torment her, sliding the leather up and down her legs and over the crack of her ass.

When the blow came, it was a shock to her system. She'd been so lulled by the gentle kiss that the first lash took her breath away. Fire spread over her ass and she nearly cried out. But she wasn't that undisciplined. She sucked in, holding in any verbal response to the strike, and then waited for the inevitable wave of pleasure that always followed.

Her eyes closed as the burn faded and became intense

pleasure. The next blow she was better prepared for and it only increased the warm haze around her, pulling her into its embrace.

He was, as he'd warned, giving her all she could take. The leather kissed her skin over and over until her entire back and ass were on fire. But she'd long since entered subspace and only a dreamy cloud surrounded her.

She was desperate for his possession, for the moment when he'd toss the belt aside and fuck her hard and fast. But he seemed determined to make her wait and drive her to the very edge of her limits.

When the blows did end, she didn't even realize it. It wasn't until he reached down and yanked her head up by her hair that she somewhat fell out of the delicious haze surrounding her.

"Who owns you, Chessy?"

His voice was rough, even cruel-sounding, and she delighted in every word.

"You do, Tate."

She was surprised she was even capable of speech at this moment.

"Who's going to fuck your sweet little ass?"

Oh God. She was verging on orgasm just imagining what was to come.

"You are," she croaked.

"Damn right," he said, satisfaction lacing his voice.

His fingers slid between her cheeks, smoothing lubricant over and around her opening. He pushed a finger in, spreading more lubricant. Then another finger was added, driving her insane.

He fucked her with his fingers for several long seconds before he seemed to be satisfied she was adequately prepared. But just when she thought he would finally give her what she most wanted, the leather descended again, jolting her abruptly from her state of anticipation.

He peppered her ass, fast and furious. She knew her behind was likely completely red. Just the way he liked it before he fucked her ass. It was a test of her endurance and that line between pleasure and true pain was certainly tested, but Tate knew her and her body. Knew just how far he could push without going too far.

Before she got to the point where she would have cried her safe word, the blows stopped and he roughly parted the cheeks of her ass and with one forceful thrust, he was inside her.

Her body protested the invasion and she went rigid around his cock, trying to expel it. He was having none of that. He gripped her hips, withdrew the tiniest of inches and then thrust to the hilt, his abdomen pressed squarely against her ass.

God, he was all the way in and her body was screaming at his rough entry. Yet, it was a delicious sensation, burning, stretching, so beautiful and pleasurable.

His hands moved up her back, caressing and smoothing away the burn of the belt. Such a sharp contrast to the roughness he'd displayed until now.

And then he began to fuck her mercilessly, riding her, plunging, thrusting. The slap of flesh against flesh filled her ears. Her body jerked, held in by the constriction of the bonds. The entire apparatus shook and swayed under the force of his possession.

"Does my girl want two dicks?"

Oh God. She was going to come before he ever got to that point.

Still, she uttered a desperate yes, knowing he'd do anything to please her.

He pulled himself from her aching body and in just a moment's time she felt the pressure of a lubricated dildo forcing its way into her pussy. He thrust gently with it, easing its path into her body. When he finally got it all the way in, he positioned his cock at her anal opening once more and then plunged into her, taking her breath away.

The fullness of having the huge dildo stuffed into her pussy and his enormous cock in her ass was simply too much. She was so close to orgasm that she didn't know if she'd be able to wait for his permission to come.

She bit into her lips and closed her eyes, summoning every ounce of discipline she owned.

Finally, finally he said the magic words.

"Come for me, Chessy. While I come all over your ass."

With his next thrust she was coming violently, her entire body clenching. He yanked himself from her and his cum splattered over her ass and back. Then he pushed himself back into her ass, thrusting as the last of his release was wrung from him.

She was catapulted right over the edge, her world exploding

around her. She must have lost consciousness for a moment because the next thing she knew, Tate was untying her and lifting her gently into his arms.

He carried her into the bathroom and turned on the shower, taking them both under the spray. He cleaned every inch of her body and then his. When he was finished, he pushed her to her knees.

"I'm still so goddamn hard," he said in a gritty voice. "You make me want you just by breathing. Suck me off, Chessy. I want to come all over your mouth."

Tilting her head back with one hand, he guided his cock to her open mouth with the other. There was no teasing or holding back. It was obvious he wanted to get off as quickly as possible.

He thrust into her mouth over and over, his movements short and jerky as if he was still hypersensitive from his earlier orgasm.

But in just a few short minutes, he let out a groan and then semen began jetting into her mouth, sliding over her lips and down her chin, disappearing into the swirling water of the shower.

He pumped his erection with his hand, squeezing the last of his release into her open mouth. Then he slid all the way to the back of her throat and rested there a moment.

His hands caressed her face, sliding into her hair and petting her. He finally withdrew just when she was at the point of needing air. He pulled her upward and gave them both another rinse before finally turning the shower off.

He stepped out first and hastily dried off. Then he pulled

her from the shower and wrapped a towel around her, gently drying every inch of her skin. He toweled the moisture from her hair and then pressed a tender kiss to her forehead.

"Did you enjoy that?" he asked in a husky voice.

She nodded, sagging into his arms.

"Good. It's just the tip of the iceberg of what's to come."

SIXTEEN

CHESSY dressed with extreme care, paying heed to the strict instructions Tate had given her. Several boxes had been delivered by courier earlier in the day and then Tate had called her from work and told her to be ready and waiting when he arrived home.

She pulled on the thigh-high stockings, luxuriating in the feel of the silk against her skin. Then she carefully unzipped the garment bag of a high-end, well-known designer and pulled out the strapless, beaded aquamarine sheath that shimmered and caught the light.

She eyed the dress dubiously because it looked small. And short. Like it would barely cover her ass. And Tate had been very explicit in his instructions not to wear underwear of any kind. The only things he wanted her to wear were the dress, the stockings, the shoes and the jewelry that had been delivered by the same courier service.

The collar, which she had not seen yet, would be placed somewhat ceremoniously around her neck by Tate right before they left for The House.

When she got to the shoes, her breath caught as she turned them experimentally in her hands, inspecting each angle of the beautiful stiletto heels. Between the dress, the jewelry and the shoes she felt like Cinderella going to an erotic ball. Somehow she didn't imagine Prince Charming in the fairy tale tying Cinderella up and fucking her in the middle of the ballroom.

The thought made her laugh out loud and she shook her head at her silliness.

She slipped into the dress, wiggling in order to shimmy into it and pull it up over her full breasts. Thank goodness for the small panel of elastic that formed a V between her shoulder blades because the dress fit her like a glove, and stretching slightly made her breasts plump up and outward.

She eyed herself skeptically in the mirror as she began the task of taming her unruly hair since Tate wanted it down. But the more she stared at the woman looking back at her, the more satisfied she became with her appearance. She looked . . . beautiful. Sexy even. Would Tate find her so?

He had impeccable tastes as evidenced by the selections he'd chosen for her to wear tonight. The dress fit perfectly and if she had to guess, what she considered to be tight in the bust was actually the intentional fit of the dress, fashioned to enhance a woman's cleavage. And the jewelry was to die for. She didn't even want to know what it cost.

After arranging her hair to her satisfaction she traipsed back into the bedroom to put on the heels that she'd left on the ottoman in front of the comfy armchair Tate referred to as her reading nest.

She only had five minutes until Tate was scheduled to be home and he'd requested she be in the living room waiting for him so he could put the collar around her neck. She winced inwardly. She found the meaning behind a collar to be beautiful and symbolic of their relationship but she much preferred the term choker, or even simply the mark of his possession. Collars were for pets but she supposed that some Dominants considered their submissives to be pets in the fondest of manners. She'd even heard a man at The House in the past call his submissive "my pet" and it was obvious from his tone that it was an affectionate term of endearment. Not derisive or degrading in the least. But for her personally, it didn't work. She much preferred Tate's "my girl" when referring to her, which was probably juvenile at best but there was no accounting for tastes. It was what it was.

She settled on the edge of the couch to wait for Tate and within a few minutes the front door opened and he entered the living room, stopping when he got his first glimpse of her.

"Stand up," he said huskily.

She complied, standing to her new, more impressive height thanks to the heels.

He didn't say anything for the longest time. He simply

drank in her appearance. The silence went on for so long that she began to wonder if she'd messed up or if perhaps she didn't look as good as she thought.

Then he crossed the room and tipped up her chin, which was now a lot closer to his with her added height, and he slanted his mouth over hers. He kissed her hungrily, as if he were starving for her. All doubt fled when she felt the solid evidence of his arousal through his slacks.

When he pulled away, his eyes were blazing with lust. "You look *magnificent*," he said in a hoarse voice.

"Thank you," she whispered. "But you picked everything out so I'd say your taste is pretty darn impressive."

"Baby, that dress would not make every woman look as sensational as you. It's you. Not the dress. One hundred percent you."

She smiled her pleasure at his sincere compliment. Then he reached into his pocket and pulled out a velvet drawstring bag with the name of a prominent jeweler monogrammed on the front.

"Sit down," he said, a quiet command.

She sank onto the couch and he pulled out an intricately designed leather choker with aquamarine stones that matched her dress to perfection. She was awed by the obvious amount of time he'd devoted to pulling together her outfit for the evening. And even more impressed with the brief amount of time he'd had to work with in order to have it all ready on such short notice.

Then he turned it over to the side that would lie against

her throat and burned into the leather were the words "My Girl."

Damn it, she would not cry. She'd shed far too many tears both in sadness and joy lately. She would not ruin the evening before it ever truly began.

"It's beautiful, Tate," she whispered.

"You truly like it?"

She was surprised at the vulnerability in his tone. She wouldn't have ever imagined him worrying over her liking a gift from him. Anything he gave her was very precious to her. But the best gift of all was simply himself.

She leaned up just a bit to kiss him and then nipped playfully at his jaw. "I don't like it. I love it."

He smiled then, and perhaps it was her imagination, but his shoulders seem to relax as if in relief.

"My girl is playful tonight, I see. That's good because I intend for us to play a lot. Let me change right quick and we'll go."

"I'll be waiting," she said.

AN hour later, Tate pulled up the winding driveway of The House that sat atop a gentle hill and looked down at grassy, green rolling landscapes. Everything about The House screamed wealth and privilege even though membership didn't require either. However, Damon Roche, the owner of The House, was the epitome of wealth and class. And he was extremely discerning when it came to membership in his establishment.

Members were carefully vetted and background checks were required for all prospective members. In addition to the care Damon took in screening the members, there was careful attention to security. Even in the private rooms members could avail themselves of if they didn't want to be in the public common room, security cameras were in place and the safety of the participants was monitored at all times. While the non-public rooms offered the illusion of privacy, in fact they were all under vigilant security surveillance for the safety of all parties involved.

Tate stopped the engine after pulling into a parking spot and then turned to look at Chessy. "Is my girl ready for her night to begin?"

"Oh yes," she breathed.

He squeezed her hand and then opened his door. She knew the drill. She waited for him to come around and open her door. He leaned in, attaching a diamond-studded leash to the loop at the back of the collar and then held out his hand to assist her in getting out.

She stumbled at first when her heel caught a crack in the pavement and Tate immediately wrapped his arm around her waist to steady her.

"Okay?" he asked.

"Yes. Just caught my heel."

He led her to the entry where a man in an expensive black suit had them sign in and Tate showed ID. It had been so long since they'd last gone to The House that Chessy didn't recognize the new doorman. But then for all she knew he could have been working here for quite some time.

Tate curled his hand around the leash and rested his hand underneath her hair that hung to the middle of her back, not making it obvious she was leashed as he led her into the downstairs social room where people met and mingled and drank expensive wine and snacked on delicious hors d'oeuvres. It was also a place for hookups. Singles looking for a night of adventure or simply people wanting to visit with other like-minded individuals who shared the same kinks and sexual preferences.

"Would you like some wine?" Tate asked as they entered the room.

Chessy shook her head in response and drank in the occupants, studying the people in attendance with her usual fascination. One of her favorite activities when they'd previously visited The House was to play the guessing game and match proclivity to person even though she had no way of confirming her guesses. But it was fun.

In a way she was relieved that she didn't recognize anyone in the room because then the inevitable question would arise as to why she and Tate hadn't been in for so long. After several minutes of circling the spacious luxurious room, Tate guided her out the door. She knew that he'd made the rounds in the social room to, in his words, show her off. It had always been a point of pride with her that he found her beautiful, that he was proud to arrive with her on his arm and that he made his claim so publicly.

"Be careful on the stairs, baby," he said when they mounted the first step. "I bought those shoes because I wanted to fuck you in them, but I damn sure don't want you falling and breaking your neck."

She laughed softly. "You'll catch me, Tate. I never doubt that."

He gathered her more closely into his side as they climbed the stairs together. But once they reached the top, he gently disentangled his hand from her hair and pulled the leash out so that it called attention to her collar. And his claim on her as her Dominant and she his submissive.

As soon as they walked through the entryway to the common room, the sights and sounds overwhelmed her. Even the scent of sex was heavy in the air. She did a quick scan of the room, looking for anyone she recognized, but all she saw were unfamiliar faces. Except for Damon Roche, who stood in the far corner, a glass of what was likely very expensive liquor in hand, conversing with another man.

It was unusual for him to be at The House these days and especially without his wife. Though he still oversaw the running and operation of The House, since his marriage he'd devoted most of his free time to his wife, Serena, and Dash had mentioned that Damon and Serena now had a daughter.

Damon glanced up as if sensing her scrutiny and nodded his head in acknowledgment of both her and Tate. Then he said something to the man beside him before excusing himself to cross the room to where Chessy and Tate stood.

"It's good to see you both," Damon said warmly. He leaned

in and kissed Chessy on the cheek and then shook Tate's hand. "James is waiting by the bench. Everything you requested is available. I hope you both enjoy yourselves tonight."

Ever the consummate host, Damon escorted them to the far corner of the room, where a tall, attractive dark-haired man stood in casual jeans and polo shirt. Butterflies danced through Chessy's stomach when the man lifted a chin in greeting as the group approached.

So this was James. The man Tate had chosen for her tonight. She was careful not to offer Tate disrespect by being too open with her admiration, but her husband had indeed chosen well. James was broad-shouldered and muscled, his arms bulging at the short sleeves of the shirt he wore and his expression was one of complete dominance. And yet he was ceding control to Tate, acting as an extension of him for tonight.

They'd certainly done this before, but none of the other men Tate had ever chosen seemed this . . . Dominant. James didn't appear to her to be a man who so easily gave up power to another man. A shiver worked its way up her spine as she studied him further. Trepidation squeezed her chest before she admonished herself for entertaining such apprehension. Tate would never put her in a position where she would be overwhelmed or hurt.

"James, good to see you again." Tate ceremoniously handed over the leash to the other man. "This is my beautiful submissive, Chessy. She is yours for the evening to do with as I dictate," he said formally. "Her safe word is 'rain.' You are to take absolute care in your handling of her. Her mouth is mine and mine alone. I expect you to treat her with utmost respect."

James looked impatient with Tate's instructions, his eyes glittering as his gaze swept hungrily over Chessy. It was as though he wanted to dispense with the niceties and get straight to the action.

James lifted one of Chessy's hands and whispered a kiss over the top of her knuckles. "It will be my honor to bring you pleasure while your husband watches."

She shivered again, the quivering sensation in her belly increasing. Why was she so nervous? This was not new to her even if it had been a while since they'd last indulged. Perhaps it was because she wanted so much for the evening to be perfect and for her and Tate to further solidify their recommitment to one another.

Tate took the hand not held by James, and for a moment she was suspended between the two men, one her husband, the other her Dominant for the evening. Tate gave her hand an encouraging squeeze but didn't put to voice any of the things she saw in his eyes.

"The others will remain on the periphery," Tate said in a low voice. "When and only when it is time for them to participate will you see them. Enjoy my gift to you, my girl. I know I certainly will enjoy every moment."

Then he turned his attention to James. Chessy blinked because Damon had discreetly removed himself from the trio and she hadn't even seen him leave.

"Undress her slowly," Tate ordered. "And then prepare her as I already instructed you."

The command in Tate's voice sent a delicate shiver of delight cascading over her flesh. Her fingers curled into fists so her trembling wouldn't be noticeable. Equal parts nervousness and anticipation vied for control.

James tugged firmly at her leash, pulling her away from Tate and closer to himself. Tate took a step back but kept a watchful eye on Chessy as James slowly began to divest her of her clothing.

"Very nice," James murmured when he was down to just her stockings and stilettos.

He ran his hand over the swell of her behind and then grew bolder, sliding his palm underneath one breast. He brushed over the nipple with his thumb and it puckered in reaction, hardening to a point.

Her breath caught and then she let out a gasp when he lowered his head to her breast and sucked the nipple wetly into his mouth.

"Delicious," he murmured. "You taste every bit as good as you look."

Heat scorched over her skin and she lifted her gaze to find Tate, only focused on him even though another man was pleasuring her in his stead.

Her action brought immediate reprimand from James. He yanked on the leash, forcing her gaze back to him. His eyes glittered in irritation.

"I am your master tonight. He is only an observer. You are to look only at me and obey my commands."

She started to launch an immediate protest because that wasn't the case. No one but Tate would ever be called her master, and it was a silly term anyway. It wasn't a word that she or Tate ever used. But something in James's eyes halted her objection. She shivered and wanted to look to Tate for reassurance, to gain his reaction to James's forceful dictate, but she didn't dare look away from him again.

James ran his palm lightly over her jaw and then turned her body so her back was to Tate, effectively preventing her from the temptation of seeking her husband's guidance. It confused her that Tate was allowing this man such leeway.

James positioned her over the bench that had an inverted, padded cutout that would cradle her abdomen. Then he stretched her arms outward, tying one wrist to one of the two posts situated in front of the bench. After securing one, he then secured her other wrist so she was stretched over the bench, her ass in the air, both arms tied tightly enough that there was no give when she tested the strength of the bonds.

James disappeared from her view and then she felt leather straps circle her ankles, securing them to the legs of the bench. She was spread wide, her most vulnerable areas accessible.

"Start with the leather flogger," Tate directed.

She took immediate comfort in hearing her husband's voice and her early apprehension eased and melted away as Tate took control of the situation. She relaxed, mentally preparing herself for the first kiss of fire.

"Administer ten blows, spread out so her flesh is evenly marked and colored," Tate continued. "When you are finished, offer her the appropriate praise and then bring her close to orgasm with your hands and mouth. Then switch to the leather strap and mark her ass so that when you fuck her ass the flesh will have been scorched by fire. As I said, her mouth is mine, and I'll fuck it while you fuck her ass. She doesn't come again until she's been flogged, untied and is being held down by the men waiting."

She closed her eyes as his words flashed like wildfire through her mind. She was bombarded by a host of decadent, sinful images, and already she could feel her body climbing to orgasm and they hadn't even yet begun.

A gasp exploded from her when the first lash landed across her ass. She'd been so absorbed in the dreamy fantasy Tate was describing that she hadn't braced herself for the first blow.

Her eyes flew open and yet she could see neither man, not James nor her husband. Only the wall stared back at her. She was positioned facing away from the rest of the entire room. For all she knew everyone was observing her flogging. That didn't bother her. She'd long since gotten over any shyness when it came to being naked in front of strangers. But she didn't like not being able to see Tate. She knew he was there, but he wasn't in her line of sight.

She wanted to see the approval and pride in his eyes. She wanted to be able to lock gazes with him and share the intensely personal connection between them. To forget that anyone other than the two of them existed, even if another man was charged with her submission.

Her jaw clenched and she winced when another blow rained down on her. James wasn't as careful as Tate was in the administration of his lashes. There was something undisciplined about James's flogging, almost as if he lacked the proper experience for the job. Or perhaps he was merely a sadist who only cared for his pleasure and didn't concern himself with the delicate line between pain and pleasure for her.

There were no words of praise or approval from James as Tate had demanded. Nor did James offer her the pleasure Tate had instructed him to. Where the hell was Tate? Why wasn't he admonishing James for not heeding Tate's dictates?

There was no break between the flogger and the leather strap. Fire spread rapidly over her skin and she bit into her lip to prevent the cry of pain. This was no longer about pleasure. Certainly not hers at least.

And then she felt an insistent prodding at her anal opening and she realized James was trying to force his way in without the aid of lubricant. This was not the way Tate had told him to do things. Why wasn't Tate putting a stop to it?

"Relax, damn it," James growled, his fingers digging into her hips. She was certain she'd wear bruises from his grasp. "You're going to get fucked and it's up to you whether this is easy or hard."

She cried out, shocked that he'd persist and that Tate had nothing to say. And then, as if to punish her for her resistance,

James cracked the strap down over her shoulder blades as he thrust more forcefully into her reluctant body.

Tears ran down her cheeks and sobs welled from her throat. "No! Stop! I don't want this," she said in a garbled tone.

Her safe word. God, what was it? Her mind was a chaotic mess of fear and pain.

"Rain," she croaked out. "Rain!"

SEVENTEEN

TATE had just uttered his last command to James when his cell phone vibrated against his side. Out of habit, he glanced down quickly to pull out the phone enough so he could identify the incoming caller, fully intending to hit ignore.

He swore under his breath before glancing back up to where James had administered the second lash of the flogger. This was an important call but it had to come now of all times? Tabitha Markham had strung him along for weeks over whether she was going to transfer her late husband's portfolio—her inheritance—to Tate's firm and he was supposed to have a firm commitment from her any moment. Apparently she'd chosen *now* to inform him of her decision.

This was going to have to be quick.

He yanked up the phone, glanced at Chessy, who was facing away from him, and then uttered a crisp hello.

"Tate? Where are you? I can't hear you."

Tabitha's voice was strident in his ear. He wasn't in the mood to chitchat. He just wanted her decision so he could get back to much more important matters. Like his wife and salvaging their marriage.

He walked a few steps away toward the corner where things were a little quieter and he could also keep an eye on Chessy.

"Can you hear me now?" he asked.

"Yes, much better. I called you because I have some concerns. You've been very hard to get in touch with lately and as my financial advisor, I'd require that I be able to get in contact with you at all times."

Tate's brow furrowed and he turned away from Chessy and James, wanting to put his fist through the wall.

"I can assure you that I am available at all times for my clients," he said tersely.

"Well that remains to be seen, does it not? If you aren't available before I become your client it hardly seems likely that you'll be available once you win me over."

Tate's fingers curled impatiently and he brought one hand up to cover his other ear so he could hear her more clearly.

"Look, either you want me to handle your portfolio or you don't," he said bluntly. "I can't talk right now because I'm out with my wife and this is our personal time. If you'd like to discuss the matter further, I encourage you to contact me during business hours on Monday."

A cry cracked through the air, freezing the blood in Tate's veins.

"Rain. Rain!" he heard Chessy scream hoarsely.

He dropped the phone and whirled in the direction of her scream. When he saw tears coursing down her cheeks and James's hands curled around her hips he broke into a run, but before he could get there, Damon and two of his security men knocked James away. Tate lunged for James.

"What the hell did you do to her, you son of a bitch?" Tate yelled.

He punched the other man in the jaw, sending him reeling, and then he turned, his heart in his throat to see Damon unfastening the last of Chessy's bonds. Chessy sagged onto the floor, curling herself into a tight ball as tears ran unchecked down her face.

Three sets of accusing eyes pinned him as he knelt down where Chessy lay sobbing.

They all looked at him, condemnation in their eyes. He'd done the unforgivable. He'd broken the unspoken rule that all Dominants lived by. He hadn't protected his submissive.

"What the hell happened?" Tate demanded.

Damon gave him a look of pure disgust. "Shouldn't you know? Where the hell were you when she was screaming her safe word? How could you have done this, Tate? This . . . This is unforgivable. I think it's safe to say you're done here."

Tate tentatively reached for Chessy, his hand over her icy

TAKING IT ALL   179

cold skin in an effort to reassure himself that she was all right. Of course she wasn't all right.

She shrank away, visibly recoiling from his touch.

"Don't touch me," she said in a voice hoarse from crying. And screaming.

Damon barked an order to one of the bystanders to bring a blanket. Tate was gutted by the utter devastation in Chessy's eyes. Worse was the fear that gripped him. He'd fucked up. Had done the unforgivable as Damon had accused. There wouldn't be—and shouldn't be—forgiveness for not ensuring his wife was safe every second of their time at The House.

The blanket was delivered and when Tate tried to wrap it around her, she drew sharply away as she'd done just moments earlier. Damon took the blanket, gently arranging it around Chessy's huddled body. Then he simply looped his arms underneath her slight form and stood from his squatting position, cradling her against his chest.

"It will be all right, Chessy," Damon said quietly. "Let me take you into my office where it's private. I'll have your clothes brought down so you can dress. Are you hurt? Do you need to go to the hospital?"

She began to quietly weep once more, each tear like a dagger to Tate's heart.

Ignoring Tate, Damon carried her swiftly from the common room and Tate followed behind, feeling the stares of the entire room as they gazed at him in disgust.

Safe, sane, consensual. He'd managed to single-handedly violate all three hallmarks of the Dominant/submissive lifestyle. And now his beautiful wife had paid for his mistake. Just another in the dozens of times he'd failed her in their five-year marriage. Apparently he could do nothing right when it came to her, which made no sense given how much he loved her.

Damon carried Chessy down the stairs and then shouldered his way into his office and gently set her down on the leather sofa, pulling the ends of the blanket around her to shield her nudity. Her shoes had fallen off at some point and she looked fragile barefoot with only a blanket and her stockings to cover her body.

Tate went to his knees in front of the couch and tried to gather her hands in his, but she withdrew them, knotting them into fists in her lap so he couldn't grasp them. She wouldn't even meet his gaze but then he could hardly blame her.

"Chessy, I'm so sorry," he whispered. "God, I'm sorry. I only stepped away a few seconds to answer a phone call. I'd already ended it when I heard you say your safe word."

At that she met his gaze, her eyes cold enough to freeze an inferno. "So that's what you were doing while I was being raped by the man you chose to dominate me? Taking a goddamn client call?"

Her words paralyzed him. The depth of his betrayal hadn't truly sunken in until now. He'd stood by while a man handpicked by him to be intimate with his wife had hurt her.

"I'm partly to blame," Damon said quietly from just a few feet away from the sofa. "I gave Tate the names of several men I thought were good choices. There was nothing in the past to indicate James's behavior tonight. The safety of my members—all of my members—is my top priority and I failed you tonight."

Chessy shook her head vigorously. "No," she said vehemently. "You aren't to blame, Damon, and I won't allow you to take any part of it. The person at fault here is *me* for trusting my husband to put me first in his priorities. For believing his promises that he'd change. I should have never allowed myself to be involved in this situation, and you can be assured I won't ever again."

Tate couldn't breathe. A hand clutched mercilessly at his throat and squeezed until he was lightheaded from oxygen deprivation. Her words sounded so . . . final. They were no less than he deserved and yet panic still shattered his nerves. His life without Chessy? Unthinkable.

A knock sounded and a moment later, Damon returned with Chessy's clothing. She stared at the items, distaste in her wounded eyes. They were evidently a reminder that Tate had arranged this evening when she wanted to do nothing but forget.

Her lips trembled and she closed her eyes, her brow knitted in an effort to regain her composure.

"Tell me what you want to do, Chessy," Damon said in a gentle voice. "I'll have a car drive you wherever you want to go. Is there someone you'd like me to call for you?"

Tate bristled and was near to exploding as he whirled to confront Damon. "I will bring my wife home," he said icily.

"I don't recall consulting you in the matter," Damon said.

"You lost that option when you abdicated your responsibility as Chessy's Dominant and allowed her to come to harm."

Tate had no response to that, which only served to piss him off even more. His hands shook violently. He was rattled to his very core when he usually met each situation with calm and decisiveness.

"I'll ride home with Tate," Chessy said so softly Tate wasn't sure he'd heard her right.

He was afraid to hope or read too much into her statement. She still wouldn't look at him. As if she couldn't bear the sight of him.

"Let me help you dress, baby," Tate said gently. "Don't worry about your shoes. I'll carry you out to the car."

She shook her head. "I can get dressed on my own. Just leave me be for a few minutes. I'll come out when I'm done."

Tate dug in his heels. "I need to make sure you're all right and I need to see for myself just what that bastard did."

"Do you care?" she threw out in a bitter tone.

His jaw clenched. "Of course I care. Goddamn it, Chessy."

She waved her hand like she just wanted it over with.

"I'll wait outside," Damon said, leaving unsaid the fact that he'd wait to see if Chessy changed her mind about wanting him to see to her ride from The House. But it was implied in his tone.

As soon as Damon left the room, Chessy allowed the blanket to fall loosely away but hunched forward protectively as if she didn't want Tate to see her. Tate immediately turned her on the sofa, swearing softly when he saw the welts on her back.

There were already bruises forming at her hips where the asshole's hands had gripped her.

"How far did he take things?" Tate asked hoarsely.

She shrugged indifferently. "Far enough."

He ran a hand through his hair in frustration. Chessy pinned him with the weight of her stare, her eyes accusing and utterly devastated. "Oh, I'm sorry, Tate. Have I annoyed you? How selfish of me that I'm not giving you my full attention."

The heavy sarcasm in her voice made his heart sink. Self-loathing filled him, brimming in his heart until hatred was a living, breathing emotion in his soul. He was utterly sick at heart, knowing full well that he didn't deserve forgiveness for what he'd done. For what he'd allowed to happen to her.

She got up, moving away from him to dress. She yanked on her clothing without care and then glanced down in disgust at the formfitting dress.

"I'm ready to go," she said.

"Chess, are you sure I don't need to take you to the hospital?" Tate asked uneasily. "How badly did he hurt you?"

Her gaze found his and she stared unflinchingly at him. "Not nearly as much as you have."

EIGHTEEN

THE ride home was silent and tense. Chessy leaned against the passenger door, her forehead pressed to the glass as she stared sightlessly at the passing streetlights. She was strangely numb. She felt empty and desolate but couldn't summon any emotion. No anger, no sorrow. Just . . . nothing.

Her marriage was over. As far as she was concerned, Tate had crossed a line he could never erase. While such knowledge would have devastated her twenty-four hours ago, right now she couldn't bring herself to feel anything but resignation.

She could feel him looking her way, but she didn't acknowledge him. Instead she pretended he wasn't even there, already making plans for a future that didn't include him.

When they finally pulled into their drive, she opened her

door before the car came to a full stop and she got out, the concrete tearing her stockings at the feet. She hadn't brought her keys so she had to wait for Tate to unlock the front door, but as soon as he accomplished that, she pushed past him in a direct path to their bedroom.

Wasting no time, she went to her closet and hauled out one of her large suitcases, flinging it onto the bed to unzip it.

"Chessy, what the hell are you doing?" Tate demanded from the doorway.

She ignored him and went back to her closet to yank clothing from hangers, returning to dump them into the suitcase without bothering to arrange them in any way.

His hand closed around her wrist and she froze when he prompted her to look up at him and meet his gaze. His features were gray, deep grooves lining his forehead. Sorrow and regret swamped his eyes. He looked tortured.

Not her problem.

She wrested her hand from his grip and took a step back, her tone as frigid as an Artic wind.

"Do not touch me."

He took an immediate step back and when she went to her dresser for underwear and bras he repeated his earlier question.

"What the hell are you doing? Where do you think you're going?"

She paused, her hands full of her intimate things. Then she turned and stared him down until unease crept into his eyes.

"I'm leaving," she said simply. "I would think that much is

obvious. But if you need me to spell it out for you, I'm packing my clothes and then I'm getting in my car and then I'm getting the hell away from you."

He flinched, his features going pale. "Chessy, please don't go. I know you're angry. God, you certainly have the right to be. But please don't leave when you're so upset. I'll go. This is your house. I'll get a hotel and come back tomorrow when we can talk this out."

"Exactly what are we going to talk out, Tate? The fact that you lied to me? That you made me promises that once again you didn't keep? Or maybe the fact that you took a phone call when your wife was helpless to defend herself against a man you chose and were supposed to have been guiding every step of the way. Let me make myself perfectly clear. There isn't a single thing you have to say that I care to hear. There's no going back. No forgetting what happened. No way to undo what's already been done. You made your choice and it damn sure wasn't me."

Tate sank onto the edge of the bed, his head bowed. His hands shook visibly and his shoulders heaved as he struggled with his emotions. Chessy tossed the rest of her clothing into the suitcase, only wanting to get it done so she could get the hell out before she broke down and completely lost it.

She grabbed an oversized bag from underneath the bathroom sink and quickly emptied the drawers of all her toiletries and then decided that whatever she didn't get she'd return for at a later time. Preferably when Tate wasn't here. His precious clients could keep him company from now on. She was done waiting around for every crumb of attention he threw her way.

After dropping the toiletry bag by the bed, she closed her suitcase and zipped it up. Tate hadn't moved, seemingly frozen and in shock that she was leaving. It didn't surprise her. Their relationship was a study in her giving and him taking. Of her never bucking his authority. Always ceding to his wishes and control.

That was all coming to a screeching halt starting tonight.

"At least let me drive you to where you're going," Tate said in a low voice. "I'm worried about you driving, Chessy. At least give me that. I want to make sure you're safe."

She gave him a scornful look and then shook her head. "That's a laugh. You want to make sure I'm safe. Forgive my amusement over the flaming hypocrisy of that statement."

Tate closed his eyes and let out a sigh. "I deserve your anger. I deserve whatever you dish out, but God, please, Chessy. Stay so we can work it out. Don't leave. I love you."

"I believe you love me," Chessy said honestly. "You just don't love me enough and you don't love me as much as I love you. I suppose I would have settled for that once. But not any longer. I deserve better."

She yanked the suitcase off the bed and slung the toiletry bag over her shoulder before heading out of the bedroom, Tate on her heels. She wished he'd just let her go. There was little point in trying to change her mind. He should know her well enough to realize the futility of dissuading her when she was set on something.

Before she would have appreciated his determination to save their marriage, but that was when she thought they had a viable relationship. Now, she just wanted to be away from him so she could vent her devastation, but she was just as determined that she not break down in front of him.

She had to be strong for herself. No longer would she depend on Tate for her emotional stability. Her faith and trust had been sorely misplaced. She would have never thought him capable of what he'd done tonight. Yes, he'd put business before her for quite some time, but never in a situation that was fraught with peril and her safety was truly at risk. In her heart, she'd always known that he'd protect her when it really counted.

How very wrong she'd been, and it broke her heart.

She kicked open the door that was still partially ajar from their entrance just minutes before and she dragged her suitcase over the step and onto the front porch. Tate tried one last time, gently capturing her arm with his hand. Though his grip wasn't bruising in the least, it was firm, commanding her attention.

She stared pointedly at him and then down at his hand, silently telling him to let her go.

"Chessy, please don't do this," he begged softly. "Stay. Tonight at least. We'll talk in the morning. I won't go into work. We'll go away if you like. Somewhere we can be afforded complete privacy. I'll do whatever it takes for you not to go."

"It's too late for that. Going away won't fix what's wrong. It only delays the inevitable. I can't force you to make me your priority and furthermore I wouldn't want to try to make someone feel something for me they don't. The truth always wins out in the end. Tonight proved that."

"If the truth wins out in the end then I'll get you back," Tate vowed. "Because the truth is I love you and that's never going away. I'll do whatever it takes to have you back home where you belong, Chessy. So be warned. I'm not giving up and I'm not letting you walk out of my life or our marriage."

"You already left our marriage," she said sadly.

Then she turned and lugged her suitcase to her Mercedes and threw it in the backseat. She didn't look back at Tate. She forced herself to open her door, slide into the driver's seat and drive away. But as she drove away, she couldn't help but glimpse in her rearview mirror and see Tate's silhouette outlined by the porch light as he watched her drive away.

NINETEEN

CHESSY had no clear destination in mind as she left her neighborhood. There were three options available to her. She could check into a hotel, go to Joss's or go to Kylie's.

She instantly vetoed the hotel because the very last thing she wanted was to be alone. Which left either going to Joss's or Kylie's. In the end she decided on Kylie because Kylie was closer and Joss was pregnant. Chessy didn't want to cause Joss undue stress, nor did she want to keep her up all night. Besides, Joss couldn't drink and Kylie could and right now a stiff drink was definitely in order.

She pulled into Jensen's driveway and parked beside Kylie's car. She sat there a moment, trying to collect her scattered thoughts. It hit her all at once. She'd walked out on Tate. She'd left him. Her marriage was over.

Tears gathered in her eyes but she gulped in air and swallowed convulsively. Then she braced herself and got out of her car. She hauled out her bags and walked up the pathway to the front door. She hadn't even rung the doorbell when the door opened and Jensen filled the doorway, his expression one of concern. Then he took in her suitcase.

"Shit," he murmured. "I'm going to kill him."

She promptly burst into tears and Jensen immediately pulled her into his arms, kicking aside her luggage and closing the door behind her.

"Come inside," Jensen said kindly. "Let me get Kylie. She just got out of the shower."

Chessy sniffled. "Thank you. I'm sorry to burst in on you unannounced like this. I just didn't know where else to go."

Jensen's expression grew fierce. "You are always welcome here, Chessy. Now sit tight. Let me go get Kylie for you."

Before he could move, Kylie walked into the living room, her hair wrapped in a towel.

"Jensen? Was that the front door I heard . . ."

Her voice trailed off when she saw Chessy sitting there.

"Oh no," Kylie whispered. She rushed over to where Chessy sat and pulled her into a hug. "What happened?"

Jensen handed Chessy a tissue but Kylie took it and gently wiped at Chessy's tears.

"It's over," Chessy said brokenly. "I left Tate."

Kylie exchanged shocked looks with Jensen. Jensen had a baffled expression as if he couldn't possibly understand why Chessy was sitting in his living room telling them she'd left Tate.

"What happened?" Kylie prompted again.

Chessy closed her eyes and then spilled the entire ugly tale. By the time she was finished, Jensen wore a murderous expression, rage emanating in waves from him.

"Un-fucking-believable," Jensen swore. "I'm going to kill him," he said, repeating the words he'd uttered in the doorway moments before. "What he did is *unforgivable*. How could he have let it happen?"

Kylie had gone pale and she looked stricken as she stared at her friend. "Chessy, are you hurt? Do you want me and Jensen to take you to the hospital?"

Chessy shook her head. "I'm fine. Okay, I'm not fine, but physically I'm okay."

"Show us your back," Jensen said bluntly. "Or if you aren't comfortable with me in the room at least show Kylie. I doubt you can see if the skin is broken but it needs to be looked at just in case."

Chessy had ignored the pain over her shoulder blades because the pain in her heart overshadowed everything else. Slowly she turned, presenting her back to Kylie and Jensen, and allowed Kylie to lift the T-shirt she'd changed into at home so she could see the damage inflicted by the strap.

She heard Kylie's swift intake of breath and Jensen's savage curse. She winced at the colorful expletives that exploded from Jensen's mouth.

"How bad is it?" Chessy whispered.

"Bad enough," Jensen said, but then he was never one to sugarcoat things. Chessy had only known him a few months, but she liked his no-nonsense air and the fact that he was always plainspoken.

"The skin's not broken, thank God," Kylie said, soothing over Jensen's more terse response. "But there are raised welts and bruises already forming."

Kylie lowered Chessy's shirt back down and Chessy turned to once again face Kylie and Jensen. She was mortified by the fact that they were witnessing the results of Tate's negligence.

Kylie opened her mouth and then closed it again, visibly uncomfortable with whatever it was she'd started to say. Then she stared directly at Chessy.

"I know you've explained some of what you and Tate do, but is this . . . normal?" she asked in a faltering tone. "I mean is this what he does to you? I've never known Joss to wear bruises but then what if I just don't see them? I guess I don't understand the dynamics of the lifestyle you and Joss live."

Jensen sighed and rested his hand on Kylie's shoulder, squeezing. "It's not something that should ever happen, honey. A Dominant is charged with the absolute safety and well-being of his submissive. He's supposed to safeguard that gift and cherish it and her. What Tate did tonight . . ." He broke off, shaking his head in confusion. "I still can't wrap my mind around it. What was he thinking? The idea that he allowed Chessy to be hurt when she was such a short distance away sickens me."

Chessy teared up all over again and Jensen looked immediately contrite that he'd caused her more upset.

"No, it's not how our relationship works," Chessy said in

response to Kylie's original question. "He's never left bruises on me. He's always been so careful and mindful when he uses a crop or flogger. I don't expect you to understand the reasons why, but the line between pain and pleasure, if done correctly, can be exciting and edgy. Pleasurable. And tonight isn't something new to us. It's something we've enjoyed before. But in the past, Tate's focus was always solely on me. He always made sure that my pleasure came first and that the man he chose never went too far. Tonight that wasn't the case. He took a damn phone call while another man had me tied and helpless and unable to protect myself."

Anger surged in her voice, becoming stronger the more she explained. Her rage surprised her. She'd expected to feel a whole host of things, but the storm of fury temporarily edged out her absolute despair.

"I want to go over there and beat his ass," Jensen said darkly.

Chessy sent him a watery smile. "Thank you, but don't bother."

"I'm so sorry this happened to you, Chessy," Jensen said, sincerity ringing in his voice. "Tate is a goddamn fool. I can't believe he doesn't recognize the treasure he has in you. But I'm glad you left his sorry ass. It's high time you stuck up for yourself."

She sighed, knowing that she'd been a doormat for far too long. Even her friends could see that and it shamed her that she'd never recognized it until now.

"I hate to ask this," Chessy said, embarrassment making her cringe. "But can I stay here tonight? I left in a hurry and haven't even figured out where I'm going or what I'm going to do for that matter."

Jensen scowled and Kylie added her own frown.

"That is not something you even have to ask," Jensen said. "You'll stay here with us for as long as you need to. We aren't kicking you out in the morning. You need friends right now."

Kylie nodded her agreement. "You're staying indefinitely," she said in an adamant tone. "I know what it's like to be by yourself in misery and believe me, it isn't pretty and it isn't fun."

Jensen flinched, knowing she was referring to the time she and Jensen had spent apart, alone and miserable after Jensen had stupidly broken things off with her.

"No, it isn't fun," Jensen agreed. "Which is why you're staying here where you can be among friends. You've always been an invaluable source of support for Kylie and I can never repay you for that. You staying is the least I can do so that we can return the favor. And we won't take no for an answer."

"Thank you," Chessy said with deep relief. As much as she hated intruding on Kylie and Jensen's newly formed relationship, she really did need her friends around her. Now more than ever. Because now the pretense would be dropped. No longer would Kylie and Joss bite their tongues and hold back their opinions. It would now be open season on Tate.

It was part of the Southern Girlfriend code of honor and etiquette, one of the first entries being that a friend will be there to bail you out of jail but a VERY good friend will be sitting in the jail cell WITH you.

And well, Chessy needed to view her husband through the

eyes of others for once. Because she had only what she'd built into her mind and so it had become truth when in fact it was all lies. It was time for the blinders to come off and for her to see what everyone else had seen for a long time. Just maybe not tonight . . .

"Uh, Kylie?" she hedged.

"What's wrong, sweetie? Is there something you need? Something Jensen and I could get you?"

"We're running low on wine and I wouldn't mind running out to restock the cabinet," Jensen said with a smile. "When my girls get together a lot of alcohol is laid to waste. I'm beginning to think the three of you could drink a whole horde of military guys under the table."

She was in turns delighted and saddened by Jensen's endearment. His girls. It gave her insight to the fact that he'd long ago accepted Joss and Chessy's role in Kylie's life and that he encouraged those friendships. Wasn't threatened by them whatsoever.

The sadness came in because Tate had always referred to Chessy as "his girl" or "my girl" and each version did something deep in her heart. It squeezed parts left untouched by years of neglect and feelings of being unwanted. He'd touched those areas, and now? They'd fade back into the bleak memories she carried of her childhood and how she was raised. Unwanted. Unloved. Because it was precisely how she currently felt about the way Tate treated her.

"I think that's a lovely idea, darling," Kylie said, her eyes growing warm as she looked up at her lover. Boyfriend seemed so 1980s and a term used for teenage kids.

"Uh, before you go, and I realize the chances of this are slim, but there are a few things I wanted to bring up," Chessy said, her chin quivering in her nervousness.

Jensen eased down on Chessy's other side, adding his support to Kylie's.

"If either of you happens to run into Tate, please don't cause a scene. Not because of me. I'd rather you just look past him. But he's your friend too and I don't expect you to dislike him just because of something that happened between us."

Jensen snorted but remained silent.

"The other thing, and I know this is complete chicken shit of me, Kylie, but can you call Joss in the morning and give her the rundown for me? I don't know if I have it in me to rehash it all over again. And I didn't want to barge over to her house at this hour and potentially upset her. She hasn't been sleeping well and her mornings have been hell with all the morning sickness, so maybe you should wait until she's feeling human to dump all of my misery on her."

Kylie patted Chessy's hand and then squeezed. "Of course I will. I don't want you to worry about a thing. Tomorrow we'll send Jensen over to pick up the rest of your things. Just give him a list so he's sure to get everything you want."

"I can go," Chessy said quietly. "I need to go. Maybe moving my own stuff will be the beginning of closure. Of acceptance that my marriage is over."

"No way," Jensen said emphatically. "You aren't going over there to face him by yourself."

Chessy smiled sadly. "Oh, he won't be there. I'm sure he has some important client meeting. Why else would he have been on the phone when he was supposed to be paying attention to me?"

"Still, I think it's a better idea if Jensen goes with you," Kylie soothed. "For that matter I'll come too. Won't take long with the three of us working. Dash can man the office by himself for the day. And when he and Joss learn what's happened, I wouldn't be surprised if Dash doesn't show up himself."

"All right," Chessy conceded.

"Now, do you want a drink or would you prefer to go straight to bed?" Jensen asked. "I'm sure Kylie doesn't mind staying up with you as late as you need her, and since I'm her boss I get to tell her she's going to sleep in tomorrow and blow off work."

Kylie rolled her eyes. "Just wait until I get that promotion, Jensen. Then we'll see who's the boss of that operation."

"Oh I know," Jensen said in a fervent tone. "Dash and I will spend the days in our offices hiding under our desks."

Chessy laughed and then because she couldn't fathom how or why she could be laughing when her entire world was crumbling around her, she buried her face in her hands and sobbed.

"Can you take her to bed, Jensen?" Chessy heard Kylie say. "Our bed. I don't want her to be alone tonight. Can you take the guest bedroom?"

Chessy lifted her head and shook it vehemently. "No. No way I'm putting Jensen out of his bed. That's where he belongs.

With you, Kylie. I would never do anything to change a thing about y'all's relationship.

Jensen smiled and tousled Chessy's hair affectionately. "I assure you our relationship will survive me sleeping in a different bedroom this one night. If it can survive me being tied to the headboard I think it's safe to say that we're pretty solid. Besides, if I sleep there, I don't have to be tied up by my kinky girlfriend."

"Jensen!" Kylie hissed. "For God's sake! Do you not have any sort of a filter when it comes to what spills from your mouth?"

"And yet that's what I love about him," Chessy said in amusement. "I suppose my taste in men isn't quite so horrible after all."

"Let's get you to bed, sweetie," Jensen said in a gentle voice. "You look like you've reached the limit of your control. Get some rest. Tomorrow you and Kylie and Joss can have one of your terror . . . er . . . uh I mean girl lunches where y'all threaten the demise of the male population. If I wasn't so pissed off at the asshole for what he did, I'd actually feel sorry for Tate about now. But he made his bed and now he has to lie in it. Alone."

"You know," Kylie said thoughtfully.

"Uh oh. I recognize that voice," Jensen said in a dry tone.

"We get up with Chessy whenever she's ready to go over and tackle packing whatever she wants to take. Then I'll call Joss, give her the 411 and have her meet us back at your place. And you can be the sweet, adorable guy who gets us takeout so we don't have any messy upsetting issues in a public restaurant. You'd be invited of course," Kylie said teasingly.

"It's a good plan and I certainly don't mind getting all my girls something to eat, but you're going to need to give Joss a heads-up before we go over there because I have to call Dash to tell him neither you or I will be in the office and I'll have to explain why. And then Joss finds out important information about her best friend from a third party, which will hurt her feelings and cause her to instantly freak and run out the door to go and help with the packing. I think we can all agree that doesn't need to happen."

"Then it's a plan," Kylie said, hugging Chessy to her once more. "Now let's go get you into bed. You look like hell, Chess. I can only imagine how exhausted you are right now. I'll stay up and talk to you as long as you want."

But as soon as Kylie returned from the bathroom after taking the towel from her hair and combing it out she saw that Chessy was already passed out on the bed, her expression one of sorrow.

Kylie's heart clenched. She knew all too well how much love had the power to hurt but also to heal. The question was, which would it do for Tate and Chessy?

TWENTY

KYLIE wrapped her hands around the mug of coffee as she stood in Jensen's kitchen. Though Chessy had slept fitfully, Kylie had barely slept at all. She'd lain awake, worried and heartbroken for her friend.

Jensen walked up behind her and wrapped both arms around her body, pulling her back against his chest as he nuzzled one ear.

"How did Chessy sleep?" he asked, concern edging his voice.

Kylie sighed. "A lot better than I did."

She set the mug on the bar and then swiveled in Jensen's embrace, wrapping her arms around him in a hug. She rested her cheek against his chest and sighed.

"What are we going to do, Jensen? This has devastated

Chessy. She was so full of hope and optimism after their disastrous anniversary night that Tate finally saw how unhappy she was and he vowed to make amends. And yet at the very first opportunity he allowed business to interfere?"

"He didn't just allow it to interfere," Jensen said darkly. "He put Chessy in harm's way over a fucking business call. He should have left the damn phone at home and devoted one hundred percent of his attention and energy on his wife. I know you have fears over Joss's and Chessy's lifestyle choices, but honey trust me, what happened last night is never supposed to happen. I would have said that Dash and Tate would cut off their right arms before ever allowing their wives to come to harm, but I don't even know what to say regarding Tate's actions. I have no idea what he was thinking. But what he did is unforgivable, and you need to prepare yourself for the possibility that this is truly the last straw for Chessy. She's going to need you and Joss more than ever. I'm proud of her for standing up for herself. It took a lot of courage to tell Tate she was leaving."

"I know," Kylie said sadly, her heart aching for her friend. "Chessy is such a good person, Jensen. She doesn't deserve this. She's so generous and sweet. She has a heart of gold but she hasn't been truly happy in a long time. I wish I could say that I hadn't seen this coming, but Joss and I have honestly been expecting this, though we never imagined it going down like it did because, like you, I would have never imagined Tate allowing anything to hurt Chessy. No matter how far he has his head stuck up his ass, I never truly thought he would allow harm to come to her. I hate him for that," she said, anger bubbling up in her chest.

Jensen squeezed her more tightly against him and brushed a kiss over her hair. "I'm not a fan at the moment either. I'd like to beat his ass for what he did."

"I'd like to watch," Kylie muttered. "Maybe you could hold him down while I kick him in the balls."

Jensen chuckled. "I love when you get all ferocious. It's very sexy."

She grinned up at him. "I love you."

He looked inordinately pleased by her declaration. His features softened in answering love and he kissed her, long and sweet. "I love you too," he said, his voice thick with emotion.

A noise from the entrance to the kitchen had Kylie whirling around to see Chessy standing there watching Kylie and Jensen kissing. She looked as though she'd been slapped, her eyes drenched with sadness.

"Sorry to interrupt," Chessy said in a low voice.

"Not at all," Jensen said in an easy tone, allowing Kylie to slide from his grasp. "How are you feeling this morning?"

"Come sit down and let me fix you a cup of coffee," Kylie urged, going over to where Chessy stood and ushering her back to the bar.

"I feel . . . numb," Chessy said in a confused voice. "Like it really hasn't sunk in. I woke up and thought I was at home and I automatically reached for Tate."

"That's understandable," Kylie soothed.

Kylie set a steaming mug of coffee in front of Chessy but

all she did was wrap her hands around the cup as though try-ing to infuse some of the warmth into her body.

"What time is it anyway?" Chessy asked wearily.

"It's almost ten," Jensen supplied. "Kylie is going to go call Joss and then we'll head over to your house so you can get what you need."

Chessy nodded, tears brimming in her eyes. "What am I going to do? I was completely dependent on Tate. It was what he wanted. He never wanted me to work. He insisted that he take care of me financially. And what did that get me? Now I have no husband, no house, no money." She buried her face in her hands, her shoulders heaving.

Kylie sent Jensen an anxious look, unsure of what to do to comfort her friend. Jensen merely shook his head and put a finger to his lips.

Jensen moved in close to Kylie and whispered near to her ear so Chessy didn't hear.

"Just give her time. She's going to be upset for a few days. Just be there for her and let her cry on your shoulder. Then we'll figure out what she's going to do. If she and Tate divorce, she gets half of everything so she'll be financially secure."

Kylie flinched. Chessy and Tate divorced? Yes, she'd cer-tainly known that there were problems in the marriage, but she honestly hadn't considered things would go this far. That Chessy would be sitting at her kitchen table crying her eyes out because she'd walked out on Tate.

"I'm going to go call Joss, hon," Kylie said to Chessy. "Why don't you jump in the shower? It'll make you feel better."

Chessy sighed but nodded and shuffled back toward the guest bathroom. Kylie waited until she was certain Chessy was in the shower before dialing Joss's number.

As expected, Joss didn't take the news well at all. Kylie winced at the expletives that filled her ear. If Joss was swearing like a sailor then it really was bad.

"I can't believe he let that happen," Joss raged. "Dash will kill him."

"He'll have to wait in line behind Jensen," Kylie said dryly.

"Poor Chessy," Joss said, tears evident in her voice. "What are we going to do, Kylie?"

"Well, the first thing is that Jensen and I are going to take her by her house after she gets out of the shower so she can properly pack what she needs. After that? She'll stay here. I'll sit on her if I have to."

"Should I come over too?" Joss asked. "I can meet y'all there."

"I think it would be best for Chessy if you came over here, after she's packed. It's going to be an ordeal for her and she'll need to be surrounded by friends. How about I text you when we're leaving her house and you can meet us here."

"That sounds good," Joss replied. "I can't believe this, Kylie. I just can't believe he let this happen."

"Neither can I," Kylie said softly.

TWENTY-ONE

CHESSY tensed when Jensen pulled into her and Tate's neighborhood. Her fingers curled into tight fists and she fought the surge of tears that welled in her eyes. Kylie turned to look at Chessy over her shoulder, her eyes brimming with sympathy.

"You'll get through this, Chessy. Jensen, Joss, Dash and I will be here for you."

"I know," Chessy said.

"Shit," Jensen muttered when he made the turn into Chessy's drive.

Chessy looked and her heart plummeted when she saw Tate's car parked outside the garage. What was he doing home? Why?

"What should we do, Jensen?" Kylie asked anxiously.

Jensen put the car in park and turned to look at Chessy. "It's up to you, honey. Kylie and I will go in with you, but if you'd rather come back when he isn't here I'll be happy to bring you another time."

Chessy squared her shoulders resolutely and spoke with calm she didn't quite feel. "No. I'll do it now. I have to face him sometime. I won't let him make me afraid to walk into my own house."

"Okay then, let's do it," Jensen said, opening his door.

Chessy climbed from the backseat and started toward the door on wobbly legs. Before she was halfway up the walk, the front door flew open and Tate filled the doorway, his appearance haggard and unkempt. As if he hadn't slept at all the night before. Relief poured from his face.

"Chessy, thank God you came back," he said in a hoarse voice.

And then he looked beyond her as if he'd been so focused on her that he hadn't even noticed that Jensen and Kylie were there.

"Chessy? What's going on?" he asked quietly.

"Jensen and Kylie drove me over so I could pack more of my things," Chessy said, proud of how steady—and firm— she sounded.

He looked as though she'd slapped him right across the face. He visibly flinched and then ran a hand through his already rumpled hair.

"You're moving out?"

The pain in his voice made her heart clench. But she steeled herself against letting him manipulate her emotionally. This wasn't about him. It was about her finally standing up for herself and doing what she should have done a long time ago.

Jensen walked up to stand beside Chessy, adding his silent support as he stared Tate down. There was open disgust in Jensen's expression. Tate wouldn't even meet Jensen's gaze. Guilt was plastered all over Tate's face and then resignation swamped his eyes and he stepped aside so Chessy could enter the front door.

Chessy walked by him, Kylie following behind. Jensen remained, however, and Chessy paused just inside the partially open door. Kylie looked questioningly at her, but Chessy held a finger to her lips and pointed at the door.

"What the fuck were you thinking, Tate?" Jensen demanded. "How could you have allowed your wife to get hurt while you were taking a fucking business call? Have you lost your goddamn mind?"

Chessy winced but Kylie looked as though she wanted to cheer.

"This is between me and Chessy," Tate said in an icy tone. "I don't need your input when it comes to my marriage."

"Someone needs to knock some sense into your head. God only knows why she's put up with you as long as she has. You had so many chances to make things right and you blew it bigtime."

"I love her," Tate said. "I've made mistakes. I wish to hell I could undo them. But I won't let her go. I'll fight for her with my last breath. I'm not going to just stand back and let her walk out of my life, even if that's what I deserve."

Jensen made a sound of disgust. "You don't act like a man who loves his wife. And you damn sure haven't put her first when it comes to any part of your life."

Chessy bowed her head, tears gathering in her eyes. She knew what Jensen was saying was true, but to hear that truth from a third party hurt. That the problems in her marriage were so obvious to others. It was humiliating.

"Come on, Chessy," Kylie said in a low voice, taking her arm to guide her away from the doorway. "It does no good for you to stand and listen to this. It'll only upset you even more. Let's get your things together so we can go."

Chessy allowed herself to be led to the bedroom and mechanically she began removing her clothing from the closet. She tossed everything onto the bed and then went through her drawers and collected all the shoe boxes from the shelves in the closet. Jensen had brought several suitcases that he would be bringing in and whatever didn't fit would just have to be piled into the backseat.

Other than clothing, what should she take? There were mementos all over the house. Things that held special meaning. And photos. Her wedding pictures. Honeymoon pictures. Though looking at them now only brought her crushing pain, would she feel differently as time passed? Would she want those things or should she leave them here, in the past where they belonged?

Oh God, should she be consulting an attorney? Was she truly going to go through with a divorce? Her heart seized and panic scuttled up her spine and rolled her stomach into one big vicious knot.

"What's wrong, Chessy?"

Kylie's concerned voice cut through her haze of dismay.

"I need a lawyer," Chessy said faintly. "Or at least I think I do. Shouldn't I file for divorce?"

Kylie's arms came around her and she hugged Chessy fiercely. "Let's not worry about that right now, sweetie. You have plenty of time to think of that. For now let's just get your stuff packed and you settled into my house. You're still in shock and you shouldn't be making any life-altering decisions in your current emotional state."

Chessy sighed. "I know, I know. You're right. It's just that I never thought I'd be standing in my bedroom thinking about hiring a divorce lawyer."

The reality of the situation came crashing down and she completely lost it. She dissolved into heart-wrenching sobs.

"Chessy?"

Tate's hoarse exclamation from the doorway made her flinch. And then suddenly he was there, his arms around her, holding her tightly as she heaved huge sobs.

His mouth was pressed against her hair and his arms were like iron around her, his strength radiating outward. For a moment she felt . . . safe. Like nothing bad had ever happened. Like she'd dreamed the entire thing and she wasn't in her bedroom packing her things to walk out on her marriage.

"Please don't cry, baby," Tate murmured. "It will be okay. I swear it. You don't have to do this. Please stay so we can work this out. I'm willing to do whatever it takes. I swear on my life. I love you."

She shook her head, prying herself from his grasp. She took a step backward, still trying to get her emotions under control.

"I can't stay," she whispered. "You made your choice, Tate. And it wasn't *me*. If the others hadn't intervened when they did, I could have been seriously hurt. I *was* hurt," she amended. "You've broken your promises time and time again. I won't continue to allow myself to be a doormat. I owe myself that much at least."

"I won't let you walk out that door," Tate said fiercely.

"That's enough, Tate."

Jensen's voice was a warning, his tone openly hostile.

"You need to back off and back off now. Let her finish packing or I'll call the police and have you forcibly removed so she can finish."

Tate went white and then a flush of red crawled over his cheeks as anger replaced his earlier entreating words.

"You need to stay the fuck out of this," he growled at Jensen.

"If you love her then you won't make it so hard for her to do this," Jensen persisted. "You say one thing but your actions don't back up your words. If you want to win her back, this isn't the way to go about it. Trying to manipulate her and then making threats won't do anything but drive her farther away. Use your head, man. Now isn't the time to push. She's at her breaking point. Anyone with eyes can see that. Give her time. And then you need to start crawling and begging her forgiveness."

His words seemed to finally register with Tate. Tate dropped his gaze, embarrassment and the knowledge that Jensen was dead-on reflected on his face.

"I'm sorry, Chess," he said in a sincere voice. "I'll leave so you can finish what you're doing. But there are two things you need to understand. One, I love you. I'll never love anyone else. And two, I'm not giving up on us. I'll do whatever it takes to get you back and to earn your trust and forgiveness, even if it takes forever."

The conviction in his statement was undeniable. Before Chessy could respond, Tate turned and slowly walked out the door. A moment later, the front door slammed and then she heard the engine start up in his car.

Kylie pulled one of the slats down in the blinds of the bedroom window and peered out.

"He's gone," she said in a low voice.

Chessy should have been relieved, but the only reaction she could summon was overwhelming sadness.

Jensen pulled her into his arms and gave her a huge hug. "Chin up, honey. We'll get you through this. I know I can speak for Joss and Dash as well, and we'll all do whatever we can to help you."

Chessy gave him a watery smile. "Thank you. I appreciate y'all. You're the best friends I could ever ask for."

"I'll start taking your stuff out to the car while you and

Kylie finish up packing. Joss is coming over as soon as we get back to the house and I'll cook dinner for us."

"If you don't stop, I'm going to cry again," Chessy said with a sniffle. "I can see why Kylie loves you so much. You're so sweet and thoughtful, Jensen."

He smiled. "As long as Kylie recognizes what a catch I am."

Kylie snorted. "If I don't, I have no doubt you'll remind me on a daily basis."

"Damn right," he said smugly.

Then he gathered an armload of Chessy's clothing and walked out of the bedroom. A few moments later, he returned carrying the suitcases from the car and opened them up on the bed.

"If there's anything in the rest of the house you know you want, tell me and I'll start packing that stuff," Jensen said.

"I honestly don't know," Chessy said softly. "I'll do a walk-through before we leave. I shouldn't be but a few more minutes. There's no point in moving so much stuff twice. Maybe after I get my own place I'll get the rest. As it is now I don't have anywhere to put everything."

Kylie rubbed her hand up and down Chessy's back comfortingly.

Her own place. How sterile and lonely it sounded. But it was something she had to face. She couldn't impose on Kylie and Jensen forever. They were still in the beginnings of their relationship and the last thing they needed was a mopey third wheel underfoot.

Maybe a town house. Something small and homey without

a lot of maintenance. There were plenty of upscale neighbor-
hoods in the Woodlands with housing ranging from apart-
ment complexes to duplexes and townhomes. She'd rent at
first until she figured out a solid plan to support herself. No
matter that she would be entitled to a settlement from Tate in
the divorce, she still needed to evaluate her career options.

She had a business degree and had job experience in a
marketing firm, but she hadn't worked anywhere in the five
years she and Tate had been married. In hindsight it had been
incredibly stupid of her to give up everything and depend
solely on her husband for support, but at the time she'd found
it wildly romantic that he was so determined to provide for
her every need.

Setting aside thoughts of divorce and her lack of indepen-
dence, she finished packing what she wanted from the bedroom and Jensen lugged it all out to the car while she and
Kylie did a sweep of the rest of the house.

On the fireplace mantel in the living room was a photo of
her and Tate looking so happy that it hurt to look at it. Her
hand hovered over it, wanting to take it, to be able to recap-
ture a time in their marriage when they'd been in love and
deliciously carefree. Before work had consumed all of Tate's
time and attention and she'd slipped in his priorities.

She closed her eyes. Could she really blame him for wanting to make a success of himself? Was she being selfish for not
being more understanding?

No. That may have been true before the night at The House.
But it was inexcusable for him to have left her at her most vul-

nerable when she was defenseless against another man's actions. But then did she share in the blame for participating in a kink they both enjoyed and had shared in multiple times before the other night?

Finally making her decision, she carefully picked up the photo and stuck it under her arm before reaching for her wedding album from the built-in shelves on either side of the fireplace.

There were other photos. Vacations. Honeymoon pictures. Candid shots that had been taken in unguarded moments. She was infused with longing for those simpler times when their focus had been each other and there were no worries about jobs or careers or anything except loving and being.

"I'm done," Chessy quietly announced as she deposited the stack of picture frames and photo albums into Jensen's waiting hands. "We can go now."

Kylie put her hand on Chessy's shoulder and squeezed in silent support. "I'll call Joss and tell her we're on our way. She'll probably be at the house waiting when we get there."

"Thank you," Chessy said softly. "Thank you both. I don't know what I'd do without such good friends. Having to do this alone . . ." She closed her eyes, unable to finish her statement.

"You won't ever have to do it alone, Chessy," Jensen said in a determined voice. "You were there for Kylie when I was a dumbass. You were there for Joss when Dash was a dumbass. So now Tate is the one being the dumbass. It all turned out well for Joss and Kylie so maybe there's hope yet for Tate."

Chessy attempted a smile but failed miserably. Compared

to Tate's "fuck-up," Dash and Jensen's paled in comparison. There was never any doubt in Chessy's mind that the two men adored their women, and even when they pulled their stupid male moves, she'd known that it would turn out just fine in the end.

Before the night at The House, Chessy had felt optimistic about her future with Tate. She'd truly believed that they'd incurred a minor hiccup on the way to happily ever after. But when a husband turned his back on his wife when she was at her most vulnerable to take an after-hours business call, what else was she to think other than that their marriage was well and truly over?

TWENTY-TWO

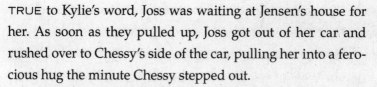

TRUE to Kylie's word, Joss was waiting at Jensen's house for her. As soon as they pulled up, Joss got out of her car and rushed over to Chessy's side of the car, pulling her into a ferocious hug the minute Chessy stepped out.

"Oh Chessy, I'm so sorry," Joss said, tears thick in her voice. "When Kylie told me what happened, I couldn't believe it. I want to kick Tate's stupid ass!"

Despite her misery, Chessy couldn't help but smile at Joss's vehemence. Her heart squeezed with love for her two best friends.

"I love you," Chessy said sincerely. "Thank you for coming. I hate to burden you when you're so miserable with morning sickness."

Joss scowled, her brow furrowing in disapproval. "If you

weren't already down and out I'd kick *your* ass for saying that. I will always be here when you need me. God knows you've been there for me countless times."

They all turned when they heard a car pull up.

"There's Dash now," Joss said. "I called him when Kylie texted me to say you were on your way and he left work to meet us here."

Chessy sighed. She knew it was inevitable that her entire group of friends would learn of the demise of her marriage, but being confronted by everyone at once was overwhelming.

Dash got out, a deep scowl on his face as he strode toward Chessy and Joss. Not even bothering to greet his wife first, he immediately pulled Chessy into a fierce hug, squeezing her against his muscular frame.

"I'm going to kill the bastard for this," Dash said darkly.

"Not if I kill him first," Jensen muttered.

Dash pulled away and gently pushed a strand of Chessy's hair behind her ear. "Are you okay, honey? Is there anything I can do?"

"I'm okay," Chessy said quietly. "Kylie and Jensen have taken good care of me and Kylie let me cry all over her earlier. At this point I'm out of tears and if I cry one more time I think my head may explode."

Sympathy darkened Dash's eyes. "I'm so sorry this happened. I wish Tate would have pulled his head out of his ass a hell of a lot earlier. There's no excuse for what he did."

"I know," she said sadly. "Leaving him was the hardest thing I've ever done, but I couldn't stay. He made a choice last

219 TAKING IT ALL 219

night and it wasn't me. If there was any hope for our marriage before, it died a quick death then. It made me realize I took too long to accept that our relationship was doomed."

"Oh sweetie," Joss said, wrapping her arm around Chessy's waist. "I'm so very sorry. I don't even know what to say to make you feel better."

"There's not much you could say at this point," Chessy said wryly. "How's the saying go? Time heals all wounds? I guess I have to hope that's true in my case. But I really wish I could press a Fast Forward button and jump to the part when everything is okay again."

"Come on inside, ladies," Jensen said. "We're standing outside where the whole neighborhood can see us. Dash and I will cook dinner while you girls relax in the living room. I'll open a bottle of wine, or something stronger if you prefer, and you're perfectly welcome to get as shit-faced as you like. Well, except you, Joss," he added with a grin. "Don't want to get the baby drunk!"

Joss and Kylie flanked Chessy, each wrapping an arm around her waist as they herded her toward the door. Once inside, they deposited Chessy on the sofa while Jensen and Dash headed for the kitchen to begin supper preparation.

True to his word, Jensen popped open a bottle of wine and poured glasses for Kylie and Chessy and then set the bottle on the coffee table with another unopened bottle in reach.

"Guess he expects us to imbibe a lot," Kylie said dryly.

"I'll drink enough for me and you, Joss," Chessy muttered. "Just keep pouring."

Joss reached for Chessy's free hand—the one not holding the wineglass. "Have you thought about what you're going to do? You know you're welcome at my house any time. You can stay as long as you want. We certainly have the room."

"I don't know," Chessy said helplessly. "I stood in my house just earlier and thought about how weak and dependent I've become. I have a degree and job experience but used neither in the five years I've been married to Tate. I have no means of supporting myself, which is so incredibly stupid I can't even begin to go there. I have to be the poorest example of womanhood on the planet. The thing is I'd be the first one to advise a woman to make sure she can stand on her own two feet and to never depend completely on a man. And yet I gave up everything because I thought it was so sweet and romantic that Tate wanted to take care of me. I was so caught up in the lifestyle we led that I never considered that I'd need to be self-sufficient. Not only does it make me hopelessly naïve, but it makes me the dumbest woman on earth."

"Stop being so hard on yourself," Kylie said in reprimand. "We'll help you get back on your feet. You can't expect to have all the answers in a day. What you need to do right now is give yourself some time. Lean on us and let us help you. Joss and I will be with you every step of the way and we'll come up with a plan."

"Absolutely," Joss said firmly. "For the next few days all you need to do is sit back and take stock. There is no hurry. We'll make a list of things that need to get done. Dash knows a divorce attorney and we can consult with him if that's still what you want to do after you've had a few days to think on it. You don't need to make hasty, emotional decisions. Then after you decide if you want to proceed with a divorce we'll figure out your job options and a place to live, although you're welcome to stay with either us or Kylie and Jensen for as long as you want."

Kylie nodded her agreement.

"You need to be sure this is what you want," Kylie said quietly. "Divorce is a huge step. You obviously love Tate and I am not disputing the fact that he royally fucked up, but are you certain there can be no reconciliation? I know he has a lot to make up for, but I also believe he truly does love you."

"I don't doubt he loves me," Chessy said in a low voice. "But sometimes love isn't enough, you know? His actions don't back up his words. Time and time again he's chosen something else over me. I've done all the giving in our marriage and he's done all the taking. I've supported him unconditionally. I've given him my submission, my heart, my soul. What else is there for me to give except forgiveness? I'm not sure I can this time."

"You make a very good point," Joss admitted. "In your shoes I honestly can't say what I'd do. But no matter what you decide, I support you one hundred percent and I'll always be here for whatever you need."

"The same goes for me," Kylie said resolutely. "And Jensen. Whatever you decide, no matter whether I agree or not, we are behind you. We'll do whatever you need us to. True friendship has no boundaries. No parameters. And certainly has no conditions. I love you like a sister—you *are* my sister in my heart—and I'll never forget how supportive you were of me when my relationship with Jensen was just beginning. You held my hand through it all. I'll never forget that or be able to repay you for your love and friendship."

Chessy set her half-empty wineglass on the coffee table and then reached for both their hands, squeezing with heart-felt love. "I love you both so much. A woman has never had truer friends than I do."

"Soup's on," Jensen called from the doorway of the living room. "You girls ready to eat?"

Chessy didn't have the heart to tell him that the very last thing she felt like doing was eating after the effort he'd gone to in order to cheer her up. With a sigh, she pushed herself up from the couch and followed Kylie and Joss to the kitchen where Dash was finishing up setting the table.

Dash pulled a chair out for Chessy and dropped an affectionate kiss on the top of her head as she sat.

"You're going to get through this, honey," he said. "I know it doesn't feel like it right now, but you're a beautiful, strong, loving woman. You'll survive."

ACROSS town, Tate stared broodingly out the window of his living room, admitting to himself that he was watching for Chessy. Hoping against hope that she'd change her mind and come home to him.

No doubt she was at Joss's or Kylie's surrounded by the unconditional support of them and Dash and Jensen. Jensen had been rightfully pissed and furious with Tate. He hadn't taken it well at the time because he'd known Jensen had been justified in his reaction. The truth was hard to swallow. It was painful and direct. And it cut straight to his heart.

He'd failed Chessy yet again. Time after time he'd let her down. He'd put her in serious jeopardy, her safety, her very life in danger, and that was unforgivable. He knew it was unforgivable and yet he couldn't face the possibility that Chessy *wouldn't* forgive him.

His greatest fear was that he'd pushed her too far this time. That he'd used up his allotment of second chances. Hell, not even second chances. More like third, fourth and fifth chances.

He rubbed his face wearily. Sleep eluded him. All he could do was sit here, phone in hand, sending her text after text, begging her to answer her phone. To talk to him. To come back home and give him yet another chance.

Each text had gone unanswered. The last time he'd tried to call her it had gone straight to voicemail, signaling that she'd turned off her phone. The rejection cut him to the core.

Tears burned his eyelids and he rubbed impatiently at them, refusing to give in to the overwhelming despair that crowded his heart.

He had some serious damage to repair. Starting with his career. He had to prove to Chessy that she could count on him going forward. Whatever it took. He'd made several calls to other financial advisors who'd expressed an interest in partnership after his last partner had bailed.

Pride had made him refuse. He wanted to become a solid

success on his own, but now he realized that he was sacrificing what mattered to him most with his stubbornness. He had enough clients to take on at least two partners. With the clients they'd bring, they'd have plenty of accounts to spread among the three of them. And he would have more time to devote to Chessy and their marriage. Provided she gave him the opportunity.

All he could do was set into motion the partnerships and hope for the best. Words were useless. Until now his actions hadn't supported his words, his promises. It was time to show Chessy instead of telling her. He refused to give up and go quietly away, allowing her to walk out of their relationship.

This would be the biggest fight of his life, but one he was fully ready to wage. There would be no holding back in his bid to win Chessy back. Her love, her faith, her trust. He wanted it all. And in return he'd give her his all.

TWENTY-THREE

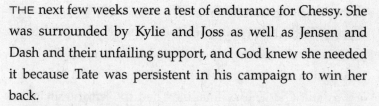

THE next few weeks were a test of endurance for Chessy. She was surrounded by Kylie and Joss as well as Jensen and Dash and their unfailing support, and God knew she needed it because Tate was persistent in his campaign to win her back.

Flowers arrived daily. Chessy had gotten on a first-name basis with the florist who delivered each bouquet. Equally prevalent were gifts. Earrings—she was admittedly an earring whore—a delicate necklace, and handwritten notes, each recalling a memory in their marriage.

She was at her breaking point emotionally. Tate had, for all practical purposes, declared emotional war. Everything he did pulled relentlessly at her heartstrings. Made her remember much happier times. If only he'd exerted half as much effort before as he was now they wouldn't be living apart in separate beds.

What was she supposed to do?

Kylie and Joss had resolutely thrown their support behind Chessy, vowing to murder Tate in his sleep if he didn't cease with the emotional warfare. It had gotten to the point where Chessy hated answering the doorbell to greet that day's delivery. Perhaps what she needed to do was move into her own place and not give out the address.

It seemed like the cowardly thing to do, but she wasn't prepared to face Tate. In the two weeks since she'd walked out on him, she hadn't seen him. Oh, it wasn't for lack of effort on his part. He'd gone first to Joss and Dash's house, thinking she was staying there. Joss had immediately called to warn Chessy that he was likely on his way to Kylie's and, sure enough, he'd knocked determinedly on the door only to be greeted—and turned away—by a scowling Jensen.

It hadn't deterred him, though. He'd continued his relentless assault and Chessy imagined had she left the shelter of Kylie's home to go anywhere, Tate would probably make an appearance and cause an embarrassing public scene. Not that he'd intend to make a scene. He'd never do anything to humiliate her. But he would likely beg her to give him another chance and then make her look like the biggest bitch who ever lived when she refused. Publicly.

So she'd remained inside Kylie's home, not venturing out for fear of running into Tate. And that pissed her off. She was a total coward. A spineless, gutless idiot for allowing him to dictate her every movement.

It was high time she took back control of her life and stopped living in fear of the inevitable confrontation with Tate. It would have to be done sooner or later. She couldn't avoid him forever. But she simply couldn't decide her own fate. One day she'd be convinced that she needed to set an appointment with the divorce attorney Dash knew and the next she'd back down from that conviction and float in the direction of not being positive of such a huge step yet. Once in motion, there was no going back. Having Tate served with divorce papers would be so . . . final. And she simply wasn't sure if she was ready for that.

And added to that, she was coming down with some sort of ugly stomach bug. She couldn't look at or smell food without gagging. She was listless, run-down and she wasn't sleeping at night. And Tate's daily onslaught was wearing on her.

Her anxiety had gotten so bad that she'd actually made a doctor's appointment so she could be prescribed medication to help calm her. She cringed at the very thought of having to be dependent on medication for her emotional stability but at the same time she was desperate for some sense of normalcy.

Since Kylie was working, Joss was coming over to take Chessy to the doctor. Chessy had protested, saying she didn't need someone to hold her hand through a doctor's appointment, but Joss had firmly told her that there was no way in hell she was letting Chessy go alone. In the end Chessy had caved under Joss's insistence and was now waiting for her to arrive.

When Chessy heard the car pull up, she went outside to meet her. Joss had just gotten out and looked decidedly green. There was a pallor to her face that made Chessy feel instantly guilty.

"Joss, you look awful, hon. Why don't you go back home and go to bed? I can drive myself to the doctor's office for God's sake."

Joss waved a hand in front of her face. "It's nothing. I promise. Mornings are just terrible for me but I can't stay in bed for my entire pregnancy even if that's precisely what Dash would prefer. I swear he's like a mother hen. One would think no other woman in the world has ever been pregnant before! He acts like I have a terminal illness. Although I will say being waited on hand and foot is a very nice perk of this pregnancy."

Her eyes twinkled merrily, some of the color returning to her cheeks. Chessy hugged her just because. Joss's good spirits were infectious. She was so sweet and kind it was impossible not to be cheered just by her presence.

"Well thank you," Chessy said. "I'm always glad to have your company. We better get going. I don't want to be late."

Joss snorted. "As if you being late will make a difference. It's not like doctors are ever prompt in seeing patients. You could probably arrive thirty minutes late and still have to wait."

"True enough, but you know I hate being late."

Joss rolled her eyes. "Is that a dig at me and the fact that I'm perpetually late for everything?"

Chessy laughed as she slid into the passenger seat of Joss's car. "Would I do something like that?"

"Yes!"

It was a fifteen-minute drive to the doctor's office though it wasn't that far away as the crow flies. But there were an insane amount of lengthy traffic lights and they caught every single one of them.

Half an hour later, Chessy sat in shock as her doctor delivered very unexpected news.

"You're pregnant, Mrs. Morgan," her physician calmly stated.

"What?" she squeaked.

Chessy felt faint and then her dizziness gave way to utter panic. Pregnant? But she was on birth control. She tried to think back. Had she taken her pills on her anniversary weekend when things had been in such upheaval? It had to have been then. She and Tate had made love that weekend. Before that it had been awhile.

"You look very distressed," the doctor said in a concerned voice. "Is someone here with you? Should I summon them?"

"No," she murmured. "I'll be fine. It's just a shock. I was— am—on birth control." Then another thought hit her and she stared anxiously up at her doctor. "I've continued to take birth control. Will that hurt the baby?"

"Well you certainly need to discontinue them," he advised. "But I doubt you've done any harm to the fetus. You'll need to get an appointment with an obstetrician so they can do a sonogram to determine your due date. And they'll want you to go in for routine prenatal care. I can give you a referral unless you already have someone in mind."

Her head was spinning trying to process the bombardment of information. Pregnant. Separated from her husband. A husband she now had to tell she was pregnant.

A few minutes later, she stumbled back into the waiting room where Joss sat. Joss took one look at her and her brow furrowed in concern. She met her halfway across the room, putting an arm around her for support.

"Chessy, what's wrong?" Joss demanded. "What did the doctor say? Did he give you a prescription for something to help your anxiety?"

Chessy closed her eyes. "What he gave me was more anxiety."

"I don't understand."

"I'm pregnant, Joss."

Joss stared at her in shock. Her mouth fell open. "Oh my God, Chessy. What are you going to do? I know how much you wanted children but Tate wanted to hold off."

"I didn't do this on purpose," Chessy said fiercely. "I know we talked about it at some point before Tate and I separated. But I acknowledged that a baby wouldn't fix our problems. I'd never purposely become pregnant with our relationship in the shape it was."

"I never thought you did this on purpose," Joss soothed.

"But hon, the timing is horrible. Tate is going to want you back more now than ever."

Tears gathered in Chessy's eyes. "I don't want him back because of the baby. I want him to want me. To put *me* first. I have no doubt he'd put his child first. Is it selfish of me to want that priority over my baby?"

"God no," Joss denied. "You should expect to come first with your husband. There's no question of that. How do you plan to tell him?"

Chessy sighed wearily as they exited the clinic and walked to Joss's car in the parking lot. "I don't know. I have to think about this. This changes everything, Joss."

"On the bright side, we'll be pregnant together!" Joss said, smiling over at Chessy as she put her car in reverse.

Chessy attempted a smile. "Our children will grow up BFFs just like us."

"Now we just have to get Kylie knocked up and it will be a trifecta!"

"Don't hold your breath," Chessy said in amusement. "I don't think Kylie has plans to be pregnant any time soon if ever. And Jensen seems content with her decision."

"And she'd make such a good mother," Joss said sadly. "I hate that her decision is based on her own terrible childhood. Her worry that she'd ever treat a child of hers like her father treated her is ridiculous. There isn't a sweeter, more generous soul out there."

"Oh I agree," Chessy said. "But I think it's good that she's waiting. Having children doesn't necessarily complete a couple. There's nothing wrong with devoting themselves to each other because, let's face it, the minute a baby enters the picture, priorities change completely."

Oh my God. The moment the words came out of her mouth, she realized that she could have well just voiced how her parents felt. That they'd devoted their time to each other, a child an unwanted intrusion. All the neglect that had been heaped upon her during her childhood was never what she wanted for her own child. In fact, even if she and Tate did get back together, her first and only priority had to be her child. Not Tate.

"Very true," Joss conceded. "And you're right. Having babies isn't a necessary component in living happily ever after. Besides, Kylie will now have two babies to spoil. She can be Auntie Kylie and the best part is, she can give them back and sleep through the night, unlike us who'll be up at all hours."

"You're not selling me on this motherhood thing," Chessy said dryly.

"Sorry. I won't say another word. My lips are sealed."

"I wish I could share this with Tate," Chessy said in a wistful voice. "Not that I'm going to keep it from him. I'm not. But I just wish things were different. That he could have gone to the doctor with me. That we were still together and he met the news with joy. This isn't ever how I envisioned getting the word that I was pregnant with my first baby."

Joss reached across the console and curled her hand around Chessy's. "I know it's not the way you wanted it to happen, but a baby is a blessing and you're going to be an awesome mom, Chessy. You can do this. We'll take childbirth classes together. I'll let you borrow all my pregnancy books and we can even use the same OB doctor and schedule our appointments on the same days."

The enthusiasm in Joss's voice was contagious. Chessy felt the first kernel of excitement since having the proverbial bomb dropped on her in the doctor's office.

She was going to have a baby.

No, it wasn't the best timing in the world, but as Joss had said, a baby was a blessing no matter the circumstances. It was a piece of Tate she'd forever have. But a baby would also tie them irrevocably no matter if their marriage truly ended in divorce. What if Tate remarried? Her child would then have a stepmother in his or her life. Someone Chessy would have to accept as a parental figure. The very thought sent a shaft of pain through her heart.

A man like Tate wouldn't have to look far for another woman. He was heart-stoppingly gorgeous, in perfect shape and he had money.

Why was jealousy gripping her at the very idea that he'd find someone else? She was the one who'd walked away. Not him. He'd spent the last weeks begging her to come back to him. But she hadn't been able to bring herself to even face him or speak directly to him.

But now it was inevitable. Because she *had* to talk to him face-to-face. She had to tell him she was pregnant with his child.

TWENTY-FOUR

WITH each passing day of complete silence from Chessy, Tate grew more and more despondent. Every day meant further loss of hope. But he still had his trump card. One he'd moved on very quickly; he planned to force a confrontation between himself and Chessy so he could prove to her that she was first and foremost in his priorities.

He'd agreed to a partnership with the two other financial advisors, splitting the client load equally three ways. Effective the next day, Morgan Financial Services would become Morgan, Hogan and Letterman Financial. Or MHL.

He'd thrown everything he had into getting it lined up as quickly as possible. It wasn't as though he was sleeping nights anyway, so he'd stayed up, working on contracts and the legalities, all the fine print of the newly formed partnership.

It was done. It would be official tomorrow but he wanted Chessy to hear it from him directly. Tonight. Before the news broke the next day. The question was how to get to her? Jensen had appointed himself her bodyguard, never allowing Tate past the doorway. Chessy wasn't answering his texts or his voicemails. And there was a giant wall of silence between him and those who used to be his friends—Dash, Joss and Kylie. Jensen he hadn't known for that long, but the others? He considered them his closest friends, but they'd made their choice. Not that he begrudged Chessy their friendship, but he missed them. Not only had he lost his wife but he'd also lost their friends.

His cell rang and he froze. His hands shook as he fumbled to get the phone from the holder secured to his pants. God, it was Chessy's ringtone. She was calling him!

He swore when he couldn't get it out right away. The very last thing he wanted was to miss her call. She may not ever call back.

"Chessy, thank God," he said when he finally was able to answer.

"Tate?"

Her quivery voice made his blood run cold. It sounded as though she'd been *crying*.

"Chessy, what's wrong?" he demanded. "Are you hurt? Tell me where you are and I'll be right there."

"I'm fine," she said, though her voice was still shaking. "I wanted to know if you could meet me tonight. At our—your—house. Somewhere private."

His thoughts scattered in a dozen different directions. Could he meet her tonight? Hell, he'd move heaven and earth to meet her any damn where she wanted. But it was the somewhere private part that bothered him. As if she had something important to tell him. Was this going to be when she told him she wanted to end their marriage and have him served with divorce papers? Or dare he hope she would agree to a reconciliation and come back home to him?

But regardless of the purpose, she'd be *here*. In their house where she belonged. That stood for something. Because once she walked in here, she was home. She'd be on his turf and she wouldn't have Jensen between her and him. No, it would be just Chessy and Tate, exactly as she requested. Definitely private.

"Unless you have work stuff," Chessy mumbled. "We can always do it another time."

He winced but he deserved that shot. "Tonight is fine. Absolutely come to the house. I'll cook dinner for us and we can talk. There's a hell of a lot you don't know about yet that will be released tomorrow but I wanted you to hear it from me first. I had fully intended to drive over to Kylie and Jensen's and pull you out by the hair to take you back home with me so I could discuss the changes I've made. Changes I hope you'll be completely on board with."

"So it sounds as though we'll both be doing a lot of talking," she mused.

"I'll listen to every subject you want to bring up. Then, only when you're satisfied with my responses, will we move on to what I want to discuss with you. It's a pretty big step. I have the backing and investors."

"Do I get a choice in the order in which we say what?"

Tate could hear the clear nervousness in her voice and she sounded as though she wanted him to speak his mind first before delving into what might bring her back to him after their long separation.

"Absolutely," he conceded.

"Okay, then listen up."

A ridiculous smile quirked up the corners of his mouth. He was already mentally going through the contents of their pantry and fridge so he'd know if he needed to run out for anything. He was positive he had all the ingredients on hand to make one of their favorite dishes.

"You're going first while we eat dinner. After and only after you've said what's on your mind will I tell you what's on mine."

Dinner was already beginning to look like one huge clusterfuck. How did one cook a meal that acted as an olive branch? And to make it the good start to try to salvage their marriage? But was that what it was going to be? Or was Chessy going to tell him it was well and truly over?

"What time do you want me there?" Chessy asked quietly, not sounding certain that she would be welcome.

Tate nearly lost his shit over that but made a visible effort to relax so he didn't come across sounding like an asshole. But there were some things that needed to be addressed.

"Baby, you do *not* have to ask what time it's okay for you to come to your own house. I don't plan to start cooking until you get here. I thought you could sit at the island and ride herd while I try *not* to ruin our supper."

This time he heard the smile in his voice and he ached all the way to his soul for one smile, directed at him. Her looking at him like he'd hung the moon. It was the way she used to look at him. Pure adoration that was there for the world to see. She was a magnet for people. They were inexplicably drawn to her just to gain a smile or a few sweet words. Men and women alike walked away as if they had just been in the presence of royalty. And well, she was in a way. She was his princess.

He'd done everything to outfit the princess, to transform her into a woman who never had need of a single item. Her credit card had no limit and he encouraged her frequently to go out and buy something for herself. She was infuriating in that regard because she always had the same answer. She didn't need anything. Tate gave her everything she wanted. How he'd loved hearing those heartfelt words come from his wife's sweet lips. What man wouldn't be absolutely agog over the fact that his woman gave not one damn over wealth or material possessions. What she wanted above all was . . . her husband. And that should have been the easiest slam dunk of all.

All he had to do was give her his undivided attention. Thinking back, yes, he'd desperately wanted to net this client because she was also entertaining other options. It was what had prevented him from giving Chessy what she deserved.

Tabitha Markham would indeed have been a coup. He had no doubt that she was being courted, wined and dined by other

financial businesses like a duck on a June bug. But he had practically told her to fuck off once he heard Chessy scream in pain
and terror. And he couldn't care less which financial advisor
she decided to go with now. If he lived to be a hundred, the
sound of Chessy's cry would haunt him to his dying day.

"I should let you go then. I still need to shower and change.
I haven't been feeling well lately and unfortunately it shows."

Tate was immediately filled with concern. "Is my girl sick?
Who's taking care of you? That's *my* job."

It angered him, this helplessness that he couldn't reach out
to his wife when she needed him most. Chessy didn't fall ill
very often at all. She always got glowing checkups from her
doctor, who announced she was fitter than the majority of
patients he saw.

But the few times a cold had gotten the best of her and one
particularly vicious bout of strep throat, Tate had been within
an arm's length the entire time. She'd wanted to sleep in the
guest bedroom because she was afraid she would make him
sick, but he was having none of that.

Every single night, or day if she were simply taking a nap,
he carried her to bed and tucked her in, ensuring all the pillows were in the exact position she liked them. And even
more generous, he handed over the remote for the TV in their
bedroom.

While she binged on the HGTV channel and watched
countless renovation episodes, Tate's head was always about
to explode, but he let her torture him with her girly shows
because he knew how much she enjoyed them.

She sounded extremely weary now and it alarmed him even more. So help him, if she didn't show tonight now that he was worried out of his damn mind, he'd go over there and haul her out of Jensen's house, police be damned.

"I'll tell you all about it tonight," she said. "I don't want to get into over the phone."

Tate's heart lurched. His stomach knotted to the point of pain and nausea welled in his throat. He had to suck in deeply through his nostrils so he didn't completely lose it.

"How soon can you be here?" he demanded.

"Uh, well I don't have anything else scheduled. I mean I guess I could come at any time. I figured I'd come when you were ready to eat."

Tate checked his watch. It was five. Certainly not out of the realm for preparing dinner. By the time Chessy drove over and they settled into the kitchen and he started preparations it would be six. Perfect timing.

"Can you head over now?" he asked, trying to keep his enthusiasm at bay and sound normal even though when it came to Chessy, anything at all to *do* with Chessy, normal wasn't part of his vocabulary for sure.

He couldn't wait to finally see Chessy one-on-one for the first time since the night she'd walked out, when she had been devastated and so damn fragile looking. As though she'd break if someone stared at her too hard. And yet he had let a brute of a man put his precious girl through the paces, warming her up for when Tate would have taken over.

Chessy could have been seriously injured. For all practical

purposes she had been raped. Just because the bastard hadn't fully penetrated her didn't mean he hadn't forced himself on her, even as she was screaming her safe word.

To still his restless mind and whirling thoughts, he began to prepare the crepes while he waited for her answer. In theory this recipe was damn good. But it was all in the execution. And Tate wasn't one to ever follow the letter of a recipe. He always improvised, adding stuff he liked and experimenting until he got the flavor he wanted. He and Chessy had always taken turns being the guinea pig and then they'd offer constructive criticism. Not enough Cajun seasoning. Too much black pepper. The lobster and crab smelled and tasted too "fishy."

There was no modesty from him when it came to this dish. He and Chessy could make themselves sick on it, eating way beyond the point where they were already full. It was always "Oh, I'll just have one more bite," and then a moan of pleasure followed by another bite and another . . . Until they groaned in agony and flopped onto the couch in a vegetative state and watched mindless reality shows to get their minds off their miserably full stomachs.

"Yes," Chessy said finally. Was there a hint of excitement in her voice or was he simply hearing what he wanted. If she had missed him only half as much as he was missing her, then he had a shot. "I'll leave in a few minutes after I shower and change. If I wait any longer, someone will want to take me, and as I said, I'd rather not have an audience for what I want to talk about."

Again that tendril of dread curled tighter and tighter

around his neck. "Tell me at least that you're okay. That there's nothing seriously wrong with you. Don't leave me to my worst imaginings, Chess. You've got me scared shitless."

"I'm fine, Tate. Truly. It's just . . . complicated, which is why I wanted to say it face-to-face."

Whatever got her back home where she belonged, even if it was only for a short time, worked for him.

"Okay then. Head this way. I'm putting together supper now."

TWENTY-FIVE

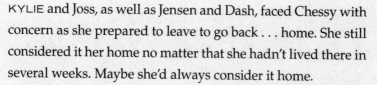

KYLIE and Joss, as well as Jensen and Dash, faced Chessy with concern as she prepared to leave to go back . . . home. She still considered it her home no matter that she hadn't lived there in several weeks. Maybe she'd always consider it home.

Moreover, when they'd bought the house, she'd picked it out with a family in mind. It was a huge house for just the two of them. Four bedrooms, three bathrooms plus a guest room downstairs, space for an office, two living areas, a formal dining room plus an eat-in kitchen and an island bar.

In her mind she could so easily see having children and raising them in that house. Most couples didn't buy their forever home right after marrying, but Tate had been financially secure enough to purchase the house and once she'd seen it—

and envisioned their future in it—she'd instantly fallen in love.

Five years later she was pregnant with the child she'd always desperately wanted but her marriage was in ruins and the house she'd once dreamed of raising a family in was off-limits. Even if she did end up getting the house if she and Tate divorced, how could she ever raise her child in a home that screamed Tate from every corner?

"I don't think it's a good idea for you to go over there alone," Dash said firmly.

He and Jensen were standing between her and the door-way, a formidable barrier, their arms crossed over their chests and stubborn looks on their faces.

Kylie and Joss stood at Chessy's side but it was clear they were in agreement with the men.

"You should make him come here. On neutral ground," Joss said in a low voice. "Or over at mine and Dash's house. We'll give you all the privacy you need but you shouldn't be at a disadvantage emotionally, and with you being pregnant you're especially vulnerable. Just ask Dash! I cry over the most ridiculous things. I swear I'm a hormonal mess. I certainly can't be trusted to make life-altering decisions with preg-nancy brain."

Dash's entire face softened with love as he gazed at his wife. "You're adorable pregnant. And you are not a hormonal mess. I love every part of you and wouldn't change a thing. You pregnant is the sexiest thing I've ever seen. I can't wait until you get bigger and I can feel the little one kick."

Chessy's hand went to her own flat stomach and tears welled in her eyes. Joss shot Dash a look of reprimand and Dash immediately looked contrite.

"I'm sorry, Chessy. That was digging the knife deeper."

Chessy shook her head. "Do not ever hold back with Joss for fear of hurting me. That isn't fair. She deserves to have someone who sees her for how special she is."

Jensen sighed. "Will you at least let one of us go with you? Joss is right about one thing. You're extremely vulnerable right now and that gives Tate the upper hand. And when he learns of your pregnancy, he's going to push hard for a reconciliation."

"I guess we'll have to see, won't we?" Chessy said lightly. "At any rate, expect me back tonight. He's cooking dinner because he says there's something he needs to tell me. Maybe he wants a divorce. But it's obvious we need to clear the air. I need . . . closure. I need to know where this is headed because I can't go on like this. I have to make plans for me and my child."

"Honey, a man does not cook dinner for a woman he's planning to dump," Dash said dryly.

"I'm going," Chessy said emphatically. "Now please let me by so I'm not late."

"Only if you promise to call if you need us," Jensen said. "One of us will be over immediately if you need help or support."

She leaned up on tiptoe and kissed Jensen's cheek and then Dash's. She hugged both Kylie and Joss before disentangling herself and headed for the door.

"Thank you all," she said sincerely. "I'm so lucky to have friends like you."

She hurried down the sidewalk to her car before she could change her mind and completely chicken out of her dinner with Tate. She had a whole horde of butterflies in her stomach and her pregnancy wasn't helping in that regard. She just hoped she could make it through dinner without losing the contents of her stomach. That certainly wasn't the way she wanted to break the news to Tate of his impending fatherhood.

Would he be happy? It saddened her that she had no clue. It had been him who'd wanted to wait when she wanted children earlier in their marriage. But he'd thought they should be more financially secure first.

But when was it enough? It seemed that no matter how much money he brought in, no matter how many clients he netted, it was never enough. He'd always put her off and said maybe next year. Or when he reached his goal of X number of portfolios that he managed. She knew for a fact that he'd surpassed his supposed goal on three separate occasions. And yet he still hadn't agreed to have children.

It was very possible that he wouldn't greet this news well at all. She may end up a single mother with an absentee father for her child.

Guilt surged through her chest for making assumptions and jumping to conclusions. Tate wasn't a horrible person. He'd be a good father. She knew that much. It didn't matter if this child was planned or not. He'd love him or her every bit as much as Chessy already did.

When she arrived at their house, she parked and got out only to be met at the door by Tate. He looked as though it took everything he had not to pull her into his arms or touch her in some way. But instead he merely stepped back and swept his arm inward in silent invitation.

Her nerves a mess, she walked inside, feeling as though she was in foreign territory rather than the house she'd made a home over the last five years.

"Come into the kitchen while I cook dinner. I've already gotten a start on the crepes."

Anticipation made her mouth water. "Crawfish and crab crepes?"

He certainly knew her weakness and his smile proved it.

"I may have made your favorite," he said slyly.

She sighed. "You don't play fair, Tate."

He shrugged in response. "I warned you, Chessy. I'm not going down without a fight. I believe in us. I love you. There's no way I'm just going to let you go without throwing everything I have your way."

Well, that answered the question of whether he was going to ask for a divorce. Was his big thing he wanted to tell her simply an opportunity to beg for forgiveness again? And how much longer could she stand up under the onslaught when she loved him with every aching breath?

She loved him, yes. Without question. But trust him? No, she couldn't say she fully trusted him any longer. Not when he'd repeatedly chosen his clients and career over her.

"Is that what you wanted to tell me tonight?" she asked.

"It's one of the things," he said calmly. "But not *the* thing. We'll discuss that over dinner. While the crepes are in the oven, I'd like to hear about you. You sounded upset on the phone and you said you hadn't been feeling well."

She shook her head. "We'll discuss it after dinner. After you've told me what it is you have to say to me."

He looked frustrated with her stubbornness but he didn't press. Instead he opened a bottle of wine and poured one glass and started to pour another until she held up her hand.

"No, don't," she said quickly. "I don't want wine. I'm afraid it will upset my stomach."

"So you *have* been ill," he said grimly.

"I'm separated from my husband," she said in a terse tone. "Do you expect me to be radiant? I've been miserable, Tate. This is never what I wanted. You chose this for us, not me."

Anger sparked in her blood and she could positively feel her blood pressure rising. She took several calming breaths, knowing it did the baby no good for Chessy to become so upset.

Tate's eyes darkened with sorrow. His hand shook as he reached for his glass of wine.

"I didn't choose our separation," he said quietly. "Never that. I fucked up. I get that. It was stupid. I just reacted without thinking. It's a mistake I'll pay for dearly for the rest of my life. I hope you can find it in your generous, loving heart to forgive me. To give me yet another chance to make things right. I don't want to live my life without you, Chessy. I can't bear the thought of it. There will never be another woman for me. You're it. And I want it all, but I want it with you."

Her heart squeezed at the sincerity and graveness in his tone. She had no doubt he meant it in this precise moment. That wasn't in question. He'd also been absolutely sincere after the night of their anniversary, and look where that had gotten them. It wasn't a matter of him speaking an untruth now. It was the question of how long that vehemence would last. A week? A month? She had no faith that he'd continue to put her first in his life and she refused to live with that uncertainty any longer. She had a child to think about now and her child deserved a full-time father, not someone who was gone all the time and never there for the important moments in life.

"I don't know what to say—to think," Chessy said, her mouth turned down in an expression of unhappiness.

"Just say you'll think about it," he urged. "I don't have to have an answer today or even tomorrow. Just promise me you'll think about it and not give up on me quite yet."

She closed her eyes but nodded, knowing there really wasn't an alternative. She couldn't very well say with any authority what would happen once he told her whatever he had to tell her, and she then told him she was pregnant. She knew he'd fight even harder for them to get back together once he learned she was pregnant, but not telling him wasn't an option. He deserved to know he was going to become a father no matter her reservations about him as a husband.

There was visible relief on his features. His eyes brightened and lost some of their dread.

"I swear you won't regret it, Chess," he said gruffly.

He turned away and cracked open the stove, peering in at

the bubbling cheese that was just turning a yummy brown. She sniffed appreciatively, her stomach growling in anticipation. She hadn't even attempted to eat today because the mere thought of food was revolting to her.

He grabbed oven mitts and slid the casserole dish from the oven, setting it on the stovetop while he closed the oven door.

"We'll give it five minutes or so to rest and then we'll dig in," Tate announced.

As he spoke, he went to the cabinet where the plates were and took two down. Then he retrieved knives and forks from the drawer and set the small table in the breakfast nook where they so often had eaten together. The formal dining room had only been used on the occasions when they entertained clients or their friends.

He carried the still-steaming casserole dish to the table and then fetched a spatula to spoon up the delectable entrée. Chessy took a cautious sniff, praying her stomach didn't rebel.

To her relief, she felt no nausea when she forked in the first savory bite. The flavor hit her taste buds like a mouth orgasm. She moaned her pleasure. This was right up there with good sex.

"Good?" Tate asked with a smile.

He knew damn well it was fantastic.

"It's wonderful," she sighed. "Best thing I've eaten in weeks."

He frowned at that. "Have you been eating, Chess? I know you. And when you're unhappy or stressed you don't eat or take proper care of yourself."

"Well duh," she muttered. "I can assure you that my marriage crumbling around me isn't exactly lighting my world on fire."

He sighed. "We're both miserable, baby. Doesn't that tell you anything? We both still love each other. I certainly love you. If we're so unhappy apart, don't you see that the logical thing to do is get back together so we can make one another happy again?"

"Because I'm afraid," she said frankly. "You've broken too many promises to me, Tate."

His nostrils flared and he went silent a moment before pushing his plate forward. He propped his elbows on the table and directed his stare at her.

"Maybe my news will prove to you that I'm trying to change—that I *am* changing. I've partnered with two other guys and expanded my firm to include them. Which means that I'm no longer a one-man show. It also means I won't have to devote so much time to work or my clients. I have two partners now to share in juggling clients and their needs. I did this for us, Chessy. Because I let my career get in the way of our relationship. I let it overrun all else. That wasn't fair to you and I'm prepared to go to whatever lengths necessary to make amends."

Chessy stared at him in utter disbelief. Tate had been so adamant about not taking on another partner after his first one had bailed. He'd been determined to make his business a success without anyone else.

"It will be made public tomorrow," Tate continued. "But I

wanted you to hear it from me. And for you to understand why I did it. I did it for you. To hopefully help you see the commitment I'm making to you. To our marriage. You mean more to me than my business, my career, money, worldly possessions. Having it all means nothing if I don't have what's most important in my life. You."

Of anything she may have expected him to say, this was not it. She was shocked at the matter-of-fact way he'd said he was taking on not one, but two partners. Tate was extremely possessive and proprietary when it came to his clients. He was a hands-on person who didn't believe in allowing anyone else to handle matters he himself could personally see to. He didn't trust other people not to fuck up.

This was huge. It was epic. She had no idea what to say to his announcement. Instead she simply stared openmouthed at him.

"I hope this will at least show you that I'm very serious about doing whatever it takes to win you back," he said quietly. "And it's only the beginning, Chess. There will be no afterhours calls. No client dinners unless you go with me. The weekends will be ours and I'm going to start taking vacation days more frequently so we can travel together."

She shook her head in confusion. "I don't get it. Why now? If you could have done this sooner, why didn't you?"

His eyes darkened with regret. And they grew suspiciously wet, which made her even more aghast. She'd never seen Tate cry. Ever. He was always the strong one while she was the emotional wreck. She cried over sad movies, happy movies, those sappy Hallmark commercials at Christmas. She cried over news stories. Hell, she cried when she was happy. But Tate?

"I should have done it a long time ago," he admitted. "I have no excuse other than I took you for granted. I took your love for granted. I wanted it all. The perfect wife, the perfect career. It was never enough. No matter how successful my firm became, I always wanted more until there was nothing left.

"Seeing what I did to you, what my neglect caused, was a huge wake-up call for me. I stood by and let another man abuse you. Do you have any idea what that did to me? I can't even look at myself in the mirror anymore. All I can see is you huddled on the floor crying. All I can remember is you screaming your safe word. Every night when I go to bed, that entire night plays over and over in my head. It's not something I'll ever get over, Chessy. I have to live with that for the rest of my life."

"I wish I could believe you," she said wistfully.

He reached across the table and captured her hand. "Just give me a chance, Chessy. One more time. I'll never ask for another. If I fail you again, I'll leave. The house and everything in it will be yours. You'll never want for a single thing. I'll make sure of it."

She closed her eyes and paused. "There's something I have to tell you, Tate. Something I only just found out. It's why I came over tonight. It changes everything and I don't know what to do."

Concern blazed over his face. His grip tightened around her hand. She took a deep breath and put it out there.

"I'm pregnant, Tate. I'm pregnant with your child."

TWENTY-SIX

TATE stared back at Chessy in shock, sure he hadn't heard her correctly. But the fear and apprehension in her eyes told him he had. Close on the heels of shock came unfettered joy—and relief. He'd been so afraid of what it was Chessy had to tell him. It's why he'd pulled out all the stops in his bid to win her back because he didn't want her to tell him she was filing for divorce.

He squeezed her hand, temporarily incapable of speech. Tears burned his eyelids and she stared at him, stunned, when one trickled down his cheek. He didn't bother wiping it away. He wanted her to realize the magnitude of this moment for him.

"Chessy, that's *wonderful*," he whispered.

"But you didn't want children," she said, her voice thick

with emotion. "You wanted to wait. Every time I brought it up, you said maybe next year. And I want you to know I didn't do this on purpose. The very last thing I would have done is bring a child into an unstable marriage. It must have happened the weekend of our anniversary. I forgot to take my birth control pills."

Unable to bear the distance between them one more second, Tate stood and walked around to her chair and pulled her up and into his arms. He hugged her tightly, his shoulders heaving with emotion. So much love welled up in his heart and soul. He closed his eyes and prayed for another chance to make things right. He had a family now. More than just him and Chessy. They had a *child*.

"Come into the living room so we can talk," he gently urged.

She allowed him to lead her to the sofa and they sat down together. He pulled her into his arms and thank God she didn't resist. He savored having her in his arms again. The last few weeks had been hell for him. Not being able to see her, talk to her, touch her. And yet he saw her every single day when he entered his house. Her stamp was on every single item in the house. It was impossible to look anywhere without seeing her reflection.

"First of all, it never crossed my mind that you got pregnant on purpose. But even if you had, I'd be overjoyed. Secondly, we've already established what a dumbass I am. I knew how much you wanted children. I wanted them too. But there were two reasons I wanted to hold off. One was me being purely selfish. I wanted you to myself a little longer and I knew once we had a child that I'd have to share you with our son or daughter. It shames me to say that, but I won't lie to you. The other reason was because I wanted to be sure I could provide for my family financially. But Chessy, I'm thrilled that you're pregnant. Is that why you haven't been feeling well?" he asked anxiously. "Is everything okay with the pregnancy? Have you seen a doctor yet?"

"I haven't seen an obstetrician yet," she admitted. "I only found out because I went to my general practitioner to ask for medication for my stress and anxiety. They obviously ran a pregnancy test when they drew blood and it was then he told me I was pregnant. I knew I had to tell you right away so here I am."

"Thank you for not keeping this from me," he said. "I want to be able to share in every aspect of your pregnancy. I want to go to every doctor's appointment and I want to see our child grow inside you. Feel him or her kick for the first time. And watch you grow rounder and more beautiful with each passing day."

"You act as though me being pregnant fixes everything," Chessy said quietly. "It doesn't, Tate. We still have so much to work out. I keep going back and forth with myself over whether to see a divorce attorney or not."

Tate's blood ran cold and he was seized by paralyzing fear. But he had to keep calm. He couldn't afford to do or say the wrong thing and drive her away for good.

"I know we have a lot to work out, but I'm willing to try. Are you?"

She bit into her bottom lip nervously, her eyes cloudy with

uncertainty. "I don't know," she admitted. "This whole thing has thrown me for a loop. I don't know what the right decision is. I just know I can't continue on like it was before. Our child deserves better. *I* deserve better."

"Yes, you do deserve better than I've given you," Tate said, not even bothering to hide the truth in her statement. "And I'm committed to giving you better. One hundred and ten percent of me from now on. But I can't do that if we're apart. I need you here. Where I can take care of you and our baby. You aren't happy. I'm not happy. What do we have to lose by trying?"

"I can't make that decision in a split second," she murmured. "I need time, Tate. I need time to think. To process this all. I only just found out about my pregnancy. I haven't had time to figure out what's best for our child or for me. Much less us."

And yet she'd come to him at her first opportunity. She hadn't tried to hide the fact that she was pregnant. That gave him hope that all wasn't lost. She'd trusted him enough to confide in him. But then she was inherently honest. Hiding anything wasn't in her nature. It was one of the things he loved most about her. She wasn't adept in disguising her emotions, her moods. He knew them all.

He wanted her back before he knew about their child, but did she realize that? Surely she did. He'd certainly not made it a secret in his relentless pursuit of her over the last weeks. But he had no way of knowing how or what she was thinking. It was new and frustrating for him. He'd always been able to count on her predictability. A quality some men might not find attractive, but for Tate, always knowing just where he stood with

Chessy and knowing she always stood with him had been a source of great comfort. But it had also been his greatest downfall because he'd grown too complacent, too confident in the fact that she was with him through thick and thin.

Never would he take her for granted again, but he had to find a way to convince her of that. Words were just words and they no longer held any power with her.

"I'll give you time," he conceded. "But please don't shut me out, Chess. Allow me to see you and our baby. Let me go to the doctor with you. I won't pressure you and I won't demand anything you're unwilling to give me. But give me a chance to show you that I've truly changed, starting with the announcement of my partnership tomorrow. I'd like us to start over. Whatever I have to do to regain your trust I'll do."

"You want to date?" she asked skeptically.

"I want us to see each other," he corrected. "I'd rather not live apart while we're doing it, but if you need time and space, I'll give it to you. But I want to see you, which means coming over, going out to dinner, you coming here so I can cook dinner for you like tonight. I'd like to go to your first obstetrician appointment and be included in your prenatal care. I want to talk about baby names and pick out baby furniture and clothing."

Her expression softened and his pulse sped up. She was caving. He could see it. But it was a hollow victory at best because he still didn't have what he most wanted. Her back in his life, his house, his bed. But he had to believe that in time those things would come. The alternative didn't bear thinking about.

"I'll consider everything you've said," Chessy finally said. "I should be going now. Kylie and Jensen are going to be worried. They didn't want me to come alone."

Tate's expression darkened. "Do they think I'm some ogre who's going to abuse you?"

"No," Chessy said softly. "But they're afraid you'll hurt me. Emotionally. And I'm not in a good place right now. As I said before the whole reason I went to the doctor was to ask for medication for anxiety and depression. Instead I found out I'm pregnant. I'm scared. More scared than I've ever been in my life. This isn't easy for me, Tate. I'm not used to questioning my every decision, but I've continued to make bad ones. I can't afford to do that now that I have a child to consider."

Tate closed his eyes, the ache in his heart making his chest hurt. "I wish you wouldn't go. I'd like you to stay so we can talk. About the baby. Our future."

"It hasn't been decided yet if we have a future," she pointed out. "I'm open to seeing you. On my terms, not yours. But ultimately the decision resides with me and I expect you to respect that."

He bit his tongue against the urge to argue. To try and wear her down. Only her complete look of fragility and fatigue halted him. The last thing she needed was more stress piled on top of her.

Patience. This was going to require patience, a trait he was very unfamiliar with. He'd never had to wait on anything in his life. When he'd met Chessy, he'd immediately known she was the one, and he'd pursued her and won her in short order.

And now he'd lost her.

"When *can* I see you then?" he asked bluntly.

"I'll call you," she said.

He made a sound of impatience. If he waited for her to call he may well wait forever.

"I *will* call you, Tate," she said quietly. "I just need a few days. I have a lot of thinking to do. Perhaps we can get together this weekend."

It took everything he had to sit there and agree when his gut was screaming at him to argue, to chip away at the wall between them until she gave in. But he didn't want a reluctant victory. He wanted it all. Chessy. Their baby. Her heart, soul and body. And he wanted it given freely. Not because he'd forced her into a corner.

"I'll wait for your call then," he finally conceded. "But promise me if anything crops up, if there are any problems with your pregnancy, that you'll let me know so I can be there."

"I have no intention of keeping anything from you, Tate."

She rose from the couch and he caught her hand, reluctant for her to leave just yet.

"Do you have to go now?"

She nodded. "I don't want Kylie and Jensen or Joss and Dash to worry. They've worried enough about me lately."

"I've worried about my girl too," Tate said in a low voice.

Hurt immediately echoed in her eyes at the endearment. He hadn't meant to land a blow. It just slipped out, a natural pet name he'd always used for her.

"Tell me something, Tate," she said, cocking her head to the side. "Do you miss *me*? Or do you miss the convenience of having me around. Would any woman do in my stead? Do you just not like being alone?"

He sucked in his breath at the hollow pain he felt in every word she uttered. It hurt him that she could possibly even think such a thing.

"No other woman could ever fill your shoes, baby. Of course I miss you. And I damn sure don't like being alone but it's because I'm not with you. Given a choice between being alone or being with someone other than you, then I'd choose to be alone."

He knew he scored points with his answer because for the first time, uncertainty flickered in her eyes. As if she were truly second-guessing her decision to remain apart from him. He could only hope that she changed her mind in short order because every day without her was a day in hell.

TWENTY-SEVEN

THE next morning Chessy was sitting in the living room, newspaper in hand turned to the business section while contemplating the evening before with Tate when Joss and Kylie both burst through the front door.

"Did you see the . . . ?"

Joss broke off when she saw the newspaper Chessy was holding.

"Ah, I guess you have seen it then," Joss finished.

"If you're referring to the article about Tate's partnership with two other financial guys then yeah," Chessy murmured. "But I knew. He told me last night."

"And you didn't tell us?" Kylie demanded.

"I was emotionally wrung out by the time I got in last night," Chessy replied. "I was too confused to rehash it all then. Hell, I'm *still* confused. I can't figure out his angle and it's driving me crazy."

Joss sat down on the couch next to Chessy, her eyes full of love and understanding. "Have you considered his only angle is winning you back at any cost, sweetie?"

"But that's just it. With Tate it's all about winning whether in business or his personal life, but especially in business. How do I know I'm not just some giant victory for him? I mean, how am I supposed to know if he's truly sincere this time? It's not like he hasn't had multiple opportunities. So what's changed now? And in his defense, he told me about taking on partners and lightening his work load so he could devote more time to our marriage before I told him I was pregnant."

"Then maybe he really does mean it this time," Kylie admitted.

Chessy looked at her in surprise because up to now she'd been Tate's biggest detractor.

"I know, I know," Kylie defended. "I've not exactly been his biggest fan. But I have to hand it to the guy. He's persistent and he really seems sincere. If it involved anyone but my best friend I'd probably wonder if she had rocks in her head for continuing to put him off. Not that it's what I think about you. You're certainly justified in being wary of allowing him the power to hurt you again. Self-preservation is a strong thing. Once bitten, twice shy, et cetera et cetera."

"I think the question that has to be asked here is what do you want, Chessy?" Joss asked softly. "Because it doesn't matter what I think or Kylie or Dash and Jensen. This is your life, your marriage. Only you can decide what's best for you and more importantly what will make you happy. Are you resisting because you truly don't trust him not to hurt you again? Or are you resisting because of your pride and you don't want to look like a gullible fool for trusting him again?"

Chessy looked thunderstruck as Joss's question sank in. "Wow. You don't ask the hard ones, do you?"

"I'd say she scored a few points judging by the expression on your face," Kylie said.

"Good God, could you be right?" Chessy breathed out. "Is it my stupid pride and me not wanting to look stupid for taking him back? Or is it truly because I don't trust him."

Joss shrugged. "Maybe it's a little of both. I certainly can't blame you either way. I wouldn't be lining up for that kind of humiliation or hurt again. But then I went through something similar with Dash and I forgave him."

"And I forgave Jensen his stupidity," Kylie said dryly. "I think it's an inherent quality in men. Some stupid gene they inherit purely because they're male. Women are so much smarter and more logical. Men? Not so much. They think with their dicks, when they're thinking at all."

Chessy and Joss burst into laughter.

"You're so irreverent, Kylie. I love that about you," Chessy said with a grin.

Kylie performed a mock bow. "Glad I can be of service. Now, let's get to the point. What do you want, Chessy? Forget everything that's happened in the past. Forget any worry over how you appear to others. Forget what me, Joss, Dash or

Jensen think. What do you want? What would make you the happiest in the world? Don't think about it. Go with your gut. Give me your answer in three seconds or less."

"I want my husband back," Chessy blurted. "I want my child raised by both its mother and father. I want Tate to share in every aspect of my pregnancy. I want my marriage back."

"Well, there you go," Joss said, satisfaction lining her face.

"Oh my God," Chessy whispered. "Is it truly that easy?"

"No," Kylie said. "Nothing good is ever easy, or so Jensen always says. He said that about me in the beginning. I didn't appreciate the sentiment at the time but that's because I was being difficult and I knew it."

Joss chuckled. "You? Difficult? Naaahhh."

"Cut the sarcasm or I'll cut you," Kylie threatened. "As I was saying, Chessy," she said pointedly ignoring Joss's smirk. "No, it's not that easy, but it can be. To quote Jensen yet again, and God, I'm starting to sound like his damn parrot! But he also says it can be as easy or as hard as we make it. The question is which do you want to make it?"

"I don't want it to be too easy for him," Chessy said hesitantly. "Shouldn't he have to work for it? If I make it too easy then it opens the door for him to take advantage of me again. To take me for granted. And, well, this may make me sound like a terrible person, but part of me wants to punish him for what he did. He deserves to be punished."

"Sweetie, I think you've made it pretty damn difficult for him over the last several weeks. Not that he didn't totally deserve it. But the guy is miserable. I'd say you're definitely punishing him," Joss said.

"Oh yeah," Kylie agreed. "Jensen told me he's looked like complete shit every time he shows up over here demanding to see you. And that he looks like a kicked puppy when Jensen tells him to fuck off."

Chessy winced. "Ugh. I don't want to strip him of his pride completely even if I *do* want to punish him for his utter stupidity."

"So, what are you going to do?" Kylie persisted. "I distinctly remember a turning point with both Joss and me when our men were being complete dumbasses and if we hadn't taken matters in our own hands, we'd probably both still be single."

"In other words it's up to me to pull Tate's head out of his ass and show some mercy," Chessy said in a dry tone.

"Well, not in so many words, but yeah, basically," Kylie said. "I know I'm repeating myself, but only if that's what you want. It's time to fish or cut bait. If you want a clean break then make an appointment with a divorce attorney and move on with your life. If you want Tate back then you need to get on the ball and tell him that. Either way, end your misery. Because right now you're in a holding pattern, stuck in the mud, not going anywhere but deeper in the mire."

"You certainly have a way with words," Joss muttered.

"Am I right?" Kylie asked with a raised eyebrow.

"Yes, you prickly bitch. You're always right," Joss said in exasperation.

Chessy laughed again, realizing this was the most she'd laughed since she and Tate had split up.

"God I love you two," she said fervently. "I have to be the luckiest woman on earth to have such good friends. Best friends."

"Sisters," Joss amended.

"Yes, sisters from another mother," Kylie agreed. "So not to beat you over the head, but for the third time, what are you going to do? Or do you need our help figuring it out?"

Chessy glanced down at the paper that was turned to the article on Tate's new partnership. She gazed thoughtfully at it and then checked her watch.

"How long do you think it would take for y'all to totally glam me out. I mean everything. Kick-ass dress. Total fuck-me shoes. Hair, makeup, the complete works."

"Not long if we get moving," Joss said emphatically. "Why? What's your plan?"

"Well, it's currently noon and according to this article the newly formed MHL investment firm will host an open house at their new headquarters in the Woodlands between one and three P.M. today. I was thinking of dropping in. Just to offer my congratulations and all."

"Oh you are evil and I love it," Joss crowed.

"I do too!" Kylie exclaimed. "Evil genius! I so admire that in a person. Usually I'm the evil bitch of the group."

"You can resume your role just as soon as I retire it," Chessy soothed.

"Well if we're going to get you all glammed out we need to

get moving. Not to hurt your feelings, girlfriend, but you look like hammered horse shit," Joss said bluntly.

"Gee thanks. I feel so much better about wowing my husband now."

"Don't listen to her. Give us forty-five minutes and you'll look like a million dollars. Just make sure you don't puke on anyone at the reception," Kylie said with an evil grin.

TWENTY-EIGHT

THE divider between the two conference rooms had been opened up to make one huge room and it was filled nearly to capacity for the open house reception for the launch of MHL Financial Services. Tate should have been thrilled with the turnout, but his heart wasn't in it.

He smiled when appropriate, exchanged pleasantries and meaningless chitchat. Answered in-depth questions about why a prospective client should choose his firm over a competitor. It was going off without a hitch. So why wasn't he more triumphant? This is what he'd been working so hard for, right?

Except that the one person who mattered the most wasn't here to share in his success.

With a sigh, he politely excused himself from the couple he'd been conversing with and went in search of one of the waiters circling with glasses of wine on his tray. Tate had made sure that only the best was served. Good wine, good champagne and he'd hired an excellent catering service and spared no expense in ensuring the food was fabulous.

As he collected a glass and brought it to his lips, he saw her. He damn near choked on the liquid in his mouth and had to cough so he didn't aspirate it into his lungs.

Chessy stood across the room so heart-stoppingly beautiful that he forgot to breathe. She positively sparkled. And he wasn't the only one to have noticed. People stopped and openly stared, drawn to Chessy's radiance. She wore a soft smile, her eyes filled with warmth as she searched the crowd. For him? Had she come for him? He was afraid to hope. But why else would she be here? How had she even known for that matter?

Her hair was arranged artfully atop her head, soft ringlets cascading down her slender neck. She wore the simple, yet elegant diamond earrings he'd given her for their anniversary one year, but what took his breath away was the collar she wore. The one she'd taken off and to his knowledge hadn't worn since that fateful night at The House.

And the shoes. God, the shoes. He wanted to charge across the room, take her into the nearest office and fuck her senseless right on the desk. Her dress, while modest, clung to her every curve, outlining in magnificent detail her spectacular figure. His tongue was dry in his mouth and he couldn't even swallow.

Then she found him in the crowd, their gazes locking. And she smiled. A brilliant, welcoming smile that nearly buckled his knees. She started forward, navigating her way through the crowd. Finally finding his own footing, he parted his way through the crowd, determined to meet her halfway.

When they drew abreast of each other, Tate simply pulled her into his arms, uncaring that they were likely causing a stir. He held on to her, closing his eyes at the simple pleasure of having her in his arms.

"I'm so glad you came," he whispered. "But how did you know?"

She drew away and smiled tenderly up at him. "I read about it in the paper. Why didn't *you* tell me about it?"

"I wasn't sure you'd want to come," he admitted.

"If it's important to you, it's important to me," she said softly.

Hope surged through his heart, hope that he was afraid to allow himself to feel.

"We'll talk about it later," she whispered. "For now, introduce me to your new partners. You have clients to court and entertain. I'll be here when it's over and then you can take me home so we can talk."

He was precariously close to breaking down and losing it right here in the middle of the crowded room. And he didn't give one damn. Wrapping his arm around her waist, anchoring her possessively to his side, he pushed through the crowd and introduced her not only to his new partners but to several of his clients.

Watching Chessy demonstrate her natural charm and effervescence was like seeing magic. She mesmerized her captive audience and had them all eating out of the palm of her hand. Why had he ever stopped bringing her to client dinners and events? At the time he hadn't wanted to burden her, but now he could see that she'd taken it as a rejection of her when nothing could be further from the truth.

He was bursting with pride over her. He saw the envious stares of the other men in the room, which is why he never allowed Chessy to stray from his side. He was publicly putting his stamp on her. Mine. Hands off.

When the event began to wind down and guests started filtering out, Tate turned to his two partners. "You can hang around until everyone has left. I'm going home with my wife."

Not even giving them a chance to argue, he herded Chessy to the door as fast as he could, ignoring her look of astonishment. She wasn't used to taking precedence over business, but she damn well better start getting accustomed to it because that was the way it was going to be from now on.

The traffic gods were on his side today and they made it home in seven minutes. Tate tucked her hand into his to make sure she didn't change her mind and refuse to come inside the house and he hurried her in. As soon as they made it through the front door, the clothes starting coming off.

He pulled impatiently at her dress, tearing the zipper when it didn't immediately open. She was as impatient as he was, ripping at the buttons on his dress shirt. She yanked his tie away and sent it sailing. He tore the delicate lace of her bra and then hooked his thumbs in her panties and sent them flying down her legs.

As soon as his dick was free of his pants, he lifted her and thrust to the hilt. Her legs wrapped solidly around his waist, anchoring her firmly against him as he walked toward the couch, buried deep in her pussy.

His hands underneath her ass, lifting and then allowing her to fall back down his erection, caused them both to groan with pleasure. Their need was desperate, a living, breathing entity that filled the room. Her hands clutched greedily at his shoulders, her body arching up and then back down to meet his thrusts.

They didn't make it to the couch.

He slid out of her long enough to sprawl them both on the plush rug and then he was back inside her, pumping and thrusting, desperate to reconnect in the most intimate fashion.

His mouth devoured every inch of flesh he could reach. He sucked avidly at her breasts, forming rigid peaks. Then he slid his lips upward, leaving a damp trail to her neck, and he sucked at the tender skin beneath her ear before licking the shell and nipping her lobe with his teeth.

She shuddered violently, already nearing her release. He could tell by the way she clenched and tightened around his cock. The sudden burst of wetness, bathing him in her sweet heat. Like liquid satin. Hot. So very tight.

He lost himself in her, thrusting mindlessly until her cry shattered the stillness. Then his own orgasm took over, rendering him incapable of thought or speech. There was so much he wanted to say and yet he was utterly blank.

He remained inside her, his chest heaving with exertion as he came down to rest on top of her, their sweat-slickened bodies hot and damp against one another.

"Was it okay to do that?" he asked anxiously. "I don't want to hurt the baby."

Chessy laughed, the sound beautiful in his ears. "It's a bit late for that concern. But no, you didn't hurt the baby. She's just fine. And so is her mama."

He closed his eyes, absorbing the beauty of the moment. When all was at peace and the world was finally set to rights.

Knowing he was too heavy for her, he slowly withdrew, his dick still rigid and wanting more. Then he bent down and curled his arms underneath her body, lifting and cradling her against his chest. He walked into the bedroom and deposited her on the bed before returning with a washcloth to clean them both.

Then he crawled onto the bed with her and pulled her into his arms. He didn't want to ruin the moment but he had to know. He couldn't bear it if this was a false alarm or he thought this was something it wasn't.

"Chessy, does this mean you're coming home?"

She lifted her head, her eyes glossy with emotion. She cupped his jaw lovingly and stroked her fingers over the afternoon shadow.

"If you'll have me back, yes."

"If I'll have you back?" he asked hoarsely. "Baby, I'm on my knees at your feet begging you to come home. But what changed your mind? I don't understand."

"I did a lot of soul searching," she admitted. "I'm miserable. You're miserable. It seems our only chance at happiness is to try to work out our differences together. I'm willing to forget and forgive if you are."

He looked at her in astonishment. "Baby, there is nothing for me to forgive and everything for you to forgive."

"I vote we forgive each other for the pain we've caused and let's start over."

He gathered her in his arms, pulling her down on top of him. "I love you so much, Chessy. I'm so damn grateful that you're willing to give me another chance when I've fucked up so many times already."

He slid his hand between them, cupping her flat belly where their child nestled in her mother's womb. "You're having my baby," he said in awe. "Do you have any idea what that does to me?"

Her eyes became troubled. "Are you truly happy about the baby, Tate? I know you weren't ready yet."

He kissed away her worried frown. "I think we've already covered in great detail what a dumbass I've been. I can't think of anything more perfect than you pregnant with my baby. I picture you all round with our child and it melts my heart every damn time. I'll be a good father and husband, Chessy. I'll get it right this time."

She gave him a smile so bright that it rivaled the sun. Her eyes filled with love, brimming with warmth and acceptance. "I know you will. I believe you, Tate. Every marriage has a bumpy road. But we got through ours. In ten years we'll look back at this, and hopefully we'll have more than one child. I'd like a large family. I want what I never had growing up. But we'll look back and laugh at how stupid we both were and how happy we are in the present. It will all seem so silly down the road."

He immediately grew somber. "I'll never make you feel unwanted again, Chess. I know how hard your childhood was for you. And I want you to know our children will never experience that. My life will always revolve around you and our children, however many we end up having."

She squeezed him tight, laying her head against his chest. "I love you, Tate."

"And I love my girl."

TWENTY-NINE

THE next day, Tate took off of work, much to Chessy's surprise. Yes, she had faith in the fact that he'd keep his promises this time to put her first, but she hadn't expected him to take a precious day off from work. But he'd told her that's what he had partners for now and that the three of them had familiarized themselves with all the MHL clients so they could respond to any needs that arose if one of them was out of pocket.

Tate drove Chessy to Kylie's so she could once again pack all her belongings, this time to move back home. Chessy had called both Joss and Kylie earlier that morning to fill them in on the developments and the fact that she and Tate were getting back together.

Both her friends were thrilled but also cautious, wanting Chessy to make certain she was absolutely sure about her decision. Once Chessy assured them she was, they were only too happy to offer her their support.

"I have a lot to thank them for," Tate said gruffly as he hauled her suitcases out to her SUV. "They took good care of my girl and didn't let her shoulder this alone."

She smiled. "That's what friends are for."

"You'll excuse me if I say I hope to hell you never need them this way again."

"I hope not either," she said with fervor.

"Don't be lifting that suitcase," Tate said sharply, when Chessy reached to hoist one of the pieces of luggage into the back. "You're pregnant for God's sake. You don't need to be lifting anything that heavy."

Chessy laughed, but delighted in his protectiveness. She was so happy she just wanted to squeeze him and never let go.

"I want to have Joss and Dash and Kylie and Jensen over for dinner one night," she said when they'd finished loading everything into her Mercedes. "Partly as a thank you and partly so they can see we're okay."

Tate's expression grew serious. "Are we okay, Chessy?"

"Yeah," she said, smiling at him.

She reached over to lace her fingers with his and squeezed his hand reassuringly.

"It's all in the past, Tate. Let's leave it there, okay?"

"You're too forgiving," he said gruffly. "But I thank God for it every single day. Not many women would forgive what all I've done. You may be able to but I'm not sure I'll ever forgive myself."

"Stop torturing yourself," she said gently. "It does little

good to keep rehashing the past. We have so much to look forward to. A baby."

Her smile became giddy as she imagined meeting their child for the first time. Having Tate right beside her in the delivery room, them both falling in love instantly with their son or daughter.

His expression softened and he too smiled. "I can't wait."

"Me either. Now, are you going to feed me or do I have to starve to death?"

He chuckled. "My girl's demanding. Want me to cook or do you want to go out? What do you feel up to?"

"Honestly I just want to go home and settle back in where I belong. We can always order takeout."

His look of intense satisfaction told her she'd said all the right things. "Damn right that's where you belong. You call in whatever you want and I'll run out and get it. And I don't want you to do a damn thing in the meantime. I'll get all your stuff out of the car and unpack it and put it away. If I catch you lifting so much as a finger, I'll spank your ass."

"That's hardly a threat," she said saucily. "I may just have to disobey on purpose."

"Then I'll have to come up with another threat. Like withholding sex for a month."

She snorted. "As if you'd last that long. Your hand isn't that good, babe."

He laughed, warmth and relief spreading over his features. "We're back," he said with satisfaction. "God, we're back!"

THIRTY

"DO you think they'll last?" Kylie asked anxiously as she sat next to Jensen on the sofa.

She was curled into the crook of his shoulder, her arm stretched across his midsection while they watched a ridiculous end-of-the-world B movie. The best kind.

He stroked her hair and then pressed a kiss to the side of her head. "What I think is that we can't control what happens in their relationship. We can only control what happens in ours."

Kylie let out a *hmmph*. "Since when did you get all sage and philosophical?"

He chuckled. "I'm just smart like that. I chose you, didn't I? That makes me the smartest guy on the planet."

"Well, there is that . . ." she said smugly.

He shifted, turning slightly so he faced her instead of sitting side-by-side with her. "Speaking of . . ."

She cocked her head, worry assailing her at the sudden seriousness of his tone and expression. Good God, surely he wasn't breaking up with her.

"I know this may be too soon," he said hesitantly. "We're still going to therapy and I know we have a long way to go, but I know my feelings aren't going to change for you. I love you. I always will. And I want to spend the rest of my life with you."

"Oh Jensen," she whispered. "Swear to God if you make me cry I'll kick your ass."

He grinned and then pulled a small velvet jeweler's box from underneath the sofa cushion. Then he slid from his perch on the couch and got down on one knee, opening the box to reveal a sparkling diamond engagement ring.

"Will you marry me, Kylie? We don't have to set a date right away. I just want your promise that one day, when you're ready, that I'll be the man you marry."

She couldn't breathe around the knot in her throat and the weight bearing down on her chest. Tears blurred her vision and she sucked in a steadying breath through distended nostrils. Her hands shook uncontrollably but he made no move to slide the ring on her finger. He was waiting for her answer.

She threw her arms around his neck, holding on to him for dear life. "Yes! Oh my God, yes. I love you so much, Jensen. There's no one I'd rather spend the rest of my life with than you."

"Thank fuck," he muttered. "You scared the shit out of me

there for a moment when you were so silent. I thought I'd screwed up and moved too fast."

"No one can ever accuse you of taking things slow and easy," she teased.

"I move fast when there's something I want. Why wait? I couldn't take the risk that some other guy would steal you away from me."

She rolled her eyes. "As if. No one else would put up with me. I'm afraid you're stuck with me."

"There's no one I'd rather be stuck with than you," he said, nearly echoing her own words.

"Thank fuck," she said, returning his words in kind. "What was it we decided? We'll be fucked up together?"

He laughed. "That about sums it up. Hell, who else would put up with us but each other? I guess that means we're perfect for one another."

"Hell yes," she said fervently.

"Don't you think you should put the ring on now?" he asked in a teasing voice.

"Oh my God, I almost forgot the ring!"

He pulled the ring from the velvet clasp and his hands shook as much as hers as he gently pushed it onto her ring finger.

She stared at it in awe. "This is huge!" she whispered. "I'm afraid to wear it, Jensen. What if I lose it? Or the diamond falls out? I'll live in terror of something happening to it."

He kissed her on the nose. "That's what insurance is for."

She wrinkled her nose as he drew away. "They insure rings?"

"Of course. You can insure anything of value. So now you

can wear it without worrying that you'll lose it. In fact, I will not be pleased if you ever take it off. This ring signals that you're mine."

"I think I can live with that," she said with a smile. "Now what can we do to celebrate?" she asked innocently.

"Oh I can think of something," he growled.

He swept her up and into his arms and carried her toward the bedroom, his mouth fused to hers.

THIRTY-ONE

CHESSY hummed cheerfully as she bustled around the kitchen putting the finishing touches on dinner. Tate had called earlier to let her know he was on his way home and he should be pulling up any second.

Just as she set the pan of baked chicken out on the table, she heard the front door open and she turned to greet him as soon as he walked through the kitchen door.

"Mmm, smells delicious," he said as he swept her into his arms, kissing her thoroughly in greeting.

"If you're ready to eat, go ahead and sit unless you want to get changed into more comfortable clothing first," she said.

He simply loosened his tie and removed his coat, tossing it over one of the unused chairs at the table, and then took his seat catty corner to where Chessy would sit. She made one more trip to the stove to carry the two pots of vegetables to the table and then she sat down with Tate.

He served up the chicken for them both and she spooned out corn onto her plate before passing it to Tate. Butter beans were next and then they both dug in.

"How was work?" she asked. "How is the new partnership going?"

Tate hesitated and glanced up, his expression growing serious. Her stomach plummeted and she braced herself for what was to come. Surely not again . . .

"I may be late the next two days," he said quietly. "We have a very important meeting with a large company who wants us to manage their private equity fund. It would be a huge account and if we ace this then it will set us at the forefront of financial firms. It could very well lead to more business."

Her brow furrowed, confused by the worry she saw in his eyes.

"Tate, are you worried that I'm going to be pissed because you're going to be late a couple of days?"

He looked chagrinned. "You have to admit the timing sucks. I just get you to move back in and give us another chance and after only a few days I have to tell you that I'll be late because of an important meeting."

She reached for his hand, hoping her sincerity showed. "I don't expect you to sacrifice your entire career in order to kiss my ass. I understand you have to work, that you have clients and important meetings. My problem before arose from the fact that it was all the time and that when you were at home, you weren't really here, if that makes any sense. You'd pulled away completely from me. We were like two strangers living in the same house. But it's not like that now."

"I hope you know it won't be that way."

"I do, Tate. I do."

His face softened with relief. The he squeezed her hand. "How are you and the little one doing?"

"We're doing great," she said enthusiastically. "I called to set up my first OB appointment today with the same one Joss uses. I was queasy this morning but managed not to throw up. I think I'm handling it far better than poor Joss."

"Tell me when you appointment is," he said seriously. "I won't miss it for anything."

"It's on the thirteenth. A Wednesday."

"I'll mark it down on my planner. What time?"

"Ten in the morning."

"How about I just plan to go into work after your appointment. I'll stick around and drive you to the doctor and we'll have lunch after."

"That sounds wonderful," she said with a bright smile.

He studied her a long moment, his gaze drifting over her features. "You look happy," he said. "I hadn't realized how long it's been since you truly looked happy. I'm so sorry, Chess."

Her heart softened at the vulnerability and true regret in his voice. "You make me happy, Tate. You've always had the power to make me the happiest woman on earth."

Left unsaid was that he also had the power to make her the unhappiest woman in the world. But he understood.

"If you're going to miss dinner tomorrow night, I may see if Joss and Kylie want to go out," Chessy said.

Tate nodded. "Tomorrow we're holding a planning meeting. Not sure when we'll wrap up but we're planning to have dinner delivered to the office and eat there. Day after tomorrow, we'll be in meetings starting at eleven with the CEO and CFO of Calder Enterprises. We'll have lunch and then give a presentation and then likely have dinner so I'll be out of pocket all day."

Chessy stood to clear her plate from the table and she dropped a kiss on Tate's cheek. "I have every confidence you'll win the account."

He stopped her, pulling her down into his lap so she had to set her plate back down on the table. He cuddled her to him, simply holding her as he kissed her forehead and then both eyes and finally her mouth.

"I love my girl. I don't deserve such blind support, but knowing you believe in me makes me feel like I can accomplish anything."

She put her palm to his jaw and then kissed him back. "Our child is counting on her father. I know you won't fail her or me."

He hugged her to him, shuddering with emotion. "I'm going to be a father," he said in wonder.

Chessy smiled. "We may not have planned her but I'm thinking she must be very strong-willed because she was conceived in nearly impossible odds."

"You think it's a girl, huh."

"Oh I'd love a boy or a girl. I've just gotten into the habit of saying *her*. I like to picture you with a precious little girl and spoiling her rotten."

"I plan to spoil her mama rotten first," he said gruffly. "I haven't been a very good Dominant, Chessy. But that's all going to change provided you still want my dominance. I'd understand if you didn't."

She stared lovingly at him. "I'm yours, Tate. You own me heart and soul. I *need* your dominance. I don't want you to start trying to be someone you're not because you're afraid that I've changed. I've been waiting here all along for you—the real you—to come back to me."

"In that case, forget the dishes and go into the bedroom. Take your clothes off and kneel in the middle of the bed."

Excitement coursed through Chessy's veins at the rough command in Tate's voice. God, he sounded just like the Tate she knew and loved so well. She wasted no time in getting off his lap and hurrying toward the bedroom. She also didn't waste any time worrying over whether their activities would hurt their baby because she trusted Tate implicitly. He'd never go too far and would always be mindful of their little one.

She undressed with little care, tossing her clothing on the floor in front of the walk-in closet. Then she climbed onto the bed and knelt in the center, facing the doorway so she'd immediately see Tate's expression when he walked in.

A few moments later he walked through the door holding several lengths of soft rope, deep red in color. His eyes caught fire when he his gaze fell on her kneeling naked on the bed.

"Lie back," he said in a husky voice. "Reach your hands

toward the headboard and spread your legs toward the foot of the bed."

She obediently complied, arranging herself so she was comfortable before lifting her hands above her head so that her knuckles just grazed the headboard.

"Who does my girl belong to?" Tate asked, the question familiar.

"You," she whispered, arching her back as he trailed a fingertip down the middle of her body, over her belly and between her legs where he stroked and petted her most intimate flesh.

Still fully clothed, he straddled her body but was careful to remain up on his knees so her belly didn't bear any of his weight. Then he reached above her head and coiled one length of the rope around her wrists before pulling it tightly upward to tether it to the headboard.

He moved off her body and then took both ankles, pushing them upward until her knees were bent and her heels rested against the bottoms of her thighs. Then he looped rope around her upper thigh and ankle, securing them together so she was spread wide. He repeated the process with her other ankle and then glanced at her to silently question her comfort level.

She gave him a reassuring smile so he'd know she was fine. How could she not be?

He stepped away from the bed and began slowly undressing. She stared unabashedly at him, drinking in his muscular body as he stripped down to his white briefs. The bulge of his erection was straining against his underwear, a rigid bow trying to push through.

Knowing what she liked, he reached inside his underwear instead of simply pulling the briefs down his legs and he pulled out his cock, stroking it as it strained upward toward his abdomen.

She licked her lips in anticipation and he groaned. Then as if deciding to be generous and give her again what she wanted, he climbed onto the bed, using one hand to turn her face toward him. He positioned his cock at her lips and tapped her cheek in a command to open for him.

He slid in immediately, his taste filling her mouth. She sucked avidly, running her tongue over the veins and the head, teasing and tracing every inch. Moisture beaded on the tip of his cock and she licked it away, humming her pleasure.

For several more minutes, he thrust gently into her mouth until she had to stretch to accommodate his burgeoning girth. Then finally he pulled free and she sucked in breaths to catch up, her nostrils flaring with the effort.

"It's my turn to taste you," he said, satisfaction edging his voice.

He crawled between her splayed-open thighs, her ankles bound to the bottoms of her thighs, rendering her completely helpless to whatever he chose to do. His hands slid over her breasts, tenderly caressing and plumping them.

"Tell me if I hurt you," he said gravely. "I know you're more sensitive now. The last thing I want to do is cause you discomfort."

"You won't hurt me," she whispered. "Just don't be as rough with them as you can sometimes be."

He cupped her belly possessively and then leaned down and kissed the spot where her womb would one day expand with their growing child. His tenderness brought tears to Chessy's eyes and her heart seized with love for this man. No, things hadn't always been easy for them, but what marriage was perfect?

Wasn't that what love and marriage were all about? Enduring the rocky roads, making mistakes and ultimately forgiving?

He nuzzled his way to her pussy, the flesh parted from the way she was bound. He licked and then sucked at her clit, causing her pelvis to clench and spasm underneath his expert mouth.

"I love seeing you this way," he said, his voice laced with desire and emotion. "Bound, beautiful, completely at my mercy. But baby, I'll have the tenderest of mercies with you."

She shivered when his mouth returned to her pussy, licking, sucking in all the right places. His tongue slid inward, licking shallowly inside her, giving her a preview of what it would feel like when his cock replaced his tongue.

"Does my girl want my dick?"

"Yes, please," she begged. "Take me, Tate. Own me. Show me I'm yours. Forever yours."

He slid up her body, positioning himself at her opening but he only inserted the head of his penis inside her, thrusting with shallow little movements, tormenting her until she was sobbing with need.

Then with one forceful thrust, the teasing was over. He seated himself to the hilt, causing her to gasp at the instant fullness. It was a delicious balance of pleasure and pain because Tate was a large man and it wasn't easy to gain full depth.

Her legs bound, her arms bound, there was nothing she could do except lie there and take whatever he did to her. He thrust into her, over and over, his hips arching, his entire body covering hers, undulating and writhing. His eyes were closed in exquisite torture, his forehead creased with tension.

His hips began slapping against her, frenzied as he pushed them closer and closer to the edge.

"Come for me, baby. Give me your release. Let me feel your wetness around my dick."

She let out a frantic cry as her orgasm crashed over her like breaking ocean waves. Her fingers curled into tight fists, straining against her bonds. She felt completely stretched to capacity, the aching fullness a delicious pleasure. The friction he caused by his swollen cock sent a surge of indescribable ecstasy cascading through her body.

And then he yanked himself from her pussy and reached down, grasping his cock. He pumped his hand up and down, his semen spurting onto her belly and then higher onto her breasts, marking her, branding her his possession.

He glanced down at the ropes of semen glistening on her skin, his eyes predatory and gleaming with satisfaction.

"My girl," he said gruffly. He cupped her belly. "My child."

She smiled up at him, exhausted by her orgasm. "We're both yours, Tate. Always."

"Let me get something to clean my girl up and then I'll untie you so I can hold you in my arms."

THIRTY-TWO

CHESSY was jittery and anxious for Tate's big presentation today. True to his word, he'd been late the night before and had been exhausted when he'd gotten home. They'd gone to bed and he'd slept with her firmly nestled in his arms.

This morning he'd been awake early and had left the house at six, dressed in his most expensive suit. He'd looked positively delicious. It was all she could do to refrain from jumping his bones, but that would make him late and she knew how important today's presentation was.

Not knowing how to pass the hours until Tate could tell her the results, she decided to do a thorough cleaning of the house since it had gone unattended in the time she'd been gone.

She dusted and got rid of all the clutter. Made up the bed

and put a load of laundry to wash. Then she went to clean the kitchen floors, since that was her biggest annoyance.

Tate had wanted to hire a cleaning lady to come in twice a week because he hadn't wanted Chessy to bear the workload of cleaning, but Chessy had refused. The idea of a stranger coming into her house gave her the shudders. She'd rather just do it herself so she'd know it was done right.

She dragged out the mop and then filled the sink with water and a cleaning agent. Then she started at the farthest point, mopping her way back toward the sink. When she was finished, she surveyed the sparkling floor with satisfaction.

She drained the water from the sink, wrung out the mop and then started toward the door leading onto the deck so she could put the mop out to dry.

She never even saw the still-wet patch of floor and as soon as her foot came down on it, she went flying, her feet coming out from underneath her. She landed with a painful thud that knocked the breath from her.

So stunned by the incident, she lay there trying to collect herself. She mentally went over every part of her body, trying to figure out if she was hurt. It seemed *everything* hurt.

She cautiously moved her arms and legs but when she tried to maneuver herself upward, pain surged through her back and abdomen. She froze, panic flooding her mind.

The baby.

Oh God, what if the baby was hurt? What if this caused her to miscarry? She was scared to death to even move.

She reached for the phone that thank God she'd kept in her

pocket. She should've dialed 911 but her first thought was to call her friends. Joss didn't answer so she called Kylie next.

"Hey girlfriend, what's up?" Kylie's cheerful voice rang in Chessy's ear.

"Kylie, I need help," Chessy said painfully. "I fell and I'm scared to get up. I'm worried about the baby."

She broke down into tears as she said the last.

"Stay where you are," Kylie commanded. "Jensen and I will be there in ten minutes."

Chessy closed her eyes in relief and then brought the phone to her side. Her very first instinct had been to call Tate. He was her lifeline. But she wouldn't do that to him today of all days. She refused to make him choose between her and a potential client who could set his firm up for years to come.

She could do this.

The wait seemed interminable but then she heard the front door fly open and Kylie's voice on its heels.

"Chessy! Where are you?"

"I'm in the kitchen," Chessy called out.

Kylie, followed quickly by Jensen, rushed into the kitchen where Chessy still lay on the floor. Jensen crouched down, his eyes full of concern.

"Where do you hurt, honey?"

"I'm not sure," Chessy admitted. "I tried to get up but it hurt so bad that I just laid back down. I'm so worried about the baby. Kylie, am I bleeding?"

Jensen looked away while Kylie gently pulled Chessy's pants down to examine her for any bleeding.

"You're spotting," Kylie said quietly.

Tears welled in Chessy's eyes. God, no. Anything but this.

"It's not a lot," Kylie soothed. "We'll take you to the ER and get you checked out. Make sure nothing is broken and that the baby is okay. Have you called Tate?"

Chessy shook her head emphatically. "No. He has a very important presentation today. This could make or break his business. I won't make him choose between me and such an important meeting."

Kylie didn't look placated by her explanation but didn't argue.

"Okay, honey, I'm going to pick you up. I'll try not to hurt you," Jensen said in a gentle voice.

Chessy tensed as Jensen curled his arms underneath her and lifted her effortlessly into his arms. She winced, her back protesting the movement. Jensen looked worried as he carried her outside to his car. He laid her in the backseat with instructions for her not to move. Kylie slid into the passenger seat and Jensen got behind the wheel and immediately pulled out of the drive, accelerating sharply out of the neighborhood.

Oh God, please, please let her baby be okay. In the short time since she'd discovered she was pregnant she'd bonded with her child. It was already a son or a daughter to her and she already dreamed of a future with a toddler running around, making her crazy. And she wanted other children. She didn't want an only child. She wanted a large family filled with love, all the things she'd never had growing up.

Her children would know how very much they were loved and wanted.

Ten minutes later, Jensen roared up to the ambulance bay at the ER and jumped out, yelling at one of the techs who was taking a smoke break.

"We need a stretcher. She's pregnant and she's hurt. I don't want to jostle her unnecessarily."

In a few minutes she was carefully loaded onto a stretcher and hustled into a cubicle in the ER where a nurse immediately began to ask her what happened and examined her for possible injuries.

"I'm just a few weeks pregnant," Chessy said tearfully. "And I'm spotting. Does that mean I'm losing her?"

The nurse patted her hand reassuringly. "Spotting is normal in the first weeks of pregnancy. But we'll do a sonogram and do blood work to check your HCG levels. I'm sure your baby will be just fine. It's you we need to worry about. Your left arm looks to be broken or at least severely bruised. We'll have to take X-rays and of course we'll take the necessary precautions to protect your baby."

Chessy heaved a sigh of relief. She didn't care about herself. She just wanted her baby to be all right.

Kylie and Jensen crowded in on either side of Chessy. Kylie put her hand on Chessy's shoulder while Jensen held her right hand. Kylie was careful not to touch her left arm.

For the first time, Chessy looked down at her arm and her mouth dropped open. It did indeed look broken. It was swollen and already bruising was evident.

A few minutes later, the tech came in and wheeled her down the hall to the X-ray room. It only took a few moments for him to X-ray her arm, but he also did ones of her ribs and her abdomen.

When he wheeled her back into the room, Joss and Dash were there waiting with Kylie and Jensen. Chessy teared up again. She loved her friends dearly but what she really wanted was her husband. She needed his strength and his reassurance but she couldn't ask him to sacrifice such an important opportunity for his firm.

"Chessy, oh my God, are you all right?" Joss asked in concern.

"What happened?" Dash asked in a grim voice.

They were interrupted when the sonogram tech came in pushing a portable sonogram machine with a wand attached. Chessy's eyes widened when they told her they would be doing an internal sonogram since it was so early in her pregnancy.

The fear and anxiety became too much. This was the moment where she'd discover whether or not her baby had survived her stupidity. She'd never forgive herself if she'd caused the death of her child.

She burst into uncontrollable sobs, tears streaking down her cheeks. Her entire body shook and the pain from her arm became unbearable.

To her utter shock, the door flew open and Tate filled the doorway, his gaze immediately seeking Chessy. He looked haggard and worried but relief flooded his features when he saw her.

But as he registered her sobs, his look turned to one of devastation. He flew over to her side, all but pushing the others away.

"Chessy, are you all right?" he demanded. "What happened? Is the baby okay?"

"What are you doing here?" she asked in astonishment, some of her tears abating as she took in the fact that her husband was here. Not at a meeting. He was here with her. "Tate, you can't miss the presentation today. How did you even know I was here?"

"Dash called me," Tate said grimly. "But you should have been the one to call me. Chessy, nothing is more important than you. Fuck the presentation. That's what I have partners for now. If we get it we get it. If not, there will be other opportunities. But my sole priority is you and your safety and our child."

Chessy burst into tears again and Tate leaned down, carefully pulling her into his arms.

"Don't cry, baby. Please don't cry. It'll be all right. I swear it. If this pregnancy doesn't work out, we'll have others. I'll give you as many babies as you want."

Her heart filled with love. Her emotions were out of control. Tate had chosen *her*. She hadn't asked him to. Hadn't expected him to leave such an important meeting. But he'd come.

"It breaks my heart that you're so overwhelmed by the fact that I came," Tate said, sorrow swamping his face. "But Chessy, I'll always choose you. I know in the past I haven't, but from now on, you are my number one priority. You should have called me but I understand why you didn't. But from now on, I expect you to always tell me what's going on with you. Especially when you're hurt and in the hospital and worried that you've lost our baby."

"I love you," she whispered. "I love you so much."

"I love you too, baby."

The sonogram tech cleared his throat. "If you'll all leave the room I'll do the sonogram and confirm whether or not the baby is still safely in her mother's womb."

"I'm not leaving," Tate growled.

He positioned himself by Chessy's side and curled his arm underneath her so he supported her upper body.

Joss, Kylie, Jensen and Dash discreetly left the room and the sonogram tech pulled up the gown they'd changed her into and quietly explained the process of an internal sonogram.

The wand would be inserted into her vagina and the images would show up on the screen of the sonogram machine.

"Let's hope for the best," the tech said with a smile. "Your spotting was minimal and it's quite normal in the early stages of pregnancy. Chances are it had nothing to do with your fall at all."

Silence descended as the tech began the sonogram. Tate had Chessy firmly anchored in his arms and he gripped her right hand, squeezing tightly. He was as afraid as she was. She could see the tension in his features, the fear in his eyes. Fear for her and fear for their child.

"There's the heartbeat! Everything looks good, little mama. Your baby is still right where it needs to be."

Chessy burst into tears again. Tate touched his forehead to hers, relief etched in every facet of his face.

"Our baby is just fine," he whispered. "But now we have to take care of you."

He tenderly wiped her tears away, kissing the damp trails on her cheeks.

"I'm so glad you're here," she said brokenly. "I wanted you here so bad but I didn't want to mess up your presentation."

"I'll always be here," he said gently. "You and our baby come first."

He'd chosen her.

Joy quickly replaced the sorrow and fear over the thought of losing her baby. She reached up with her uninjured arm and caressed Tate's face.

"You chose me," she whispered.

Tears brimmed in Tate's own eyes.

"I know I can't erase the past, Chessy, but I can affect the future. And from now on, you come first. Always. I need you to believe that."

"I do," she whispered.

"I love you," he said gravely, sincerity brimming in his tear-filled eyes. "And as soon as they release you, I'm taking you home and you're not going to lift so much as a finger while you recover. I'm taking the rest of the week off and depending on how you're doing, I may take off next week as well."

She was stunned, sure that shock registered on her face.

He caressed her cheek, love and tenderness radiating from his eyes.

"I chose you, Chessy. I'll always choose you."

She smiled, ignoring the pain in her arm. She had everything in the world that mattered to her right here and now. Her baby was safe and her husband was here. Everything was good. Finally, she was at peace.

And she did believe Tate. All the doubts of the past, all the betrayals and disappointment melted away, leaving love and trust in their wake.

EPILOGUE

KYLIE decided to wait until after Joss's and Chessy's babies were born before she and Jensen married. Joss and Chessy had complained that they could hardly be bridesmaids when they were big as a house. Jensen wasn't happy with the delay. He wanted Kylie to be legally his as soon as possible and he didn't care if they had an actual wedding or not. He'd threatened to kidnap Kylie and elope to Vegas but in the end he caved when Kylie told him how important it was that she be surrounded by her "family" on their special day.

Joss gave birth to an eight-pound, nine-ounce baby boy. They named him Carson, in recognition of Joss's first husband and Dash's best friend.

Not long after, Chessy delivered a seven-pound, two-ounce baby girl. She smugly told Tate that she'd been right all along and that she knew she was having a daughter. Tate had coddled her the entire time. He'd taken her home from the hospital on that horrible day when she'd feared the worst. Her arm had indeed been broken and she'd worn a cast for two months. Tate hadn't allowed her to so much as lift a finger, and also true to his word, he'd spent much more time away from work and with her.

When the cast had been removed, and with her having an adorable baby bump, he'd taken her away for an entire week where they'd done nothing more than lounge on a beach and make love in the hotel room. It had been utter perfection.

Two months after Chessy gave birth, Kylie's wedding day arrived. The weather was perfect, heralding a magnificent day.

"You look beautiful," Tate said as he watched Chessy put the finishing touches on her makeup.

The bridesmaid dress was gorgeous and to Chessy's delight she was actually able to fit into the same size she'd worn before her pregnancy. The only problem was that her boobs were huge. Tate wasn't complaining about that at all.

"You don't look so shabby yourself," Chessy said, admiring the black tuxedo he'd donned in order to be one of Jensen's attendants.

Tate picked up Caroline and when she started to fuss, he reached for her pacifier. Once inserted, Caroline sucked contentedly and immediately settled into sleep in her father's arms.

It had been decided that Joss and Chessy would carry their babies with them down the aisle to stand for Kylie at her ceremony. Chessy just hoped that neither child started fussing through the service.

She needn't have worried. The babies were perfectly content in their mothers' arms. Joss and Chessy watched Kylie and Jensen pledge their love and the start of their lives together as man and wife and they both started crying.

Tate heaved an exasperated sigh and handed over a handkerchief to Chessy.

"And to think we were worried about the babies crying," Dash muttered.

Rings were exchanged and then the minister pronounced them man and wife. Jensen pulled Kylie into a scorching kiss that made Chessy blush. Tate didn't know it yet, but tonight was the night she planned to tell him her doctor had told her she was perfectly able to resume sexual activity.

To everyone's surprise—and delight—Jensen swept Kylie into his arms and carried her down the aisle instead of the traditional side-by-side walk down the aisle after being pronounced man and wife.

The others hurried after them and caught up to them in the vestibule of the church.

Kylie hugged Joss and then Chessy. "Thank you for being here," she whispered. "It made my wedding so much more special to have the people I love the most around me."

"I wouldn't have missed it for the world," Chessy said. "We love you, Kylie. And I'm so glad you're happy. You deserve happiness and I think Jensen is perfect for you. I wish for you a long life of love and happiness."

Tears glistened in Kylie's eyes. "I don't know what I'd do without you and Joss. I love you both."

"I think Jensen is getting a wee bit impatient," Joss murmured. "He's ready to take you on your honeymoon!"

Kylie blushed but turned only to be swept into her husband's arms—again. He carried her to the waiting limo and put her inside. Then he turned with a grin and waved at his group of friends.

"Thank you all for making this so special for Kylie. I know she won't forget this day and neither will I."

They all waved as Jensen got into the limo with Kylie, and as they drove away, Tate reached for Caroline and nestled her on his chest so her head rested on his shoulder.

Chessy leaned in close so no one could hear her as she whispered to her husband.

"My OB gave me the green light to resume sexual relations," she murmured.

Fire blazed in Tate's eyes, desire and lust brimming. He gave her a predatory look and then glanced ruefully down at their baby.

"I'm going to set a record in getting her down for the night. And then you and I are going to be up a very long time. I may just have to call out of work tomorrow."

Chessy laughed, the sound joyous and carefree. Everything was simply . . . perfect. She had her husband back, Kylie was happily married and Joss and Dash were new parents. Everyone was . . . happy. What more could she ask for?